WHITE WOLF MOON

MIKE GRANT

Copyright © 2012 by Mike Grant

Second Edition – September 2016

ISBN
978-1539013082

All rights reserved.

White Wolf Moon is a work of fiction. All names, places, characters, and events in this book are fictitious. Any resemblance to actual persons, living or dead, events, or locales is purely coincidental.
(At Second Glance Books, its owner and staff names used with permission.)

No part of this publication may be reproduced in any form, or by any means, electronic or mechanical, including photocopying, recording, or any information browsing, storage, or retrieval system, without permission in writing from the publisher.

WHITE WOLF MOON

Jenn MacAvoy peered through the windshield at the sidewalk tables, breath erratic and knees shaking. All the time she'd spent building the courage to confront him had been a waste. She was completely terrified now. More terrified than at the gallery where she had stood so close to him, deciphering the final clues he'd unwittingly set before her.

Holding the battered book of poetry in her trembling hand she studied the photograph on the back cover then stared at the man sitting at the table closest to her.

His once blonde shoulder-length hair was now grey and framed a well-tanned face. Although it appeared that he hadn't slept or shaven in days his features were true to the forty-year-old picture with the same brass rimmed granny-style glasses riding low on his nose and a drooping moustache burying his upper lip. His long legs wrapped in well-worn and torn denim were stretched straight under the table, a large white dog taking residence beneath his knees. An equally worn flannel shirt bore unwitting testimony to a slight paunch but overall she would still consider him slim. A beaten wide-brim leather hat completed the sixties persona of the man she had sought out.

He read a folded newspaper while he ate, occasionally peering over his glasses to study his surroundings. Three times his narrowed blue eyes had paused when they met hers. Each time his expression turned darker, more intent.

He knows she's been watching.

Jenn turned off the ignition, took a deep breath then gathered herself to face him.

Peter Michaelson couldn't see her face in the shadowed interior of the car catching only glimpses as she raised and lowered her head, the late afternoon sun highlighting her blonde hair with every movement.

The small older maroon four-door was typical of imports, nearly impossible to discern either make or model. Other than the cryptic graphic logo at the center of the grill they all look alike. Not like in the old days. You could spot a Chevy or Ford a mile away. Of course we don't have miles anymore either. This car however had become easy to spot. He'd studied the vehicle on several occasions, finding it parked at many of his haunts with the driver nowhere to be seen.

The car bore an Alberta license plate on the rear. It was dusty, not unusual in Kamloops, and was shy the right front hubcap. A copy of Quill and Quire sat atop a handful of tattered paperbacks in the back window deck and a small hand-made dream catcher swung from the rearview mirror. A drive-through coffee cup permanently occupied the holder on the console along with various gasoline and grocery receipts. On the passenger seat sat a scattered pile of CDs by groups he hadn't heard of and a Thompson Rivers University bag obviously stuffed with books. The driver's seat was always in a forward position so he'd already established that his stalker was shorter and judging by the sunglasses on the dashboard, female.

As he watched her close the door and walk towards him he sensed…something.

"I found you," she said, walking past him to the chair at the opposite side of the table.

"I wasn't lost." His voice was low, cold.

"Mind if I sit down?"

"Yes," he muttered, his eyes not leaving the newspaper.

She slid the chair out, moved it directly across from him and sat quickly, her foot prompting a slight whine from beneath the table. She looked down at the white face and piercing blue eyes.

"Cool dog. What's his name?"

"Ginn."

"Oh, she's female?"

"Since birth."

"What kind of dog is she?"

"Canadian."

"Uh-huh. She looks kind of like a wolf."

"Only when you walk on her wild side." He sighed, arching his neck from side to side.

An ambulance passed quickly by, the siren encouraging a restrained howl from beneath the table. She waited until the sounds faded then extended her hand.

"My name is Jenn MacAvoy."

He looked up over the newspaper and smiled to himself. Her green T-shirt had 'Look Up... Look Way Up' stenciled in subtle but noticeable gold lettering across her breasts. She was young, slight, bright...and familiar. Her shoulder-length hair was disobedient, choosing to fall wherever it pleased. Those aqua eyes were distinctive and sharp. Perhaps contacts? No, but there was something familiar about them. Her smile was pleasant but tight and forced. Her extended hand trembled slightly indicating a lack of confidence but deep down she harbored the determination to overcome it. If he would only ease her nervousness.

She pushed her hand closer to him. "My name is Jenn?"

"Is it?" His eyes met hers, his hands still clutching the newspaper. "Then I'm Peter Michaelson. With that out of the way I'd like to finish my dinner?"

"I know your secret Peter and I'll keep it but I really need to talk to you."

"Secret?"

"I'm finishing up my Journalism at the university and I was thinking that an interview with Evan Morris would be a great final project."

"Good luck with that."

She leaned back in her chair and drew a deep breath. "My research took me halfway across the country and then back here. You are Evan Morris, right?"

"Miss MacAvoy..." He pulled his hat down over his eyes. "My name is Peter Michaelson. I'm a photographer and jack-of-all-trades." He studied the thin black braided leather collar about her neck. "Now if you don't mind, my chicken is getting cold and my beer is getting warm."

"Yes I've seen your work." She reached and touched the collar. "Some of it is brilliant."

That's where he'd seen her, the gallery. "Some of it?"

"Yes, some I didn't care for."

He sipped his beer then leaned forward and set the bottle on her side of the table. "And just what qualifications do you possess that make you expert enough to judge my photographs?"

"None really." She smiled timidly. "I just know what I like."

"Knowing what you like and knowing what is good are two different things."

"I agree. But art is personal." Jenn sat up and pushed the bottle towards him, resting her elbows on the table. "Just because some critic says its good doesn't make it palatable to everyone. Finding something you like is what's important, right?"

His spine tingled. She wasn't going to be easily intimidated.

"Right, best of luck on your crusade Miss MacAvoy," he said, "but for now I'd really like to finish my meal and go home."

He disappeared behind his hat and newspaper.

"Fine." Jenn stood and noisily pushed her chair back under the table bringing about another whine from Ginn. "I'm sorry I disturbed you," she said. "Perhaps another time?"

She walked past him and out onto the sidewalk, glowering over her shoulder. Peter rested his elbow on the railing surrounding the tables and watched her step in front of her car.

"Miss MacAvoy?" he called.

Jenn stopped as she opened the door then glared across the roof, saying nothing.

"A good journalist needs to be persistent and assertive," he said, "yet patient and understanding."

"I'll keep that in mind," she growled. "Good-bye Mister Michaelson."

Ginn sat up and pushed her nose through the metal bars. Peter reached and scratched the top of her head then watched the maroon import pull out into traffic and disappear down the street.

Those eyes...his heartbeat quickened.

"For now," he whispered, patting the wolf.

Chapter 01

Marie Morris was intently reading a book in her large armchair on the back porch. Like her husband she lived in a gentler, more comfortable time. Her greying-blond hair lay lightly against a faded blue denim vest worn over a rainbow-colored tie-dyed T-shirt. Her knees peeked through torn jeans adorned with embroidered roses on each pocket. She glanced up as the hound and the hippie rounded the corner of the house, casually strolling along the fieldstone walkway. He'd always ambled but lately his steps had been slower and less pronounced. She sensed a growing restlessness in the man with whom she had spent forty years but true to form he wouldn't discuss it, choosing to hide behind his perfected knack for irreverent chitchat. Tonight he appeared even more distant as he stood with his hands in his pockets and shoulders hunched, staring across the river valley.

Marie rested the book in her lap. "Don't you two look schwacked," she said. "Bad day?"

"Interesting day." Peter climbed the steps and looked out over the yard watching Ginn roll in the tall grass. "Lawn needs mowing…the hound has grass stains."

"Run her through on gentle then fluff dry. Throw in a fabric sheet or the bugs'll stick to her."

"Be easier to mow the mutt," he mumbled. "What's the book?"

"What You Need…Eliza Clark." She began reading again. "You'd like it, she's from Toronto."

"And that's why I'd like it?"

"She writes real in an interestingly bizarre way. The Buddy character reminds me a little of you."

"How so?"

"He's scruffy and eccentric…lives for the moment, does what he wants when he wants. He's got this girlfriend, kind of…her name's Dorene…or Abby. She's a door-to-door stripper who wears electronic Godzilla slippers and wants to be a famous back-up country singer."

"Where does the bizarre part come in?"

"Never mind."

Peter propped his hat back on his head and rubbed his eyes. "Danny called while you were off beaching. They buried Jack this morning."

"Jack died?"

"No…they just got fed up with his incessant whining."

She slipped the bookmark between the pages and stared at the cover. "I guess the 'Dead End' tattoo on his ass takes on a whole new meaning now."

"Self-fulfilling prophecy…a lifetime later."

"What happened?"

Peter turned and leaned back against the railing. "Heart attack apparently. Danny, Carl, and Steve are coming down on Saturday. They figure we should hold a memorial for old Jack."

"Drunkapalooza. Why?"

"I don't know…a salute to old times?"

"It's not like they've made any attempt to get together over the last thirty years."

He half-smiled. "We haven't either. You still talk to Andy a fair bit though."

"Not much lately, I should call her. You think they'll bring the womenfolk?"

"I imagine. As I recall they're all pretty much whupped."

"Are you okay with this?"

He pulled his hat back down over his eyes. "I don't know."

"Why weren't we invited to the funeral?"

"None of us were, just the family." Then he smiled. "I suppose it could be that Andy was worried that Danny would somehow find a way to honor Jack's wishes."

"Which were?"

"To be cremated and have his ashes tossed over Shirley McCafferty."

"And she is?"

"A girl we went to school with."

"Had a crush did he?"

"Hell no, they hated each other to no end." He stood upright and stretched. "He just wanted to piss Miss 'Pinnacle of Perfection' off one last time."

"That'd do it."

Peter sat on the couch opposite her. Kicking off his sandals and resting his feet on the railing he watched a tree float down the North Thompson River. He put his hands behind his head and looked about the yard, finally focusing on the back corner of the garden.

Marie stared into his face. There was no outward emotion, no sign that the death had affected him in any way. "You thinking about Jack?"

"No…hoppers."

"Okay." She sighed. "Why?"

"Haven't you noticed how many we've got this year?"

"It's not just us Peter. Everybody has lots of grasshoppers this year."

"Yes, but ours are more organized…militant."

"Of course they are."

"Go look." He pointed across the yard. "They're mostly huddled over by the fence. It's like they're preparing to invade Marion's place."

"I'm not sure where to take this conversation. Ginn hasn't been chowing down on them as much lately. Perhaps that's why we have so many."

"Same as spiders. Maybe she's getting too old and slow to chase long-legged things."

"So are you but that doesn't stop you."

"Point taken." He grinned. "Speaking of which, we met a pretty nice young lady tonight."

"Imagine my surprise," Marie whispered, opening the book again. "Should I be concerned?"

"Right. Her name is Jennifer MacAvoy. She's a journalism student up at the university."

"Student? So she's youngish?"

"Yesish," he said flexing his toes against the cool breeze. "Probably about twenty."

"And what's she like?"

"Attractive, perky, smart. Actually she reminds me a lot of you when we got together."

"Nice save. How did you three meet?"

"She interrupted my dinner." He folded his hands across his stomach and watched a large log bobbing down the river. "She's after an interview with Evan Morris as a writing project."

Marie closed the book, her smile gone. "She recognized you?"

"Oh yeah."

"How?"

"Don't know, didn't ask. You know the red car that's been out on the road a few times?"

"That was her? She's your stalker?"

He nodded. "If I have to be stalked…."

"So what are you thinking Peter?"

"I'm thinking that maybe it's time."

"I've been telling you that for years…why now?"

"I don't know. It feels right, I guess."

"And it wouldn't have anything to do with this attractive perky smart Jennifer?"

"For some reason she feels right too." He watched the sky gradually turning orange. "When she asked me if I was Evan Morris I realized I was. Sounds stupid really."

"No, not stupid. I hope I get the chance to meet this young lady."

"You will…she's persistent. She'll show up here sooner or later."

Marie stood and walked towards the door. "I'm getting an early night…you should too."

"Wanna work the corners off the fitted sheets?"

"We did that last month," she replied. "Besides you've spent a lot of time tossing and turning lately."

"Exactly, we might as well put the energy to good use."

She wrinkled her nose and shuddered. "You smell like beer and Cajun."

"Sexy Seniors summer issue says that's an aphrodisiac."

"Don't believe everything you read." She opened the door then turned. "Double-check the locks before you come to bed?"

"Yeah, I won't be long."

"Goodnight...Evan."

"Sleep warm." He watched Ginn prance around the yard chasing the unseen insects that drifted up from the lawn everywhere she ran. How do you get grass stains out of a wolf?

Why would you want to be just a back-up country singer?

The honking of a pair of geese drew his gaze skyward. Just dark shapes against a deepening sky they moved with lumbering grace along the shore then dipped behind the scraggly pine and spruce separating the beach from the residential lots. The mountain across the river was peppered with scars of the fires, blackened trunks stood boldly against the new green of fresh grasses.

He felt good.

Marie calling him 'Evan' was a coming home of sorts but how did he really feel about facing his past?

It doesn't matter. No one will remember him anyway. Even if they did, times have changed.

Then he wondered why he even cared. Evan was just a part of who he is. The part from which he had chosen to run and hide. Marie had said it was because the idea of success frightened him; that he took pleasure from the journey but feared the destination. He didn't understand her explanation but it was better than anything he could come up with so he let it be.

Tonight he had another problem. Jennifer MacAvoy. Maybe she wasn't a problem. Maybe she was an answer. Now if he could just figure out the question.

The low moaning of the wolf brought him back to now. An invisible flutter above his head sounded the departure of the bats from beneath the eaves.

Ginn stood on the riverbank quietly calling out to nature, reminding all those who would listen of her role in the natural order...an order that included death.

They were all dying now, those he grew up with and worked with through the years. He guessed that a part of the natural order was that those left would accept each passing with less emotion. He and Jack had been close at times and had Jack been the first to go

Evan would have been devastated. But death had now become almost routine.

There was something wrong with that.

Chapter 02

Marie placed her breakfast dishes in the machine and pushed the door shut. The morning sun was sneaking a peek over the mountains and already warming the kitchen. She smiled as he lumbered to the coffeemaker and poured his first of the day.

"Good morning Evan."

"Good," he mumbled.

"Evan Morris. Sounds nice doesn't it?"

"Nice." He lifted the sugar jar and wrestled with the top. "Why is the sugar lidded?" he asked as he handed her the jar.

Marie gave it a quick twist then handed it back. "Ants."

"Thanks Jaime," he muttered. "Isn't that why you built motel row outside?"

"They're not checking in."

"Maybe you should offer free dirty ant movies, or get a bigger sign. I hear they have lousy vision."

"Maybe."

"I'm leaving the top loose…I doubt they'll be able to lift it."

"Probably not. I left you some bacon. It just needs to be warmed."

"Later."

She watched him walk to the fridge and pour cream into the cup. "You were pretty restless again last night," she said. "What's up?"

"I don't know. Too many ideas running hot laps in my head I guess."

"Good or bad?"

"Doesn't matter...at my age I'm just thankful I get one now and then."

"We are still talking about ideas, right?"

"That too..." He began walking towards the back door. "I'll be on the porch."

"Think maybe you should get dressed first?"

"Then I'll be on the porch second."

He wandered down the hallway and into the bedroom, stopping to look in the mirror. Yesterday he'd seen Peter Michaelson...today, Evan Morris. The absurdity was that they really did look like two different people. Yesterday's Evan was young and firm with a boyish charm that bode well with the ladies. The Evan in the mirror was...Peter.

"Quarter for your thoughts?" Marie asked from the doorway.

He squinted into the mirror. "Where has Evan Morris gone?"

"Long time passing," she sang. "He's still in there screaming to get out."

"He doesn't scream, he vocalizes firmly...and the Evan I remember wasn't quite as pudgy."

Marie giggled as she stepped in beside him. "You're not pudgy."

"Don't say love handles." He sighed. "I hate that. Look at my belly button."

"I'd rather not."

"It's smiling. They're not supposed to smile. They're supposed to look surprised." He squinted into the mirror again then put his hands on his chest. "And I have breasts. When the hell did that happen?"

"February twenty-sixth, sometime between the presents and the cake. A happy sixtieth surprise package from old Mum Nature. Boom-boom."

"Oh."

"They're cute. They match your girlish ass."

"Girlish ass and boobs?" He shook his head. "If this keeps up you'll become redundant."

She restrained her laughter as he turned full circle in front of the mirror, checking himself out. Finally he stopped, put his hands on his hips and stared.

Marie put her arm around his waist, avoiding the love handles. "Now what?"

"Why is my hair thinning on top and thicking on the bottom?"

She glanced at his buttocks. "You're right. What's up with that?"

He lifted an old pair of jeans from the top of his dresser and quickly pulled them on. "The whole Goddamn world is upside down," he muttered.

"Why this sudden interest in your appearance?"

"Dunno. Evan really was good looking though wasn't he?"

"Yes he was. 'A right handsome lad' Mum used to say."

"What about Peter?"

"He's okay but that Evan. Wow!"

"Thanks. Your mum really said that I was handsome?"

"No." Marie checked her hair in the mirror. "Are you doing anything today?"

"I do things every day."

"Any important things?"

He reached a flannel shirt from the closet. "Define 'important'."

"Want to go back to bed?"

"Is that a trick question?"

"Yes." She wrapped her arms around his waist. "I'm heading into town. You should be able to get some more sleep while I'm gone."

"What's up in town?"

"Hopefully my little Russian tank commander. He's waiting in unit 112."

"Oh," he whispered. "Does he have a sister?"

"Yes, Olga. She's a gunner."

"I'll just bet she is. So why are you really heading to town?"

"I'm changing your display at the gallery." She patted his shoulder. "You seem pretty funked up this morning?"

"Funked up?" Closing the last snap on his shirt he smiled curiously at his reflection. "Funked up...I like that."

"Seriously Evan, what's going on?"

"I don't know. Why don't you go perform a little foreign policy on tankboy while I try to figure me out."

"You haven't got that much time left. Let me kick-start you…Jennifer MacAvoy?"

"Mostly, I think."

"Olga's closer to your age."

He grinned. "Well then, she just won't do will she?"

Chapter 03

Ginn leaned heavily against his leg as Evan surveyed the scene from the edge of the riverbank. The valley was cloaked in a light haze, the tang of wood smoke in the air. Waters rushed deep while early morning strollers sauntered along the beach at the bottom of the ten steps leading down from his property. It was already hot and would get unbearable by late afternoon. That would be the time to retire to the air-conditioned darkroom. There in the orange-glow tranquility he felt most at home although today for the first time in years he would be Evan Morris.

'Interesting,' he thought. Peter is the commercial part of his life and while his name also appears on the art, the concepts were all rooted in Evan.

He reached down and patted the wolf. "I'm beside myself girl," he said. "Shall we walk?"

With a quick bark Ginn scurried down the steps and onto the sand, Evan close behind.

Dobson was on the beach, plodding along with the certainty of a drunk in a canoe. Every day he'd follow his bleeping metal detector hoping to uncover a buried cache of something that wasn't there yesterday. He was bedecked in the usual vibrant pink plastic sandals, knee-high black socks, perfectly pressed khaki walking shorts, loose blue cotton shirt, and Special Forces camouflage hat. Dobson always tramped the same trail, circled the same trees, and consistently managed to get his garden-clogs stuck in the same mud.

Evan once asked Marie to tie him up if he ever grew that old and strange. In a preparatory move she had knotted a leash to the back porch railing.

He walked the beach wondering how long it would take before the water lapped at the bottom of his steps. The snowcap was still melting, trees and other debris careening down the North Thompson. It wouldn't flood this year apparently, but they've been wrong before.

Flood.

That would be the best description of what he was feeling right now. He was in over his head, drowning in emotions and memories.

Evan Morris was a different time and over the years he'd become a different person. He liked Evan and occasionally missed him but he was still just a distant memory of someone he once knew.

Then there was Jack. He too floundered somewhere in the murky muck and weeds at the bottom of Evan's stream of consciousness. They'd disappeared together and even though there were times they were in different worlds on the same planet, they were a lot alike.

He heard voices from behind but before he could turn two girls jogged passed him.

Bikinis were already out in force. One little, two little…too late.

Evan picked up a stick and tossed it toward the girls. "Fetch," he called to Ginn. She quickly bounced after it, barking all the way. This prompted the bikinis to turn and visit.

And that was as close as he was going to get.

By now Jack would have pulled a five-dollar bill from his pocket and approached the prey by asking if either of them had dropped it. Even if they had said 'yes' he would have considered it a fiver well spent.

The subtler approach usually worked best for Evan. He had few girlfriends in his youth but many girl friends. They knew he was shy and safe. Word got around the female population quickly…if you needed somebody to talk to he was the one. He'd share but he wouldn't dare. The times he had consoled girls after they had broken up with their boyfriends were many. Years later he found out about rebound sex but by then he wasn't quite as trustworthy. Throughout his youth he had tried being cool and tried being a little on the bad side but eventually he discovered that simply being Evan was enough. His soft-spoken manner worked well with many women.

Those days are gone. Today he's a sixty-something guy with boobs and a hairy girly-butt. It takes a pretty special woman to appreciate him now.

Marie.

She has to be special. Over the years she's put up with more than any woman should have to and she's remained strong throughout. He isn't easy to live with, never has been. There were times he wanted to kick himself out of the house.

In a way he had.

Ginn lay beside him as he sat down on the sand. Another bikini strolled by but this one passed unnoticed. He was wondering what Evan would think of the man he'd become? How would he have handled the last forty years? What would he have done differently?

"Christ." He shook his head then looked at Ginn. "You're sitting next to an idiot."

She whined.

"Thanks, but you're just being kind."

He looked up when he heard the drone of a water bomber soaring north up the valley. The shifting winds had carried more smoke down the river. The haze was thicker now, the bite to the nostrils sharper. He thought of the fires three years before when the mountain across the river had burned. He and Marie spent that evening sipping wine in the hot tub watching helicopters dip long-tethered scoops into the water then release their load onto the flames. He had seen artistic merit in the red chemical retardant the bombers laid down, the mountainside resembling a thousand hectare canvas at the mercy of a squadron of aerial impressionists.

"Cool dog, what's his name?"

Evan snapped back to now. "Uh, Ginn...her name is Ginn."

"Oh, is she friendly?"

He looked into the face of an attractive young lady and smiled his professional smile. "Yes, she is."

She bent and petted the wolf. "Hi Ginn, I'm Cassie," she said then giggled as Ginn lifted a paw.

The hound was a chick magnet.

Cassie held up a digital camera. "May I take a picture of her?"

"Of course you may. Sit pretty girl."

Ginn snapped to attention.

"She's Samoyed, right?" Cassie asked as she took the photograph.

"She's an anomaly."

"A what?"

"A happenstance…a mix." He reached and stroked Ginn's neck. "Vets have checked her out and opinions range from Samoyed to Malamute and Husky. I lean toward the Samoyed. The only thing that's certain is that a lot of her is wolf."

"Her eyes remind me of my Siamese cat."

"Damn, we've been exploring the wrong species."

Cassie took another photograph then frowned, studying her subject from nose to tail. "Isn't she a little fat for a wolf?"

Ginn put her head to one side and narrowed her eyes.

"Shh," Evan raised a finger to his lips. "Don't say 'fat' in front of the w-o-l-f. She's 'big-boned'."

"Sorry," she whispered, "but all the wolves I've seen are, you know…skinnier?"

"Whites are generally heavier than most but in her case a lot of it is fur and easy living."

"But she seems so cuddly and tame."

"Do you really want to see the wolf?"

Cassie half-smiled. "Sure…maybe."

Evan leaned toward Ginn and whispered in her ear. Instantly she dropped her head. With eyes wide and ears flattened she bared her teeth and growled savagely.

Cassie snapped the picture. "Okay, that's all I need," she said softly then stepped back and quickly walked down the beach.

'Déjà vu,' he thought.

Jennifer MacAvoy.

She will resurface…he'll have to deal with her sooner or later. She was taken aback by his reaction to her intrusion but she has the determination to give it at least one more shot. She wasn't going to just go away.

Neither was the ghost she was chasing.

Chapter 04

Marie was back on the porch with her book and coffee when Evan and Ginn walked into the yard. He stopped briefly to pull two scraggly plants from the garden then crossed the grass to the house. He climbed the stairs, holding up his catch. "These weeds?" he asked.

"No."

"Oh." Unceremoniously he tossed the greenery over the railing into the flower patch and sat beside her on the couch. "You weren't gone long?"

"You were. Got your figuring done?"

"No. How was tankboy?"

"It's not the size of the gun…Olga says 'hi'."

"Hi back." Evan dropped his hat onto the couch beside him. "I fixed the string on the back gate."

"I noticed. I'm proud of you dear."

"No need for sarcasm."

"It wasn't sarcasm…just an affectionate yet objective evaluation of your mechanical abilities, that's all."

"Been watching Doctor Phil again have we?" He kicked at the leash suspended from the railing. "Dobson was on the beach again. Has he ever found anything?"

"Other than the washing machine, I don't think so."

"Washing machine?"

"It's in his back yard beside the saucepan windmill. He painted it blue and turned it into a planter."

"You've been in his yard?"

Marie raised her eyebrows. "Come now Evan, a guy can only wink and click at you so many times before you just have to follow him home."

"Click?"

"A cluck…really."

"Uh huh…."

"You know…that naughty little noise dirty old men make with their tongue."

"I don't cluck." Evan frowned. "It works?"

"Only if he's a sexy dirty old man."

"Dobson's sexy?"

"He has a certain confidence that women are drawn to. Plus that wink…I swear Evan, he can melt you with that wink."

"He wears day-glow pink plastic sandals for Chrissakes."

"I know," she said, "but it speaks volumes about how comfortable he is with his sexuality."

"I guess…although the man needed a metal detector to find a washing machine. That has to speak at least a chapter."

"I'll admit he's a queer old duck but he's nice."

"In a queer old duck kind of way. You finished the book?"

Marie showed him the number of pages she had left. "Nearly."

"Cool cover photo…" He moved in for a closer look. "And cute author on the back."

"I'm thinking of suggesting it at the book club tomorrow night."

"It's Wednesday again? I need to do laundry."

"Is it just me or are you rambling more than usual lately?"

"Yeah, not really I suppose." He reached and pulled off his shoes. "Did Buddy get lucky?"

"Page eighty."

"Did Dorene's slippers light up?"

"They don't light up, they just growl."

"Of course…flashing Godzilla slippers would just be silly."

"You've got King Kong slippers."

"So?"

"Nothing. Are we finished?"

He rested his feet on the railing. "Finished what?"

"Abbot and Costello?"

"Yeah…I'm really funked up Marie."

"That's what happens when you meet an old friend after a few decades. It's always a shock."

"Evan?"

Marie nodded. "It's got to be tough but I really like that you're back. It reminds me of some pretty good times."

"What's wrong with these times?"

"Nothing…they're just a different good, that's all." She placed her hand on his. "Worried about the weekend?"

"Just curious. I'm almost sure I know how I turned out but the rest of them…."

"Does it matter?"

"Not really. You've talked to Andy a fair bit, anything to share?"

"Not much. She used to mention the old gang occasionally but the last few calls she's only wanted to talk about us."

"Not even Jack?"

"Not recently."

"Give me something to work with here Marie."

"She did joke about Danny recording the ball drop every year."

He frowned. "I thought that only happened once."

"What?"

"The ball drop."

"What are you talking about?"

"What are you talking about?"

"New Years at Times Square," she said. "The ball dropping?"

"Oh."

"What did you think I was talking about?"

"Nothing. Why would he record that?"

"Come now Evan, this is Danny."

"Right." He closed his eyes. "So all I have to work with is a ball dropping fetish. I'm not sure even I could stretch that into more than a few minutes."

"Once they get here everything will be fine."

"I guess." He leaned back and put his hands behind his head. "These times really are pretty good aren't they?"

"Yes they are and that's more than likely what's funking you up. This Jennifer has come along and ripped the lid off your coffin."

"I'd appreciate it if you could rephrase that."

"All I'm saying is that she's unearthed a part of your life that you thought was safely tucked away."

"Then you could have simply said that she untucked me."

"You're stalling Evan. Seriously I think you should be working on how to deal with your journalism student. If she's as persistent as you think she is you'd better decide what, if anything, you want to tell her." She leaned and kissed his cheek. "When was the last time you shaved?"

He rubbed his chin. "Evan had a beard…maybe I should let it grow out again."

"Maybe. How do you think he would he have handled the young reporter-in-training?"

"I'll ask him later, we're showering."

"People will talk."

"Not these days. I'm a sexy old man, right?"

"Sure, okay." Marie stood and handed him the book. "Page eighty…I'm heading inside."

He flipped through to the page but closed it just as quickly and stared out into the yard. Marie was right…these were good times. She was also right about Jennifer.

Marie was usually right about everything.

He hadn't been sure they could make it work back then. She was more stable than he was, more sensible. All relationships require a little give and take on both sides but it seemed she always gave a little more. She understood him better than he understood himself, always accepting his tangents and attitude although not necessarily without question or with agreement. She was the grounding that he never had and she was the light he'd always needed. She'd stood by both Evan and Peter throughout each of their lives. She'd pushed them gently and sometimes not so gently when required. Most times she didn't push at all.

The only time they had gone horse-back riding was one time she shouldn't have pushed.

Marie had grown up with horses, attended the summer camps, and was quite comfortable around the beasts. He didn't much like them. He didn't trust anything that was bigger and hairier than he was. When they arrived at the stables Marie told the handler that it didn't matter what kind of horse she rode but that her friend would need a 'for kids and fraidy-cats' mount.

Evan should have known from the formal introduction. Her horse was 'Sugar Sue'…his was 'Diablo'. Who calls a laid-backer Diablo?

Marie encouraged him to climb aboard, to start off with a slow walk, to gently kick the horse in the ribs, and to yell 'giddy up'.

Then she'd encouraged him to lie still in case anything was broken.

"When you fall off you've got to climb right back on," the handler had said as he tested for feeling in Evan's legs.

Evan succinctly told him what he could do with his horse but didn't hang around long enough to see if he'd attempted the suggestion.

Diablo was about the only time that Marie had steered him wrong. Looking back it was no big deal.

He tucked the book under his arm and walked into the house. She was in the kitchen leaning over the sink. He tiptoed up across the floor and hugged her.

"We've read page eighty have we?" she sighed.

"No, I just wanted to say I love you."

She stood upright and returned the hug. "And I love you. What brought this on?"

"All the good years that I think I finally appreciate."

"It's about time."

Chapter 05

The smells and solitude of the darkroom welcomed him as they have so many times over so many years. In the dim orange glow the small room seemed as borderless as the imagination that creates the images. He sat on the battered wooden stool that put him at the right height for the old enlarger. The antique no-frills machine had served him well throughout his career. It is the photographer who makes the photograph, not the newest camera or printing equipment. Even in the digital age it's still all about the heart of the image. These days there are so many 'pretty' pictures but so few truly unique and meaningful photographs.

He stood and moved through the dim light to his old recliner, kicked it back then rested his head against the scarred leather. Images from decades of darkness were tacked to the wall above the concrete block and plank shelf that housed his old photography books. A discarded kitchen counter ran along one wall providing the perfect work center. It was there he created his magic, sliding the exposed paper into the chemicals and watching the image materialize into a realization of his vision.

'What an artsy thing to think,' he thought. Then he closed his eyes.

Today was not a day for magic. This room was more than a means to an artistic and monetary end. It was a part of him; his thoughtful spot, nowhere near the hundred-acre wood.

Memories of Evan Morris were beginning to claw their way through the age-induced fog like a photograph in the developer, fuzzy at first but gradually becoming clear and sharp. He concentrated on the image of a young man who wanted it all but not bad enough to take it. He was the 'out' kid on the block, the one who never made sense and didn't care much for other kids. He was the tallest in the class, the one who'd rather doodle than play hockey, and the one who wouldn't raise his hand…even when he knew the answer. Evan was almost as much of an outcast as the smelly kid in the back row by the window. He was quiet, shy, and non-confrontational with, as all of his report cards had said, a good mind if only he'd apply it.

Elmer Cameron's grade twelve art class was where things had changed. Evan appreciated art but he wasn't good at it and never professed to be. He had the imagination but not the talent to put his visions to paper and admired those that did. For him the class was only a means to an end, that last subject needed to give him enough credits to get out of school. Cameron knew this and spent the first three months belittling anything that Evan attempted.

The last class before the Christmas break Cameron took the ridicule too far. "Mister Morris," he had said, "In pursuing art you are wasting both my time and your life. You are creatively worthless and have no more talent than does the lantern that you are so sadly attempting to sketch." Then, to a roomful of restrained giggles, Cameron suggested that after the holidays Evan should enroll in the Home Economics class because as an artist he would make someone a wonderful housekeeper.

When his father asked why he was home from school before noon Evan explained that there was this little known rule forbidding the practice of pouring India ink over a teacher's suit.

Dad grinned and asked what his usually reserved son was going to do about it.

"When the time comes I shall pour one more bottle over his grave," had been his reply.

Evan's brief trip on the road to ruin had begun. He never went back to school, preferring instead to spend his time with the guys in the band playing teen clubs and gymnasiums and partying with what little money they made. It was a rough and tumble life and one in which Evan had flourished. Fast cars and faster women filled his emotionally empty existence.

He was reborn on a cold, wet and windy November day at a hillside cemetery. Evan had viewed the funeral from afar, observing the handful of mourners repeatedly checking their watches. He had read the obituary. Other than a surviving brother in England, Cameron had passed away a solitary man. The list of pre-deceased relatives filled the remaining half of the announcement. Evan later found himself crouched over Elmer Cameron's marker, opened inkbottle in hand, but unable to make good on his promise.

"Lay at peace beneath the stone…as in life, in death alone," he had whispered as he sat on the wet grass and wept for someone he had loathed.

The next day he would lay flowers.

He started writing again and on a dare and a promise of beer he presented some of his poetry to an appreciative though ill-informed audience in one of the many small coffee clubs that had become part of the Edmonton landscape. After the first reading he realized that he had found a world in which he was the most comfortable. As a poet of sorts his quiet withdrawn manner was not only accepted but expected. He now realized he had also lived two lives back then, straddling the line between the old and the new Evan…the bad and the good. He relished those rapid-fire nights of partying with the guys but they eventually became an occasional release rather than a lifestyle. He remained close with Danny and Jack after the predicted and long overdue demise of the group but when he finally left it all behind they too had disappeared.

The three of them had talked about getting back together to celebrate all those lost, forgotten, and non-existent glories. They planned a reunion road trip one day…maybe hitting a few of the old familiar towns across the border and reliving some of the good times.

But one day never came.

Now it was too late.

Chapter 06

Evan poured his 'sunset' coffee and tossed a cursory look about the kitchen. It seemed tidy to him but then his brain always wrestled with tidy. He couldn't understand how sliding the toaster back against the wall made the scene any more aesthetically pleasing or any less messy.

He stepped out onto the porch and sat beside Marie on the couch, settling in to catch the arrival of night. "You talked to Andy?" he asked.

"She's thinking about coming down this weekend."

"It might be good for her."

"Might not. She sounds like she's dealing with it well though."

Evan looked around the yard. "Where's Ginn?"

"She's in the tub."

"Ah yes, the natural evolution of the wolf. Why would she be in the tub?"

Marie winked at him. "Grass stains…pre-soak?"

"Seriously."

"It's cooler in there."

"It's cooler out here now."

"She doesn't know that…she's been in the tub."

Evan snapped his fingers twice. Moments later Ginn pushed open the screen door, paused for a scritch behind her ears then ran down the steps onto the lawn.

"By the way…" He blew lightly across his coffee and took a cautious sip. "You didn't comment on my stir-fry."

"Didn't I?"

"No." He blew across his coffee again.

"What were the orange chunks in the sauce?" Marie asked.

"Really old yellow chunks."

"It was good."

He frowned. "Even a coerced compliment should contain some emotion, don't you think?"

"It really was great Evan…probably the best wok you've ever wokked! Okay?"

"It'll do," he mumbled.

"You tidied up the kitchen?"

"I didn't move the toaster."

"For a photographer you have a terrible sense of balance."

"Too many beer in my younger days." He took another cautious sip. "You remember the old culinary rule about the chef never having to clean up the kitchen?"

"Vaguely." Marie picked up her book, opening it at the bookmark. "At Second Glance," she said, "side two, cut three."

"What?"

"Your song 'Life at Second Glance'. The store's bookmark reminded me of it."

He stared into his coffee. "You know all the times I've been in there I've never thought of that."

"I hadn't until tonight. It's such a beautiful song. Maybe it really is time for Evan Morris to resurface."

"This is another of your sign thingies isn't it?"

"Perhaps…" She began reading. "I do think you'd enjoy this one."

"She's really a good writer?"

"Oh yes, although she's no Francine Jennings."

"But then who is?" He shrugged, watching the sky turn dark. "Night's coming quicker now."

"No it isn't, just earlier." Marie put the book on her lap. "You okay?"

"I'm just trying to put the day in focus." He stared into his coffee again. "Isn't quicker and earlier the same thing?"

"No, and isn't 'isn't' aren't?"

"The thing is singular."

"But the quicker and earlier parts aren't, are they?"

"Who's Francine Jennings?"

"She was in my grade twelve English class. We studied erotic literature from the turn of the century. She wrote a scathingly hot piece for an assignment, that's all."

"Oh. Scathingly hot?"

"I'll say. It was about these two guys and a girl who worked in a costume shop."

"I've heard enough."

"Okay." Marie picked up the book again. "If you're going to the market tomorrow we need lettuce and tomatoes."

"You studied erotic literature in grade twelve?"

"Didn't you?"

"Not in class. I can't believe there wasn't some sort of parental outcry back then."

"There was but it was too late. We'd already been smuttened."

"Uh huh." Evan stared into the sunset, thoughts of Jack filtering through his mind. The old days…why do they always seem so much better than the new ones? When the old days were new they didn't seem better, the days before them did. And these new days are just…confusing.

"I can't believe he's gone," he muttered.

Marie sighed and again put the book on her lap. "You ready to talk now?"

"How could they stay in business selling costumes?"

"They rented them, but that wasn't the point. The guys wore a pink donkey costume and she was the farmer's daughter. Its fantasy Evan…you do remember fantasy don't you?"

"Certainly not pink donkeys."

"The farmer's daughter?"

"Never."

"Naughty schoolgirl?"

"I think you're right, it's 'aren't'." Evan stood and stretched. "We're going to grab a shower and go to bed." He turned as he opened the door. "Lettuce and tomatoes, right?"

"Right…night guys."

Chapter 07

Evan shuffled through the crowded farmers market nodding and smiling politely to those who acknowledged him, usually by asking how Marie was. Perhaps they assumed that if he was walking among them he was fine but they never asked…just assumed. This Wednesday morning ritual was not unlike the Sunday flea market routine. Most faces he recognized…some he didn't but they all remained nameless to the man they called Peter. Too many to remember, none he really wanted to know any better.

    He stopped at the first table and put on his glasses. The lettuce was wet and crisp with that fresh smell that only wet, crisp lettuce has. He picked two and slipped them into the weathered canvas bag he had bought to save the world. He thought of Marie and the first few years they were in the house. Every day she'd be out in the garden painstakingly thinning the lettuce, feeling the tomatoes, and pulling out the 'baddies'. It still amazed him how she could tell which were weeds and which weren't. He finally convinced her that it was better to enjoy the fruits of someone else's labor than to have her hands forever soiled. Plus she'd have the time to pursue other interests.

    Marie had taken up soap making.

    With head held high Ginn pranced proudly beside him. A foolhardy tethered terrier bent on building a reputation barked and growled, straining at his leash in a futile effort to confront her. With wolfish amusement she glanced briefly at the suicidal nuisance then sauntered on, awaiting the reassurance that it was right to just walk on by.

Evan reached down and firmly patted her side. "Good girl," he said, although she already knew that.

A longhaired kid in weathered jeans and a bright orange shirt strummed a beaten guitar and sung 'For What It's Worth' with a sense of conviction that only someone who hadn't been there could. Evan gave him credit for trying and dropped a dollar in the hat before continuing his way through the market. The confused strumming blended awkwardly into a polka being played on an equally beaten accordion. The musician, an elderly gentleman dressed like a ranch hand from an old black and white western, was enjoying himself far more than any rational person should.

They stopped at a display of raspberries. Those ruby morsels defied description when cuddled up to a large scoop of frosty ice cream. If there was anything he'd like to grow in the yard it would be raspberries but he'd never had success with them. There were fields of raspberries on his grandparents' farm when he was a kid…canes as tall as he and heavy with fruit. He'd spend countless magical hot summer days filling metal buckets with those red gems containing the nectar of the Gods. Most of them would make it back to the kitchen where Gram would preserve them in what he used to refer to as her jam sessions.

That was a half-century ago. They were all gone now…the canes, the buckets, and the magic. These days his trips down memory lane take a lot longer. Disappearing dreams and faded memories echo through what once seemed like a full and frantic life.

He took three trays, gave the lady her money then carefully set the containers in the bag before moving on to the next table. This one was covered with more lettuce, tomatoes, cucumbers, and green beans. He settled at the end with the tomatoes but his thoughts had started to drift.

Jennifer. Her familiarity was troubling. He really couldn't remember her from the gallery but that was the only place they could have met. He felt he knew her and, past lives theory aside, this wasn't possible.

She was a student and that interested him. This wasn't someone out to gain a bonus in the pay envelope by exhuming a secret so long buried. She was doing this to help begin a career, to further herself…and she had already done her homework.

She deserved to be heard if nothing else.

Evan sorted through the tomatoes, selected six then paid the robust vendor. As he pocketed the change he realized that if Jennifer had found him others might.

Paranoia strikes deep.

With his hat pulled down against the morning sun he wound his way along the crowded sidewalk, resisting the urge to turn to see if anyone was following.

Into your life it will creep.

They reached the Rover. He held the door open for Ginn and glanced back down the street.

Chapter 08

Jenn approached the house with not so much reservation as curiosity. Far enough out Westsyde Road to be considered country it reminded her of an old faux-painting that used to hang in her mothers' living room. Huge trees and heavily populated flower gardens surrounded the single-level greying wood structure. A five-foot concrete dragon stood guard at the back gate, the claws sunk deeply into a tree trunk pedestal, the wings stretched wide. A small metal plaque between the feet read 'Path to Evermore', another clue to verify her findings.

She followed a staggered fieldstone walkway overgrown with grass along the side of the house, through a rose trellis and into the back yard. Lush vines of every sort covered fences surrounding what was surely the most eclectic display of plants, shrubs, and garden whatnots she could possibly imagine. She turned at the corner of the house and was greeted by a reception line of bright yellow and orange gnomes standing guard amid the daisies bordering the walk. These weren't your average variety garden gnomes. Much more detailed and realistic they stared up at her with wide blue eyes and knowing grins as she walked toward the porch.

"You must be Jennifer," Marie called from the doorway.

"Yes." Jenn pointed at the petite pottery people. "These guys seem so real…so creepy. Weird smiles or what?"

"It's because they can see up your dress. Peter made them that way. They all have names but the only one I know for certain is Pokey, the one by the step with the excess frontage in his coveralls.

The two staring at each other at the far end are gnome-o-sexual. He's a big believer in tolerance, especially in Evermore."

"I see." She giggled nervously. "Is he around?"

"He's gone to the farmers market but he'll be back soon. I'm Marie."

Jenn stopped at the bottom of the steps. "As in 'Last Night with Marie'?"

"He's right you are bright…and cute. Can I get you something to drink Jennifer?"

"No, thanks." Jenn continued her way up the steps. "I usually go by 'Jenn'. How did you know it was me?"

"He said you'd find your way here." Marie patted the chair beside her. "Come sit and tell me how you did it."

"In a way you did. Then he confirmed it."

"Mysterious, tell me more."

Jenn explained how, as a complement to her journalism degree, she had elected to study creative writing. As a combined final assignment she decided to research a Canadian author and, if possible, conduct an interview. Her mother mentioned a writer that she'd known in Edmonton. She thought he now lived in Kamloops and while he wasn't a household name, it might provide an interesting story. She sent her daughter a well-worn copy of his book of poetry and a record album. The book contained a short bio that provided enough information on Evan Morris to launch the project. An on-line search uncovered his only tour itinerary but it ended in Saskatoon in 1969 and nothing more was ever written about him.

"I did find a couple of fan-based sites but they also ask the 'where is he?' question. It's as if he vanished off the crust of the earth." Jenn unfolded her notes and held up a photocopied newspaper article. "Then I found this write-up from the Star-Phoenix where he mentions a girl he'd met in Kamloops named Marie and he speaks of how much she inspired him."

"So you figured he'd come running to me?"

"He just seemed to be that kind of guy, y'know?"

"He is that kind of guy. Go on."

"My roommate D'Arcy is studying photography and when Peter had that exhibition at the gallery she talked me into going with her. One of the prints was a black and white of two lilies."

"Sisters."

Jenn nodded affirmatively. "I recognized the text under the photo from the book Mum had sent me. Then I remembered her telling me something about a scar that Evan had from a camping weekend when he was a kid. Peter was at the table signing prints and chatting with people so I went over to say hello and there it was, just above the joint on his left thumb."

"My God," Marie said, "Holmes in a halter-top."

"The brochure said that cheques were to be made out to Peter Michaelson Photography. I searched Business Licensing at City Hall and discovered that one Evan Morris owns it. Address, phone number…it was all there." Jenn shook her head. "What a great way to disappear. He can call himself anything he wants and as long as the money goes into the business account nobody is the wiser. Oh, and Evermore…also from his book. Everything just nicely fell into place."

"You mentioned fan-based sites?"

"Yes, they've gathered some of his writings and songs…and a few old photographs."

"I'm surprised he doesn't know about those. You've done well Jenn, I really admire your tenacity. What's your mother's name? Maybe Evan has mentioned her."

"She was Claire Archer back then."

"Ah." Marie smiled. "You seem awfully young to have a mum her age."

"I was a surprise. Fortunately for me she didn't believe that having children after forty was a bad thing. I don't know how well she knew Evan. She didn't really get into that much detail…although she did remember the scar. Maybe they were friends or classmates or something."

"I'd ask Evan."

"Ask Evan." Jenn took a deep breath then said, "I'm so nervous about all of this Marie. Before the restaurant I felt pretty confident but when I actually met him everything I'd planned to say went out the window. Plus after his reaction I'm not sure he'll want to talk to me."

"He'll talk to you Jenn."

"Are you sure?"

"Pretty sure."

Jenn stood and leaned on the railing, looking into the yard. Her eyes followed the path from the side of the house then to the riverbank. "Paths that lead to Evermore, paths that twist and turn, then not so surprisingly twist and turn some more." She pointed to an iridescent blue blur skipping from vine to vine along the fence. "That's a hummingbird!"

Marie appreciated the young girl's excitement. "You've never seen one?"

"No and never so many butterflies all at once. This is really beautiful. His life…your life is so idyllic. I feel like an alien, like I don't belong…like I'm going to mess everything up." She turned and faced Marie. "I am trespassing aren't I?"

"Yes but Evan will decide whether or not to prosecute you." Marie smiled. "Don't over-think this Jenn, just let it unfold. He'll let you know what the rules are. He's not going to give you anything he doesn't want you to have and he's certainly not going to let you take it."

"I'm just not sure how to handle this."

"You've started the process now follow it through. You have no idea about what you're going to ask him?"

"Honestly, no." Jenn leaned back against the railing. "I did have, but not anymore."

"Good, you're starting with a blank canvas. Let him paint his own portrait and trust what you see. Don't interview, just chat…and listen. I imagine he'll ramble and double-talk your ears off but I have a hunch he'll give you everything you need if you're willing to weed it out."

"Why?"

"Because you're Jennifer."

"I don't understand."

"You don't have to. Now would you like some tea, or a cold drink?"

"Tea would be nice."

Jenn followed Marie into the living room. Facing her were floor to ceiling windows framing a view of the front garden while a large rough-stone fireplace dominated the corner to her left. The dark wood mantelpiece supported a collection of family photos and an abundance of plants. To her right a large television screen sat atop a shelf unit filled with electronics, tapes, DVDs, and more plants. Overloaded curio cabinets, well-stocked mismatched bookcases and black and white prints filled the remaining wall spaces. On top of a patterned thick pile area rug sat plump black leather furniture surrounding a large wooden coffee table cluttered with ornaments, books, and remote controls.

"Wow," Jenn said, "this is unexpected."

"What were you expecting?"

"I don't know but this wasn't it."

"Evan is definitely the old hippie-type but he does take his pleasures seriously."

"Funny," Jenn said, "I wouldn't have thought him a big TV fan."

"He's a fan of big televisions but doesn't watch a lot. Some hockey games and the news but usually he just settles in with movies, all kinds. He's into science fiction-fantasy mostly…aliens, dragons, King Kong and the like but he doesn't mind relaxing with an occasional chick-flick."

"Really? That surprises me."

"I imagine there's a lot about him that'll surprise you. I've known him for over forty years and there are still times I realize I don't know everything…and he gleefully reminds me of that every chance he gets. Take a look around while the kettle boils, I'll get the cups."

Jenn walked slowly down the hallway studying the photographs that covered virtually every inch of wall. To her left the bathroom, larger than she thought it might be and quite modern. To her right a bedroom, more photographs then another bedroom to her left, the master obviously. The room at the end of the hall had to be his study with shelving from floor to ceiling filled with who knew what. The fragrance of vanilla hung lightly in the air. But for the labored ticking of an old wall clock the room was quiet and close.

When Marie called that the tea was steeping Jenn walked back to the large country-style kitchen. "Interesting room at the end of the hall," she said.

"Evermore, I guess…his refuge. He really values his time alone. That and the darkroom are his favorite places. Ask him to show you around, it's pretty interesting in there. Cream?"

"Please," Jenn said as she joined Marie at the counter. "Where did he get all that stuff?"

"Flea markets, yard sales…wherever there are tables with piles of non-descript stuff you'll find Evan. It's his addiction. He wandered back from the hospital thrift shop with a doll a while ago. I looked at it and couldn't believe he'd even paid a buck for it. The face was cracked, her arms were broken and her hair was matted. She was a mess. He spent quite a few evenings fixing her up, painting her and stitching her clothes." Marie smiled at her young guest. "I think her name is Jenny?"

"And the weirdness just keeps growing," Jenn mumbled. "Why would he buy a doll? Is it an antique maybe?"

"It's old but not worth anything. He just felt sorry for her."

"Pardon?"

"He was pretty sure that nobody else would buy her in that condition so to save Jenny from the trash he gave her a home."

"I don't know whether to laugh or cry."

"That's just the way he is. Like I say he still surprises me every once in a while."

Jenn pointed out the window into the driveway. "That's new," she said.

"What is?"

"The big grey thing. It wasn't there when I arrived."

"Ah yes, the Land Rover. He says that only the cockroaches and the Rover will survive Armageddon. He's probably right. It's built like a tank…from the fifties, I think."

Evan marched into the kitchen and opened the refrigerator. "Fifty-two, kind of."

Jenn turned and faced him. "Kind of?"

"It's all new Ford underneath, engine, drive train, suspension." He tossed the groceries into the fridge and pulled out a bottle of water. "I'll be somewhere," he muttered and turned back to the hallway.

"That was in-depth," Jenn whispered as she heard the back door close.

"He's mostly bark," Marie said. "Grab your tea and let's sit at the table."

"Sure makes me want to go ask him for an interview."

"He's not going to make it easy for you Jenn."

"Why?"

"You've disrupted his little world. He's not sure what to make of you."

They sat on either side of the dinette, Jenn by the window watching Ginn run across the back yard. "I think it's pretty simple. Either he will or he won't let me do this."

"For Jennifer MacAvoy it might have been simple but when he finds out that you're Claire's daughter it'll get complicated. You're a link to his past and lately the past has been weighing heavily on him...especially now that one of the gang just passed away."

"My timing couldn't be worse," Jenn said, staring into the tea. "Maybe I should just forget the whole thing."

"First I believe your timing couldn't be better and second...you've gone to a lot of trouble to get here. You can't stop now."

"But he's a little scary Marie."

"No, you're scared of him but he's not really scary. He can be crusty and blunt to a fault but not scary."

Jenn bit her lip, her finger circling the rim of the teacup. "This person who died, they were close?"

"Yes, he and Jack were high school friends and two of the founding members of Bogwump, which is probably the reason you have a story to begin with."

"What?"

"They started out as the Bogwump Five. Jack was painting their name on his drums and asked the rest of them whether to use the number five or spell it out. After hours of deliberation and beer they were all so hopelessly undecided and drunk that they choose the path of least resistance and dropped it altogether."

"They were a band?"

"I use the term loosely. I've never actually heard them play...just some tapes that Evan kept that should have been declared toxic waste years ago."

Jenn smiled. "So I could ask him about Bog...what?"

"Wump. But be warned fair young maiden...do not foolishly venture too far lest he make you listen to those tapes. If you think Evan is scary...."

"What exactly is a Bogwump?"

"A nocturnal hedgehog-like little pig that lives in rotted tree stumps and eats slugs and fungus."

"Nummers." She grinned. "There's no such thing, right?"

"I've never seen one but Evan claims that swamps and barber shops are infested with them."

"I'm guessing that's why he doesn't go to barber shops?"

"Or swamps. The Bogwump was one of many bizarre creatures he invented for a children's fantasy book. Yet another undertaking he never quite got around to finishing."

"There's so much about him that nobody knows."

"And probably never will." Marie stood and cleared the cups from the table. "Some of the old bunch will be out for the weekend…I'm sure Evan wouldn't mind if you were here. You could get the whole story of Bogwump and maybe gain some insight as to how they underwhelmed the music industry."

"My little project is growing."

"Maybe you should get a start on it before it gets too big? He's probably at the back by the river."

Chapter 09

Evan sat on the bench at the edge of the yard overlooking the river, his legs stretched out, arms crossed, and hat pulled over his eyes. Ginn lay at his feet, lifting her ears when she heard the young girl approach.

"Evan?" Jenn whispered.

"That's going to take some getting used to," he whispered back.

"Sorry, I thought maybe you were in siesta mode."

"Nope. We're just trying to decide what we're going to do with you."

"We?"

"Yup, me and the wolf. She's figuring we should afford you only the best of hospitality."

"What do you figure?"

"That we should boot your inquiring little ass out of here."

"Oh. Do you mind if I sit down?"

"Does it matter?"

"No." She laughed nervously as she sat. "So what are you going to do with me?"

"I've decided to go with the wolf for now."

Jenn reached down and scratched Ginn between her ears. "Thanks. Is she really a wolf?"

"Some of her."

"Where does one go about getting a wolf these days?"

"Ginn's from the SPCA. She and two siblings were found tied to an old truck on a farm up river. They weren't much more than pups. They'd been starved and beaten…so much so that her brothers had to be put down."

"That's awful. How did she end up here?"

"Marie and I were dropping off some cat food when we heard the commotion in the back. I walked through and saw Ginn backed into one of the cages, eyes wide and teeth bared. Nobody could get near her. She was amazing. I loved the spirit, the savage beauty. I asked what they were going to do with her but I already knew the answer. I suggested she be turned loose in the wild but that wasn't an option so I volunteered to take her. There wasn't one person in that place that thought it was a good idea but they tranquilized and muzzled her and we brought her home. I had to agree to keep her contained and that I'd call them when I'd given up and they'd come out and take care of her. She lived in the storage shed for a month or so. I had to wear a padded suit just to go in and feed her. I must have spent hours talking while she growled and snapped at me. Eventually she came around. You should have seen her the first day she ran free. That alone was worth all the fear and bruises."

"She seems pretty docile now."

"But she's still wild by nature. I've been told I shouldn't trust her but I figure if she knows I do we'll get along fine."

"No kidding. You don't use a leash?"

"Tethering doesn't promote trust now does it?"

"I guess not. Has she ever tried to run away?"

"Never."

"I'd never leave here if I had a choice."

"You don't have a choice."

"I have the wolf on my side."

"For now."

Jenn stared at him. Not once had he taken his eyes off the river to look at her. His voice was calm and controlled but he seemed as nervous as she was, his legs keeping time to an unheard rhythm. "What did you talk about?" she asked.

"When?"

"You and Ginn…in the shed."

"Small-talk mostly. I read to her, sang some quiet songs. Why?"

"Just curious. So what did you sing?"

"Nursery rhymes, Beatles…anything that came to mind. Where are you going with this?"

"Nowhere really, I'm just trying to understand your other side. Pretty much all I've seen is guarded and a tad cranky."

"You think I'm cranky?"

She shrugged her shoulders. "A little, maybe."

"Sometimes I'm downright miserable."

"So I should appreciate cranky?"

He drew a deep breath. "Jennifer…do you understand what you're doing here?"

"Trying to get a degree?"

"No. Here…me. This part of me has been buried for nearly forty years. I'm living in peace in my own Eden then along comes some sweet thing that wants to blow it all up for personal gain."

"Gee, no wonder you're cranky. You think I'm sweet?"

"Ginn."

Ginn jumped to her feet.

"Mad face," Evan said quietly.

Instantly Ginn lowered her head and hunched her massive shoulders. With ears laid flat and teeth bared she growled a guttural growl, her cold blue eyes glaring at Jenn.

"Good girl." He reached and patted her head.

"Good girl?" Jenn screamed, "I just about pee my pants and she gets 'good girl'?"

"A little demonstration. As you said, everybody…every living thing has more than one side Jennifer. That other side is often the other side for a reason. Sometimes what you see is what you get and sometimes you shouldn't want what you don't see."

"Isn't this the part where the high priest or something sends Grasshopper out into the world to spread the word?"

"You really are becoming a source of frustration."

"I'm sorry Evan and you're right, I am doing this for personal gain. Tell me what you want."

"There's nothing you could possibly have that would equal what you want from me."

"So that's it? We're through? Make the wolf put on a mad face then throw me out? I've worked damn hard to get to this bench. I've mustered up more courage than I ever thought I had to come and talk to you. Let me tell you something Mister Evan Friggin' Morris…if that doesn't mean anything to you then you and your psycho wolf can go straight to hell!"

For the first time he turned to her, squinted then smiled. "Wow…that's what I wanted to see."

"So now you've seen it." Jenn glowered then stood. "Thanks for your time."

"Did I say I wanted you to leave?"

"Now who's being frustrating?"

He arched his back and stretched his arms forward. "Ask me some questions."

"What?"

"You're asking me to give up secrets that I've kept forever so you can get a degree. I'm putting a lot on the line and I need to know that you have the desire to see it through. I don't understand why but with certain parameters I'm prepared to give you some latitude here."

"Even after my little tirade?"

"Because of your little tirade."

She sat back down beside him. "Really?"

"It takes a lot of guts to blast me the way you just did. I figured you had it in you but I had to be sure. By the way, nicely done at the restaurant."

"What?"

"With the bottle."

"I studied a little psychology," she said shrugging her shoulders. "And let's face it, you weren't overly subtle. You should have expanded your borders by laying the newspaper out…less obtrusive and obvious."

He smiled. "Well Miss MacAvoy, it appears you may be a bit of a challenge."

"So you'll do the interview?"

"Consider this off the record. I assume you've prepared some questions?"

"Uh, yes…of course."

Evan dropped his head to one side, raised an eyebrow, and smiled at her. "Well?"

"Well what?"

"Questions?"

Jenn closed her eyes. Right or wrong she had to ask and now was the time. "Do you remember Claire Archer?" she blurted.

He straightened up and pulled his hat back off his eyes. "Okay, I didn't see that one coming. Yes I do, why?"

"She's my mum."

"You're Claire's daughter?"

"It usually works that way."

"I know, of course…I don't know what to say."

"You don't do a great interview Mister Morris." Jenn giggled.

He laughed a real laugh. "Maybe that's why I've been hiding all this time. Really? Claire's daughter?"

"Yeah, pretty freaky huh?"

"No kidding. How is your mum?"

"She's good. She asked me to say 'hello' if I managed to find you. Hello?"

"Hello back." He slowly shook his head. "Jennifer. That's her middle name."

"I know."

"Of course you do. I'm sorry, I'm just…" He looked closely at the beaming face before him. "That's why you seem so familiar, you have her eyes."

"That's what everyone says. I'm surprised you remember."

"I'll never forget."

"How well did you know her?"

"We were…close." He stood and offered his hand. "Let's walk the wolf. There's so much I want to ask you."

She took his hand and let him pull her to her feet. "Excuse me but isn't that my job?"

"Patience and understanding, remember? First, I'd really like to know how you got here."

They walked slowly down the steps to the beach, Jenn telling Evan what she had told Marie earlier.

"I can't believe Claire remembered the scar," he said as their feet sank into the sand.

Jenn shrugged her shoulders. "I think she remembers more than she tells. It kind of makes me want to dig. Then again maybe I shouldn't."

"You've worked hard to get here Jennifer. You should be proud of yourself."

"I'm not done yet. I still have to snag an interview with the mysterious Mister Morris."

"Think you will?"

"I don't know. He's making it as difficult as he possibly can."

Evan's eyes were drawn to a redheaded girl jogging past them near the water, her well-tanned young body barely clothed in a rainbow-colored bikini.

Jenn stopped and glared at him. "I saw that, you scoped her!"

"Just wondering where she keeps her cell phone."

"Certainly not where you were looking, I can't believe you did that!"

"All young ladies have cells these days. I'm merely curious."

"Give it up Evan…you just like looking at girls."

"I admit it." He smiled. "But it's the same with cars."

"What?"

"You know you can't get a new one but you always check out the latest models."

"So what's the verdict on the redhead?"

He donned a thoughtful expression. "Great options package, sporty."

"You're a dirty old man."

"I'm male, it's genetic predisposition." He grinned wickedly. "But yonder rainbow-rider is far too young."

"I thought you old, uh, older men liked young girls."

"At my age 'young' would be thirty-five."

"So what does that make me?"

"A child?"

"Thanks. So if a young girl, say that one, hit on you…you'd walk away?"

"The Marie factor aside, I don't really know. It hasn't happened in modern history. I must admit the thought is somewhat pleasant but unfortunately I don't have that kind of energy or stamina anymore." He lowered his gaze. "The official medical diagnosis is acute LOFS."

"What?"

"L-O-F-S, Lazy Old Fart Syndrome. I'll take a sleepy forty-year-old any day...not as much work."

"You really can be disgusting."

"It's part of my charm."

"That it is. So did you have to work at it back when?"

"No."

"That's it, a simple 'no'? Care to elaborate?"

Evan looked out over the river and smiled. "No."

Jenn stopped walking and began to laugh. "I can't believe I'm talking like this, and to my mother's old friend."

"Like what?"

"Just...talking. How did you and Mum meet?"

"I was doing a reading at the university coffee shop. She was with a male friend. He left...she didn't. I took his spot at her table and we talked until they kicked us out. We went to her room and chatted until dawn."

"Chatted?"

"Until dawn. Then I fell asleep on her couch."

Jenn picked up a small branch and tossed it for Ginn. "What did you talk about?"

"I don't remember. I was so captivated by your mother that it didn't matter."

"This was when?"

"1965."

"That was before the book?"

"About a year before the book, two before the album."

"But you just said you were doing a reading?"

"It was a casual drop-in scene. Anybody who wanted to take the stage could do so. I wrote my stuff long-hand on loose-leaf paper."

"Oh." Jenn kicked at a large piece of rusted metal protruding from the sand. "I can't believe the junk on this beach."

"Old truck," he said, "they're all along here, mostly still buried. Years ago someone decided to build a berm to help control the flooding. In some places they used flattened car bodies as a base.

I guess nobody thought of what would happen later on." He ran his fingers over the rust. "There's beauty here if you look for it."

"It's just rust."

"The textures and richness of the shades is nature's paint on a man-made canvas. If you learn to look you'll find beauty and form in everything...even this old Ford truck."

"Okay all I see are bits of crunched metal. How can you tell it was a Ford?"

He nodded toward the bank. "There's the tailgate."

"I guess that would be the 'learning to look' part."

"Observance is the key to everything." He pointed towards the river. "For example...."

Jenn looked down the beach and saw the rainbow redhead talking into her cell phone. "Okay, you win that one."

"I win more than I lose."

"I bet. What did she look like? Mum, I mean. I've seen pictures but it isn't the same."

"She was beautiful, the little turned-up nose and pouting lips...her long blonde hair falling freely about her shoulders. That night she wore a brown vest, suede I think, over a puffy-sleeved white blouse and the obligatory floral print peasant skirt."

"Child of the sixties."

"I sat at the table and just stared into her eyes. There was no other moment but that moment and nobody else in the world but her."

"Sounds like you were really smitten."

"Alas my smitteness was ill-fated."

"That can't be all there is to the story."

"Oh no, we were involved for a couple of years. We and another couple even did the drive to San Francisco that summer to see what the all fuss was about."

"Right, she has photos. Hey, you might be in some of them!"

"Probably. She really got wrapped up in the whole scene. I on the other hand did a lot of shopping."

"Shopping? You're in San Francisco at the height of hippiedom and you shopped?"

"Mostly all I saw was a bunch of kids with no ambition and a lame excuse to get high and make out in the park. It certainly wasn't the campfires and kumbaya we'd heard about."

"Tell me more?"

"Another time."

Jenn wondered if he was already shutting the door or just setting out the guidelines; giving just what he wanted, when he wanted. He too was going to be a challenge.

They talked little on the way back to the house, mostly comments about rising water levels and pine beetle devastation. Suddenly he clapped his hands then chased Ginn along the sand and up the steps. Their relationship was interesting. The savage beast tamed by...what? Jenn didn't understand it but she felt it.

By the time she got into the yard Evan was already in a chair on the porch, his feet up on the railing. Ginn turned circles in the grass before settling in for a nap.

"What took you so long?" Evan asked as Jenn sat on the couch opposite him.

"I wasn't chasing a wolf."

"Next time we'll let the wolf chase you."

"No, that's okay..." Her attention was drawn to a distant dog howl. "A wavering voice drifted across the river," she recited, "blending yet distinctive..."

"Like an oboe in a symphony," Evan added. "You really have done your homework."

"I've spent many an evening reading your stuff," she said quietly, her gaze drifting across the yard. "I love this place but I guess I should be heading home."

"Stay for dinner...Marie works wonders with dead cow."

"Sounds yummy." Jenn glanced at Pokey at the bottom of the steps. "She tells me you made those little guys?"

"Yup. Store-bought gnomes are like...so Monday."

"What about the dragon at the gate?"

"Uh huh. If you go on a hunt you'll find all kinds of lizards, frogs, and snakes around the yard."

"But they're all made out of clay, right?"

"Right...except for the snakes."

"They're real?"

"No, mostly."

"But some are?"

"Yup. Just like Bert and Cummings."

"And they would be?"

"Bats."

"Bats?"

"Up there, to your left." He pointed to a dark recess in the corner of the porch roof.

Jenn turned cautiously and squinted into the shadows. "They're alive?"

"Last I checked."

"You think maybe Marie needs a hand with dinner?"

He laughed. "Perhaps you'd better go find out."

Chapter 10

Marie didn't turn as she worked at the kitchen counter. "So, did you get him?"

"I still don't know…" Jenn leaned against the pantry. "But he did invite me to dinner."

"That's a start."

"Need a hand?"

"You could set the table if you like," Marie said, dropping a handful of green beans into a saucepan. "Cutlery is in the drawer on the left."

"Sure smells good." Jenn crossed the kitchen and opened the drawer. "I haven't had home-cooked since I moved here."

"Evan likes his roast and potatoes."

"And bats."

"Oh, you met the happy couple?"

"How do you know they're happy?"

"They're bats, what do they have to be pissed-off about?"

Jenn stopped counting out silverware and giggled. "I just got it!"

"What?"

"Bert and Cummings. This place is bizarre."

"My dear 'tis not the place, 'tis the laird."

"No kidding. You have snakes out here?"

"Not as often since Ginn's been on patrol but occasionally one sneaks past her."

"He set her on me you know."

Marie smiled. "Yes, I saw that."

"You could've come and helped."

"You didn't need any help Jenn, you're in. Peter...Evan doesn't usually let anyone get as close to him as you already have."

"Yeah? Why?"

"Big question. He works mostly on feelings and he told me that you felt right to him. He's an extremely private person...a quiet person, but if the feelings are good you'll catch glimpses of the other sides. He usually only lets people see what he calls 'show time'...presenting only what's expected of him and nothing more."

"We talked about sides when we weren't analyzing bikinis."

"Has he figured out where they hide those cell phones?"

Jenn laughed. "No, he's going to have to keep working on that one I'm afraid."

"Oh the burden he bears in the name of science. I gather you asked about your mum?"

Jenn placed the last setting on the table. "Yes."

"And?"

"Marie...I'm not sure I want to talk about this."

"It's okay Jenn. I know more than you think, probably more than he thinks, but I shouldn't say anything. It really is up to him to tell you what he wants to tell you."

"You didn't know Mum?"

"No, she was before my time. Most of what you're looking for happened before I knew him."

"How did you meet?"

"My parents ran a motel on the highway coming into town. I'd spell dad off on the desk so he could eat or watch a hockey game. Evan checked in late one night and asked where he could get a decent dinner. I told him and he invited me to come along."

"That's it?"

"Pretty much. Dad took over behind the desk then Evan and I walked across the parking lot to the restaurant."

"Your dad was okay with you leaving with this stranger?"

"I was twenty-one at the time so he couldn't really say anything although he certainly wanted to."

"He didn't like Evan?"

"Lord no. The first impression definitely set the stage. Evan was wearing this floppy grey hat with a white shirt, black jeans and longcoat. He had a droopy moustache and about a week's worth of beard. I was quite taken by the mystery man but he really did look like the evil priest in a Gothic horror movie. Dad and the 'God-damned long-haired hippie' really didn't get along back then. Evan tried but dad wanted none of it."

"Did they ever sort it out?"

Marie smiled, shaking her head. "Evan eventually became the son he never had. It was incredible, much like the taming of Ginn. I honestly don't know what turned it around."

"Maybe he sang your dad some nursery rhymes?"

"Yeah, right."

"There's something I'd like to ask you…you don't have to answer though."

"Sounds interesting."

"'Last Night with Marie' was in the book that my mum gave me. According to what Evan just said the book was released while he and Mum knew each other so I can't figure out how you were in it."

"You are a thinker. Your copy must be the second printing. The publisher added some pages so I was sort of an afterthought. He and your mum had parted ways before we met, I assure you." She checked her watch. "Let's get this meal over with. I have book club tonight."

"At least you've got something to look forward to. I've got a laundry and cleaning day tomorrow, whoopee."

"No classes?"

"Not until Monday. I'm hoping to get all the chores done then kick back for three days and maybe try to nail Evan down for my project."

"You could kick back here Jenn, we've a spare room. Now that Evan knows you're Claire's daughter I'm sure he'd enjoy having you around. It might be easier to get him to talk if you're in his face for a few days."

"Maybe. I can't think of a nicer place to relax." She bit her lip. "What about you Marie? Are you okay with me staying here?"

"I wouldn't have suggested it if I wasn't."

Chapter 11

Jenn entered his study with trepidation. The door was open after all. If he minded company then he'd close it. Still she hesitated before stepping further into the room.

The green glow from the shade of his desk lamp just added to the antiquity of the scene before her. The myriad of shelves containing books, records, toys and Lord knows what else surrounded a large desk in the middle of the room.

Behind the bankers light he tapped quickly on the keyboard of a laptop. With his long grey hair and glasses he presented the impression of a candlelit wizard hiding behind his book of spells, shrouded in darkness. She stared at him. He looked different now than he did at the restaurant. His blue eyes had lost the chill that greeted her that first time yet she still felt unsettled.

"Come in Jennifer," he whispered without looking up. "There's a comfy chair just waiting for you to curl up in." His voice was quiet, yet commanding rather than inviting. He stroked his unshaven chin. She heard the 'scritching' from across the room.

Slowly approaching him Jenn felt like a schoolgirl called to the principal's office. "The only other person to call me Jennifer was my grandfather," she softly said.

"A man of obvious breeding." He shook his index finger at her. "Jennifer MacAvoy. Now that…is a writer's name."

Her eyes tried to take in all there was but as she found her way to the large leather armchair in front of his desk she realized it was impossible. Souvenirs and mementos of his life cluttered every corner.

"Marie's off to her book club," she said, snuggling into the deep padding. "Man, it's like a flea market in here. Do you always wear flannel shirts?"

"Do you ever board a long train of thought?"

"Mum wonders pretty much the same thing. So...the shirts?"

"They make me feel pretty."

"They make you look like a lumberjack."

"Ah, but a pretty lumberjack. No, I don't always wear them. I usually grab whatever's closest in the closet."

"Ah yes, the dreaded LOFS." She caught the fragrance again. "Is that a vanilla I smell?"

"Tobacco. I confess to relaxing with a pipe-full and a glass of wine occasionally." He brought his elbows to the top of the desk, rested his chin in his hands and peered at her over his glasses. "What's up?"

"Marie suggested I stay here for a couple of days. Are you okay with that?"

"Of course."

"That was easy."

"It was an easy question." His tone was suddenly lighter.

"Okay then," Jenn said, "I'll come back tomorrow prepared to stay awhile."

As he leaned back in the chair she noticed a leather strand around his neck. Hanging from it was a pendant; a bird with turquoise and silver wings spread. She studied the detail. "That's really nice. Navaho?"

He lifted the pendant. "Damned if I know. We found it buried in the sand on a beach...California somewhere."

"We?"

"Your mum and I."

"Quite a find. Do you always wear it?"

"No. I'd tossed it in the drawer years ago. I uncovered it tonight while I was looking for something else."

"So you've found it twice. That must be some sort of lucky sign?"

"Must be. Let us compare accessories. That collar...your mum's?"

"One similar to it. You remember hers?"

He closed his eyes and sighed softly. "Yes, I remember."

Jenn rested her head on the back of the chair. "I'm beat. This whole experience has been draining."

"I imagine it has."

"Do you realize how strange this is?"

"For both of us."

"I mean you could have been my father."

He keyed 'save' on the computer then clicked 'shut down'. "It wasn't meant to happen that way."

"How do you know?"

"Because it didn't."

"Right, I guess." She watched him close the screen on his laptop. "How much does Marie know about you and Mum?" she asked.

"Everything I told her."

"And did you tell her everything?"

"I don't remember…probably. She and I had a history cleansing one night over a bottle of wine. We talked at length about those from before. Claire is part of that history."

"I'm not sure I could do that…tell my husband about old boyfriends."

"But those old relationships are part of who you are now."

"Everything is part of who I am now."

"True."

"Say something long?"

"Long? What do you mean?"

"You have such a pleasant voice. It makes me feel comfortable. Please?"

Evan rolled his chair back, cupped his hands behind his neck and looked up. "Then kneeling by the gentle stream she'd whisper all her rhymes and dreams to swans that sparkled in the sun while birds no bigger than her thumb started here then darted there then quickly flew to who knows where."

Jenn promptly raised her hand. "And somewhere in the darkened woods a sleepy dragon yawned and stretched and then with dragonly disdain he closed his eyes to sleep again. He'd studied her with some regard and though he'd much prefer her charred, the energy that it would take to simply bring her to a bake was much more than this snoozy beast could spare." She smiled proudly. "'And She Sang'... I love that one."

Evan smirked. "And you memorized it. I'm both impressed and flattered."

"And surprised?"

"Not really. I believe that you're a pretty amazing young lady...your mother's daughter."

"Does that mean you like me maybe a little bit?"

"Maybe a little bit."

"Enough to give me the interview?"

"Enough."

Chapter 12

"Good morning," Marie said as Evan walked into the kitchen. "I'd turn around and go get dressed if I were you. Jenn just pulled into the driveway."

"What…already?"

"You said she was persistent. I'm guessing that talking to you trumps doing laundry."

He pulled a mug from the dishwasher. "I'm honored."

"She seems nice?"

He grunted then lifted the carafe from the coffee maker. "Is that a new shirt?"

"One of your old ones." Marie glanced out the window then back across at Evan as he opened the fridge door and reached out the cream. "At the path?" she said.

He put the jug away and let the door slowly close. "I had a pink shirt?"

"No, it was white. You washed it with your red socks."

"I have red socks?" he asked, stirring sugar into the coffee. "Where are they?"

"In my sock drawer. You never wear them anyway."

"Why would I…I didn't know I had them."

Marie looked out the window again. "Bottom of the steps?"

"Christ she walks fast," he mumbled. "Can I have my socks back?"

"No. Are you actually intending to flash the poor little thing?"

Evan muttered under his breath as he quickly walked down the hallway to the bedroom. He stepped into a clean pair of jeans and reached into the closet. Flannel was again closest.

Not today.

He searched until he found a black T-shirt with 'Let It Be' lettered in white above a line-art Arctic wolf. He pulled it on then sat on the end of the bed.

Claire's daughter. Freaky wasn't the word. How much should he tell her? How much would Claire want him to tell her?

Jennifer. How so like her mother she was. That look on the beach with the sun hugging her face and the wind tickling her hair was the same look he'd seen on another beach in California so many years ago. His angel of the bay. Her smiles and laughter were once again so close yet so far away. With each memory the emotions also returned. He felt the tingling on his flesh and a warm emptiness inside. This was not going to be easy.

He stood and glanced a casual glance in the mirror then grinned. "Lord it's hard to be humble," he sang to himself.

After a quick stop in the bathroom to harvest the stubble on his cheeks and chin, he was prepared to face his yesterdays.

Jenn was already sitting at the dinette when he walked back into the kitchen. "Good day sunshine," he mumbled, sitting across from her.

Jenn smiled. "Wow, black...you dressed up for me."

"You're half right," Marie said. "Now if you two will excuse me I have to go pluck a few weeds before it gets too hot." As she passed Evan she ran her hand down his cheek. "I see you did the same?"

Jenn stared at him as he sipped his coffee. The morning sun accented the lines of life scattered across his face. For the first time she saw his age. "How are you?" she asked.

"Mmm...."

"Marie just told me you have a couple of grandkids?"

He set the mug on the table. "So does she."

"Uh-huh. So do you feel like a grandpa?"

"No but every once in a while I feel like a grandma."

"I just keep tossing you the straights don't I?"

He smiled. "Yup."

"Not a morning person?"

He shrugged his shoulders and squinted into the back yard.

Jenn started to stand. "Okay. I'll go help Marie with the weeds."

Evan looked back into her eyes. "You haven't mentioned your father or any siblings in our chats."

"I didn't really think about it," she said, sitting again. "My brother Justin is thirty-six, my sister Donna is thirty-four. Dad's retired from his own law office. Need more?"

"I'm sorry I don't mean to interrogate you Jennifer, I'm just curious."

"That's okay. She did all right Evan."

"I'm happy for her, even if she did marry into the establishment."

"Oh Dad's one of those defenders of the down-trodden types, loved taking on the system. He was pretty good at it too although he worked for a helluva lot less money than his peers."

"Good for him." Evan grinned. "Somehow that fits." He lifted himself out of the chair and ambled to the sink. "Maybe you could go give Marie a hand. I'm going to take Ginn for a stroll and when I get back we'll talk about this interview."

"Sounds good." She stood and walked to the door then turned. "Thanks Evan, you don't know how much this means to me."

He nodded at her. "I think I do."

Chapter 13

Jenn studied a small pile of plaster pieces encircled by plastic flowers in front of a white-rock cairn, obvious remnants of a squirrel figurine. "What happened to this poor li'l guy?" she asked.

Marie looked to where Jenn was pointing then grinned. "The Wilkinsons supposedly had a squirrel problem in their yard so they got one of those plastic owls and sat it on the fence between the houses, like that would fool them. Evan hated that thing to no end so he bought a squirrel lawn ornament. One night he snuck out here and parked it beside the owl. Six o'clock the next morning we hear this loud crack and look out the window. The owl was swinging off its perch and the squirrel was nowhere to be seen. The old man had somehow managed to put a bullet through both of them. The owl just split in two but the squirrel exploded. Evan kept finding pieces of the deceased all over the lawn. He felt that a shrine was in order, even wrote a eulogy for the ceremony."

"He's twisted you know."

"I know."

"Does the old man still have his gun?"

"He died a number of years ago."

"Oh. Does his wife still have his gun?"

Marie giggled. "No fear, the cops confiscated it after the massacre. Besides if she did Evan would have been down there beside the squirrel long ago."

"Doesn't like him much?"

"Not in the beginning but after the old man died Evan helped her around the yard. One night just after we got Ginn she set up this terrible howling and wasn't about to settle down for anyone. Marion came over the next morning to complain and said if it happened again she'd call the cops. Evan gave her a copy of his book and signed it 'to my dearest neighbor'. He asked her to keep his secret and a secret is a sacred bond, or that's how he put it."

"Buddies ever since?"

"He's her second favorite old hippie. Every so often the two of them have a long visit. Evan just lets her go on and on about her husband…how he was so into the beads and flowers."

"She's probably lonely." Jenn held up a plant. "This is bad, right?"

"That's why he does it. Wrong."

"Sorry. Does Evan do any of this…the weeding and stuff?"

"He mows the lawn and he did a bit of weeding when it was vegetables but flowers, not so much. He figures they're just weeds that caught a break from society."

"Is there anything he's done in the last forty years I shouldn't ask him about?"

"Now that's a confusing question."

"I guess it is. Marie, I still have no idea how I'm going to do this."

"Isn't that what you paid good money to learn?"

"Of course and in theory it's simple but Evan isn't making it that way. I can't get an angle on how to approach this. Every time we talk it's like he's a different person."

"You have no idea how many times I've wanted to turn him upside down and give him a shake to see how many people fall out. That's Evan."

"He's that complex?"

Marie laughed. "He's a lot of things but 'complex' isn't one of them. He's probably the easiest man to figure out."

"How so?"

"Evan likes the simpler stuff. Cheese is cheddar and coffee is coffee…none of that frothy crap they serve up these days. His idea of continental cuisine is cruising the drive-through in a Lincoln. He has no airs about him whatsoever when he's on his own time."

"What you see is what you get?"

"Not exactly. There are people who've only seen the serious, quiet side and others who think he's a stand-up comic. What he wants you to see is what you get."

"What does he want me to see?"

"I have no idea. As I said yesterday, don't push it. Let him map it out for you."

"He'll do that?"

"He's already started."

Jenn held up another plant. "Bad?"

"That one is." Marie pointed to Jenn's feet. "The one you're standing on isn't."

"Oh." She stepped back. "What do you mean he's already started?"

"You being out here chatting with me?"

"He planned that?"

"Not planned but an exercise of convenience. He probably figured you'd ask me some questions to get a bit of an idea of how to do this…a little background."

"So I really am in?"

"You're in Jenn."

Chapter 14

Evan sat at the bottom of the steps leading from the beach up into the yard. Beside him Ginn was digging in the sand for whatever it is that wolves dig for. He heard Jennifer and Marie chatting and laughing in the garden above. No doubt he was part of the banter but that was okay.

In fact it was good.

Jennifer brought a lightness that had been absent in his life. Not that there was anything wrong with his world, simply that something was missing. Her being Claire's daughter only added to the good feelings he was experiencing.

His memories of Claire were warm and filling. He smiled when he recalled the trip to the stock car races in Boise that ended with an impromptu and chaotic romp to San Francisco. He'd reminisced about that adventure often but not recently.

"That was fun," Jack had said as the aroma of oil and rubber still filled the night air. "What say we go eat?"

"What say we all go to California?" Claire shouted, "San Francisco!"

There was a moment of silence while three other minds fought to process the notion.

"Surely there's a restaurant closer." Andy finally quipped.

Claire pushed. "Aw come on guys, we're halfway there already."

"True," Jack said. "Why don't we find one of those closer restaurants and discuss this."

They climbed into the van, drove to the highway then pulled in at a roadside diner. The parking lot was lit by a row of yellow bug bulbs along the twisted rain gutter providing a warm if somewhat jaundiced environment in which to make this potentially life-altering decision.

"Okay," Evan said, "let's get a burger and then decide what we're going to do. When we come out we'll either go north and head home or west to San Francisco."

The red vinyl bench of the booth was scarred in random duct tape patterns, the blended bouquet of grease and onions hung heavily in the air and Roy Orbison was 'Crying' softly in the background. Evan had wanted to plug the jukebox but an 'Out of Order' sign was taped to the shattered rounded glass. Life's musical score was being provided by a turquoise and gold plastic radio that sat above the cash register.

The diner was typical of the day, as was Doris. The waitress appeared haggard as she shuffled across the plank-wood floor to their booth. A long strand of black hair, obviously tired of the teasing, hung down the right side of her face drawing attention to her pale make-up and blue eye shadow. The form-fitting white uniform highlighted a body that had seen better days although Evan figured she couldn't have been much older than he was. They each ordered a burger and cola and added two sides of fries to share.

The four of them sat under the buzzing pink neon 'OPEN' sign counting their money and calculating the odds of survival while crazy George screamed about his 'Saturday Morning Madness clearance on overstocked used cars' on the radio.

Going home had been the leaning but about the time that Andy and Jack were fighting over the last french fry Doris heard the Mama's and Papa's and turned up the volume. They all joined in singing 'California Dreamin'' and in the end, even though it made no sense to any of them, they headed west. The battered old baby-blue Econoline that would provide their transportation and accommodation had been held together by rust and ran on faith but it got them to the heart of the Sixties culture.

A book could be written about that experience but words are hearsay, even if authored by someone who was there.

The only way to really be there was to be there.

And they were, for one brief week during the summer of 1967.

The summer of love.

He had told Jennifer about the laze-abouts and losers but there were some lovely people too…with flowers in their hair. Claire was one of them.

She could have been the poster child of the times. They all wore the uniform but few bore the attitude. Flowers, peasant dresses, and the obligatory long hair were in abundance but the essence of that moment was discriminating, choosing only a select few to feel the real magic. Not many believed as Claire believed.

Not many loved as Claire loved.

And now her daughter was stirring her own magical concoction. He drew a deep breath then stood and climbed the steps.

"Where's Ginn?" Marie asked as Evan wandered into the garden.

"Digging for her peace of mind," he mumbled. "Jennifer, let's take a ride."

Jenn stood and brushed the dirt from her hands. "Am I allowed to ask where?"

"Yes, but it will count as one of your interview questions."

"Okay, I won't ask." She looked at Marie questioningly.

Marie shrugged her shoulders and continued gardening.

Chapter 15

Evan said little as they drove downtown, mostly small talk…comments about the traffic or the height of the river. He seemed distracted and distant yet calm.

Jenn was letting him lead, as Marie had suggested but she grew increasingly uncomfortable until he finally pulled into a parking spot at Riverside Park.

He turned off the engine. "Here is where Marie and I decided to get married."

"Okay," Jenn whispered.

"I'm telling you this because…I honestly don't know why I'm telling you this."

"Evan…."

"Let's walk."

They climbed out of the Land Rover and walked toward the trees.

Evan pointed to the river. "By the pier there's a bench that overlooks the swimming area. That bench could be my tombstone, as Evan Morris. It was there I decided to slip away, to put myself behind me." His eyes were drawn to a movement on his right. "You're about to meet Annie," he quietly said, nodding towards a figure sitting at the edge of the park. "She's basically harmless."

Nobody knew her real name but Annie and her rusted shopping cart filled with boxed and green-bagged treasures were fixtures in this part of town. She sat hunched on the concrete barrier at the exit of the parking lot, leering through thick black-rimmed glasses. Her head darted from side to side like a paranoid crow protecting fresh road kill. Atop a mop of frizzled blond hair sat a large straw hat decorated with artificial flowers of every description.

Her hands searched frantically through the pockets of a tattered yellow nylon jacket while between her lips an unlit cigarette bobbed, emphasizing unheard words to invisible listeners. She had company in her world, albeit ghostly figures from her fifty-something past or new spirits seen by only the lonely. She found her lighter and with shaking hands touched the flame to the end of the cigarette, took a deep breath and smiled a quizzical, contented smile. Then she saw them and waved.

"Evan," she shouted. "Spare some?"

He reached into his pocket and pulled out a five-dollar bill. "Annie," he said, "this is Jennifer."

Annie squinted into the sun. "My God man, she's just a child! Does your wife know about this little thing?"

"Yes she does." Jenn smiled. "Hello Annie, how are you?"

"Been better, been worse…been second, been first."

Evan handed her the money and patted her shoulder. "We're off on a bit of a walk. We might see you later?"

Annie slipped the banknote into her shirt pocket. "Doubt it…I've got things to do. Nice seeing you Jennifer."

"Likewise Annie," Jenn called over her shoulder as Evan guided her into the park. He led her to a bench overlooking the spot where the North and South Thompson Rivers met.

"Right here," he said.

"What?"

"Marie and I. She saw it as some sort of spiritual sign, to decide to get married right here where the rivers join. We sat on this bench and watched…"

"Wait," Jenn interrupted. "She called you 'Evan'."

"Pardon?"

"Annie…she called you 'Evan'."

"That's my name isn't it?"

"But it's a secret."

He shrugged his shoulders. "Obviously not much of one…did you hear anything I said?"

"Yes, rivers join, sign, Marie…how does Annie know who you are?"

"I told her."

"Before or after you were Peter?"

"After. It wasn't that long ago actually. I was at a thrift shop checking out old vinyl and I found a copy of my record. Fifty-cents. That's what it cost me to catch the bus to and from the studio back then. At first I was pretty pissed but when I took a look at the wear on the groove…somebody had played that sucker a lot. It's like the book. I've managed to find a half-dozen copies at yard sales, flea markets and used book shops. The more beaten and dog-eared they are the better I feel. Does that make sense?"

"Of course, but Annie?"

"She was looking at puzzles or something on the opposite side of the aisle. I flipped the album to check out the back and she saw the picture." He looked down at Jenn and grinned. "She took it from me, tore it right out of my hands. She told me that she used to have one but she'd lost it somewhere along the way. She even had it signed by 'Mister Morris' at the record store."

"Your whole life is the Twilight Zone."

"I told her I was Evan Morris. She didn't believe me so I showed her my driver's license, bought her the record and signed it for her."

"That was nice."

"'To my youngest fan, luv ya…Evan'. Apparently that was how I signed it back then."

"You don't remember signing it for her?"

"It was in the middle of the promo tour and I had been to every book and record shop in every town and city in the province. It's all just a blur but of all the signings I do feel badly about not remembering that one."

"You would." Jenn stood beside him then they started to walk across the grass toward the beach. "Your driver's license says 'Evan Morris'?"

"All my ID does. Legally that's who I am. I registered Peter Michaelson as a company and just started using that name. Marie still goes by 'Morris'."

"So you really haven't tried to hide."

"Maybe just a little."

"Do you mind if I use this?" She held up a hand-recorder. "It's okay if you'd rather I didn't."

"No that's fine. It's pretty tough to write and walk at the same time. That's why I've got one of those. I'm not a big believer in multi-tasking. Walking, breathing and…that's about it. I trust you'll sort through the material and use only what's pertinent to your assignment?"

"Yes of course, but I'll still let you read the final draft, okay?"

"Okay."

She pressed the 'start' button and held the machine between them. "You called the bench Evan Morris's tombstone. Why did he have to die?"

"Direct and to the point, I like that…but I don't really know the answer."

"I have a theory that it was Marie. The call of love was stronger and won out over the fame."

"Fame? I was a long way from it, but I suppose that would be a romanticist's view. Alas 'twas not beauty that killed the beast but the winter in Saskatoon. I woke up one morning in my hotel room and realized I was alone and had been for three months. I'd drive all day, grab some supper, do my shtick then get a few hours sleep and do it all over again. I looked down on the parking lot and saw the old van covered in snow. I knew what little money I was going to make that evening would be diminished greatly by a battery boost. I'd already had enough of the life so I decided to play out my obligations and go home."

"That doesn't answer my question. You didn't have to disappear."

"Probably not but I felt it was important to totally separate my lives."

"And Marie agreed?"

"Hell no, she was against it from the start. She still goes on at me about it. That's why she likes you…she has an ally."

"I like her too but I'd rather not be in the middle."

"I'm not sure there are two sides for you to be in the middle of anymore."

"You said you went home but Kamloops wasn't home was it?"

"No." He reached his arm across her shoulder and pulled her close. "But your mum and I had parted a month before I left on the tour. There wasn't anything left for me in Edmonton so I turned southwest and kept driving until I ended up here."

She tensed as she felt his arm tighten around her. "In an interview you credited Marie with your inspiration."

"That's right. She was working at the motel that I checked into during the first month of the tour. I wrote 'Last Night with Marie' while I was here. When I called the publisher to see how things were going he said they'd be running another five hundred books. He asked if I had enough material to add a flat to the next printing and I did. Some of the newer stuff was inspired by Marie."

Jenn nodded. "Was my mum any part of that?"

"Pretty much the whole first printing."

"So why did you two break up?"

"Like I said I think it was more a parting of the ways. We just didn't seem to be able to synchronize our idiosyncrasies. We split as friends and I'd like to think that on some level we still are. I wish I'd kept in touch."

"I would have liked that too. Did you ever try to get back together?"

He paused. "That would have to be a secret."

"Trust me?" She turned off the recorder.

"I phoned her a few times the first year. With each call the distance seemed to grow longer."

"You were with Marie at the time?"

"Technically, yes. Nothing in stone as they say, but I'm not sure she'd like to hear about it."

"I won't say anything, promise."

"I know."

Evan rambled on about geese as they walked the path along the rivers edge. Jenn chose to just listen and enjoy the moment. His arm across her shoulders felt a little more comfortable now but she was still unsure of what he was thinking. They had to climb the pedestrian bridge over the railway yards to get to downtown. At the top of the tall yellow structure Evan stopped to watch the train shunting below. Jenn had kept walking and was sitting at the bottom of the steps reviewing what she had recorded when he caught up to her.

"Little boys and trains," she said. "Never grew up?"

"Nope, growing up is the first step to growing old."

"Sooner or later we have to do both."

"If that's the way you feel then that's the way it'll be."

"Do I have a choice?"

"Of course you do. Right now I choose to be twenty-five."

She smirked. "Funny, you don't look it."

"But I am."

"And the reason would be?"

"Sure I'm physically sixty." He touched his chest. "But in here it doesn't count for much. When I turned sixty, fifty-nine didn't disappear. It'll always be part of who I am. Every year I've lived is buried somewhere in this battered old body which means I'm still fifty-nine, and forty and thirty and twenty…"

"Stop, I get it!" Jenn laughed as she stood to continue their walk. "So you've decided that it's a twenty-five day?"

"That I have." He put his hand on her shoulder again.

"Okay." She nudged him lightly with her elbow. "Then I choose to be fourteen and you're flirting with trouble young man."

He quickly dropped his arm to his side. "I'm sorry. I hope I didn't make you uncomfortable."

"A little, but it's okay… I don't plan on being fourteen forever."

Chapter 16

Evan admired the way Jennifer had put him in his place although he still felt embarrassed as they crossed Lansdowne Street and strolled up Third Avenue. She was definitely Claire's little girl.

She turned on the recorder and held it towards him. "What have you been doing all this time?"

"I've tackled pretty much everything from construction to telemarketing. The money from the initial sales bought us the house so we really only needed enough to live on."

"You made enough to buy a house?"

"A shack would be more accurate. After all these years it's finally the way I want it. We were out in the country back then…it was pretty cheap."

"But lately it's been the photography?"

"Mostly."

"Did you ever think about going back to writing?"

"Never stopped."

"Thinking or writing?"

"They tend to go together."

"Like Bert and Cummings?"

"Like. I wrote a lifestyle column for the local paper for a couple of years, a few magazine articles…I've kept busy."

Jenn clicked the recorder off. "I phoned Mum last night. She asked about you, how you were doing yadda, yadda."

"I trust you told her I was still the energetic robust stud she fell in love with?"

"Sure, something like that. I didn't realize how involved you two were."

"What did she say?"

"Nothing really, it was in her voice. You said 'she fell in love with'...did she?"

"Yeah." He paused, looking into her eyes. "How about a cold drink?"

"Sounds good."

They stepped through the opening in the green metal fence surrounding the sidewalk tables where they had first met and sat in the same place. Evan pulled his hat back off his eyes. "God it's bright out there," he moaned.

Jenn placed the recorder on the table. "Tell me about those days?"

"A lot of what you hear is mythology. Sure there were good times...plenty of them. But the sixties were also about segregation, assassinations, Vietnam, civil disobedience...it wasn't all flowers and love."

The server stopped at their table and asked Jenn what she wanted.

"Would a beer be okay?" she looked at Evan.

"Two would be better, thanks Tara." He smiled at Jenn. "You don't need my permission."

"Okay. Seriously Evan, I think the way to try to understand you would be to understand the environment that created you."

He lowered his gaze to a coaster on the table and smiled. "The sixties didn't create people...people created the sixties. To really understand you have to go back to the fifties. Elvis had almost as much to do with creating the atmosphere and attitudes of the sixties as Dylan did but in my opinion James Dean was the one that kick-started the whole revolution."

"James Dean?"

"Rebel Without A Cause?"

"No, I know James Dean but how was he responsible for anything to do with the sixties?"

"Until 'Rebel' everything was pretty much Beaver Cleaver."

"Excuse me?"

"A television series, 'Leave It to Beaver'. It depicted the sterile American family with hair always in place…apple pie cooling on the sill and such perfect children. The only thing vaguely resembling rebellion was Eddie Haskell and he was just an idiot. All the shows were like that. Then along came James. It was like he gave permission for kids to have opinions and emotions. It was okay to stand up to your parents or society in general and say what you thought."

"Thanks," Jenn said as two bottles were set before them.

Evan traced a line in the condensation that formed when the cold bottle hit the heat of the day. "You have to remember that what most people cherish as the 'love' part of the sixties was actually only from about 1966 to 1969. That was the time for peace and spirituality. The first half of the decade was a sociological and cultural stew. The peace movement started in there somewhere but it wasn't as much about love as it was protest. Everything was experimental from ideologies to drugs, music to art. Gently stir in JFK, the war, riots, and dead students then simmer for a few years and low and behold…enlightenment is served to all those eager to feast."

"I sense sarcasm."

"A little. Do you drink at home?" He tilted the bottle and sipped.

"Mum let me have wine at Christmas from the time I was about sixteen. What about drugs?"

"No, but I know a guy or three."

"Not me, ever. I was wondering…you know?"

"Twice. Once on the San Francisco trip then once back home."

"It didn't open up those creative floodgates?"

Evan laughed out loud. "Christ no. I felt sick and my knees wouldn't work…what a waste."

"No bells and lights, no revelations?"

"Just the realization that it was all pretty useless."

"Mum?"

"Other than those times I don't think so." He lifted the beer. "This on the other hand…."

"Mum's more of a wine drinker now."

"Actually she was then too." He leaned toward her and whispered, "We both preferred a bottle of white and strip checkers to a case of beer and naked Twister."

"It sounds like there was a lot more to this romance than I've been lead to believe."

"Sounds like."

"What's your favorite colour?" Jenn asked sheepishly.

"Is this the start of the in-depth interview?"

"Change of topic mostly."

"Blue, I suppose."

"But that's so ordinary."

"No," Evan said, "taupe is ordinary. Blue is classic…Blue Velvet, Blue Eyes Cryin' in the Rain, Moody Blue, Blue Moon…"

"Okay…On Taupe Of Old Smoky?"

"Uh huh…"

"Taupe Gun, or that mouse from Ed Sullivan Taupe-O-Gigio?"

"Ed Sullivan?"

"Golden Days on Sunday afternoon television."

He gazed across the table. She was more like Claire than he needed her to be. The smile, the eyes, her quickness and spirit had all been handed down. Jenn exuded everything that had attracted him to her mother all those years ago and she was making it too easy to slip back. The disconcerting part was how comfortable he felt with her and the unsettling feeling that she was growing more at ease with him. Generations separated them yet something was bringing them together.

Jenn looked up and caught his stare. "You okay? You look a million miles away."

"A million years maybe. Drink up…it's time to move on."

Evan handed Tara a ten-dollar bill, pulled the brim of his hat to his eyes then stood and guided Jenn to the sidewalk and back toward Third Avenue.

She had to slow her pace to stay beside him. "You don't hurry for anything do you?"

"No need, it'll still be there."

"What will?"

"Everything…anything. If it isn't I didn't really need it anyway."

"This trip to Frisco, tell me more."

"First of all it's San Francisco or simply 'the City'. The natives used to get touchy if you called it 'Frisco'. It was our first road trip together, first of many." He smiled, picturing the four of them. "Jack, Andy, Claire, and Evan on the road to who knew where and who really cared?"

"Jack and Andy? Three guys and my mum?"

"Jack and Andrea. They eventually married, until death did them part."

"That's right, sorry. Tell me more about the trip."

"We'd gone to the races in Boise with the intention of finding a campsite and heading home the next morning. Then your free-spirited mum suggested we go to San Francisco."

"It was her idea?"

"Yeah, she fit into the whole culture thing pretty well, better than the rest of us. As we drove along the highway we realized we had no idea where we were going or what we were doing. When we crossed the California state line we stopped and picked up this turnpike troubadour and his lady."

"Turnpike troubadour?"

"Kids who'd hit the road with their guitars, bongos or flutes…they'd busk in every town along the way earning money to get them to Utopia. Between towns they hitched rides. Charlie was his name, he played flute and Beth played cute and tambourine. They were standing by the road, him fluting away and Beth sitting on an old battered suitcase with a 'Take Us To Heaven' sign taped to it. I remember she was wearing this heavy purple velvet skirt that was probably curtains in better days. He wore brown cords with a white shirt and sheepskin vest. I was surprised they hadn't passed out. It was the middle of June and at least ninety degrees."

While they were stopped for the light on Third Avenue Evan overheard two seniors on sidewalk scooters comparing the options and power of their rides in much the same way as they might have fifty years ago. He imagined the two of them bragging about what was under the hood of their Chevy or Ford in the parking lot of the neighborhood burger joint and although trickle-charged amperage had replaced horsepower, the intensity was still there.

Jenn stepped in front of him and extended her arms. "Hug?" She smiled.

Evan resisted then reached for her. "What's this all about?"

"When I told you that Mum had said to say 'hello' I left out the part about giving you a hug. I really wasn't comfortable with it then."

"But you are now?"

"More today than yesterday."

Chapter 17

The light changed and as they walked across Third Avenue the speakers at the record store belted out the Beach Boys. "Now that was the true California sound," he told Jenn.

She listened and recognized the song. "Mum and dad went to their concert a few years ago."

"I did too, last year. I guess we all try to hang on to those good vibrations."

"But you can't go home again."

"Not to live but it's nice to visit every once in a while."

"What made you start writing?"

"I don't remember really. I was about ten. I loved the old Whitman books based on the television shows of the time. The first story I wrote was 'Fury Meets the Lone Ranger'."

"The Lone Ranger I know…"

"Fury was this big black horse. He and Silver didn't like each other at first but eventually they worked it out to save Tonto."

"Wow, covering all those social issues at ten. You were so ahead of your time."

"I was?"

"The metaphors, black and white solve their issues then help the Native American…so politically correct of you."

"I hadn't thought of it that way but then I don't necessarily think in metaphors."

"Really? I read so many things into what you've written."

"Most people do, as with any writing. I admit I throw a few things in here and there but generally people put their own spin on the words. It's like the old subliminal seduction obsession with photographs a while back. A book came out suggesting that there were dirty words and naked women in all the images we were exposed to. People looked and found all kinds of things even though there was usually nothing there."

"How could you see them if they weren't there?"

"If you send your mind off in a direction to find something eventually you'll find it. I still get a giggle when I think of all those puritans that found the word 'sex' in places it wasn't. If they only knew that most of it was the crop of their fertile and somewhat dirty imaginations. Just look closely at the shapes of clouds, patterns in natural stone or even tree bark…you'll find all kinds of hidden images or words. Random patterns can be patternized by a good imagination."

"Patternized?"

"Poetic license."

"And isn't 'random pattern' an oxymoron?"

"Whatever. It's the same with words. People read what they want to read as much as they see what they want to see."

"But this isn't a bad thing."

"Of course not. It doesn't matter what your interpretation is as long as you identify with the work. Years ago I read a quote rightly or wrongly attributed to Bob Dylan. Someone asked him what he meant by some of his lyrics. 'They're just words, man,' was his response. John Lennon supposedly said something similar, as have so many writers throughout history."

"So you're saying that they never had anything in mind when they wrote those lyrics, metaphorically speaking?"

"No, I'm not saying that. They did…and often. I'm just saying that not everything is not how it appears."

"But sometimes it is not how it appears?"

"Right."

"I am? I fear I am a tad confused."

Evan laughed. "Take poetry…if you appreciate an Edna St. Vincent Millay poem because it captures the essence of your feelings for a lover, that's good, it has meaning for you. Then you find out it was written in a morphine-induced delusional funk and that she meant something entirely different, does that change your appreciation of the piece?"

"It shouldn't but I suppose it would."

"They're just words. Words can mean nothing or everything, something or anything. The mind applies whatever leaning it wants and that leaning changes with age and experience. I realize now that the rooster crowing at the break of dawn was just an insomniac fowl and the walrus was…well, it was John…apparently."

"Didn't John say Paul was the walrus?"

"He fibbed."

"So Lennon and Dylan influenced you?"

"They influenced everybody, more so John Lennon with me. He was the word-meister. He played with the English language in a way that I'm not sure anyone else could in both his books and music. There are so many great writers and artists that you can't help but be influenced by each of them to some extent."

"I'm gathering it was Charlie and Beth that introduced you to the hippie culture?"

"In a way I guess. They were in the back of the van, he played notes that I don't think ever existed and she got topless and propositioned Jack."

"But Andy was with Jack, right?"

"Not a problem, she hit on her too."

"Geez, I've lived a sheltered life."

"We learned pretty quickly that up until that day we had too. It was an eye-opener for all of us. When we drove into Oakland everything changed. Your mum and I had slipped across the border into the northern States before but this was Oakland and this was California. It was an incredible feeling. It was hot…we had the windows down and the radio blasting. The Beatles had released 'Sgt. Pepper' a couple of weeks earlier and it was still on every station we punched in. We knew all the words by the time we hit the Oakland Bay Bridge."

"I think I've opened the floodgates."

"Yes you have. It's good to remember."

"It sounds like a wonderful time."

"Some of it was. There were moments when nothing made sense but it was okay. You were with other people who were equally confused and somehow that brought everyone together."

"So now you're in San Francisco…"

"Later Jennifer…" He pointed toward a shop. "We've reached our destination."

"You want to try calling me 'Jenn'?"

"No."

"Fine."

Chapter 18

She turned off the recorder and followed him into the store. Her eyes widened as she studied the tightly packed shelves and stacks of books imprisoned by bright yellow and red walls. "Man, they have a lot of books in here!"

"It's a book shop."

"Has anybody ever slapped you around?"

"Not recently."

"It sure is colorful. I feel like I'm back on holidays in Madrid."

"I know what you mean."

"Sure you do. Hey look at these guys!" She knelt as two small white dogs bounced toward her. "They are so cute."

"It's all an act. The big one is Molly and the little guy is Ben."

"I assume you don't bring Ginn in here?"

"Hell she loves little dogs, usually with a side of kibble and a shake."

"So I guess cats would be dessert?"

"No, they terrify her. Go figure, a hundred-and-thirty pound wolf scared of cats." Evan dramatically set a clenched fist on his forehead. "Oh the shame of it all."

"Maybe that's her feline side…kinda like men have a feminine side?"

"Don't go there. I'm having enough trouble with my masculine side lately."

"So why are we here?"

"I need transmission fluid."

"That slap is a lot closer than you think."

Evan spread his arms in a sweeping motion around the store. "It's a book shop Jennifer, go look at books."

"I have books."

"Get more."

"I don't need more."

"Everybody needs more."

"I have a small room."

"They have small books."

She sighed dramatically. "To think I was actually looking forward to spending time with you."

"And I with you. What are you reading now?"

"Required…Karlyn Craig's 'Invisible Bars'."

"What kind of bars are we talking here?"

"Prison, smart-ass…true crime. She drowned her six year-old daughter in a lake and was sent up for life. It's all about how she found God in jail."

"What was He in for?"

"Kill," she pointed Ben at Evan, "or at least maim."

"You're required to read that sort of stuff?"

She shrugged. "It's well written, she's received all kinds of good reviews."

"Cool and all it cost her was her daughter. Do they ever force you to read the classics?"

"Some of them," Jenn said. "I really liked Salinger and Kerouac."

"Kerouac died in 1969."

"You're just a little cornucopia of information aren't you?"

"I pay attention."

"No kidding. I could have used you for 'Show and Tell' in my history class."

"Harr."

"So where's the poetry section?"

Evan pointed to a set of shelves behind the sales counter. "There be the poets, I be in Sci-Fi."

Still clutching Ben, Jenn studied the many poets on the shelves. Some names she recognized but most she didn't. Then again there was only one she was interested in at the moment.

She stepped her way through the aisles, winding around an incredible mass of books of every size and sort. She stopped at the literature shelves and knelt by the end of the alphabet. While searching for Vonnegut she found something else of interest.

"I can't believe I missed that," she muttered, holding up a book.

"Missed what?" Evan leaned on the end of the shelf wearing a Cheshire-cat grin.

"Ginn…Virginia Woolf?"

"Really? Is that coincidence or what?"

She tossed the book back on the shelf and stood glowering at him. "You really are starting to piss me off."

"He does that to everybody."

Jenn turned to see a woman wearing a vibrant yellow shirt and a bright orange floral print skirt; her blond hair draped across her shoulders.

Evan stepped forward to introduce them. "Jennifer meet Patricia, this is her store."

Jenn held out her hand. "Actually I'm Jenn," she said.

"And I'm Pat, nice to meet you. Did he kidnap you or are you really with this guy willingly?"

"I see you know him well."

"Yeah. So Evan, if you're adopting I've got one about her age I can let you have. It's better to get two, they keep each other company."

"Evan?" Jenn shook her head from side to side. "Some secret identity…I've spent months tracking you down on the internet, digging through old newspapers and legal documents when all I had to do was ask anybody in Kamloops where the hell Evan Morris was."

"Not just anybody…" Evan chuckled. "Jennifer is the daughter of an ex-girlfriend from a couple of lifetimes ago. She's interviewing me for a class assignment."

"Studying primitive man?" Pat asked.

"Yeah, I'm debunking Darwin's theory." Jenn smirked. "Journalism and creative writing, the two birds with one stone thing.

I'm guessing you don't have any of this guy's books hidden away somewhere."

"Honestly I've never seen one. He keeps promising me a copy but he never delivers. I figure it's all just urban legend."

"He's urban legend. Where are your craft books?'

"Follow me."

Evan watched the two of them disappear around the corner, their laughter drifting through the store. He moved back to the poetry shelves where a thick Irving Layton biography dominated a stack of thin, self-published works. He initially thought that it was sacrilege that Layton should be lumped in with those unknowns but then he thought better. Layton himself would have been the first to congratulate them for the perseverance and gumption they possessed to get even this far. Irving would have been right.

He leafed through the biography cluttered with fluorescent yellow highlighting and penned margin notes…a student perhaps. He was always curious about what other people deemed significant enough to underline or otherwise deface a book. He quickly browsed a few of the 'important' paragraphs. All of it had to do with the writing and not the man. As with all authors Layton was more than what he wrote and the more was usually far more interesting and insightful than the percentage of his soul bared in the work. Evan dropped the book back on the stack and turned toward the young lady sorting books at the sales counter.

"Excuse me Jess…" He pointed to a large paperback in a stack beside her. "That book 'Savage Beauty'…is it for sale?"

"Hey Evan, who's the cutie?"

"You are."

"No…" She smiled shyly. "The other one?"

"Her name is Jennifer. We met in the chat room at almostcroaked.com. She liked my sense of humor and my mature yet undeniably boyish charm."

"But then she met you?"

"Yeah. Things kind of went downhill after that."

"This would be the hill you're over?" Jess grinned.

"That would be the one. The book?"

"Does Marie know about the email-order bride?"

"Why is everyone so concerned about Marie?"

"Because she's really nice."

"And I'm not?"

"You have your moments. I hear she created quite a stir at the book club last night."

Evan shrugged. "It's what she does sometimes...about the book?"

"It came in not ten minutes ago."

"So not did I. It must be fate."

"Must be..." She picked up the book and read the cover. "'Savage Beauty, The life of Edna St. Vincent Millay'. Man, she had a big life."

"You have no idea." He took the heavy paperback from her. "I've been looking for this for a while."

"I read some of her poetry when I was a kid."

"When was that, Tuesday?"

"Do you have any friends?"

Evan winked at her. "None that know me all that well."

"Tell me about Edna."

"She was probably the tip of the women's lib spear, boldly going where no woman had gone before. She was the definitive child of the sixties...thirty-years ahead of her time."

"I can see why you'd identify with her."

"I'm not sure identify would be the word although I certainly would have loved to have met her. She had a passion so rare back then...outspoken and freethinking. Unfortunately that freethinking got the better of her. I think the cry would have been 'Sex, Drugs and Syntax'. But I do admire her."

Jenn sidled up to his elbow. "So are you done?" she asked, dropping a handful of books on the counter.

Evan sifted through the titles. "Leathercraft, beadwork?"

"Not for me."

"She's still into all that?"

"Big time, I've got all kinds of custom accessories, so have my friends."

Evan nodded. "I have a vest and a serf-shirt she made me in those medieval times."

"Serf-shirt?"

"Blouse actually. Butt length with big puffy sleeves. No buttons, just a cloth belt that tied around the waist."

"Sounds very Luke Skywalker."

"I guess you're right. It's still the most comfortable shirt I own although it's pretty much worn out now."

"You really don't throw anything away do you?" Jenn studied the large paperback on the counter in front of him. "Savage Beauty. That's how you described Ginn a few days ago."

"So it is."

Pat stepped behind the counter and sorted through the books. "Off your credit Evan?" she asked, adding up the prices.

"Yeah, how's hubs?"

"Gone fishing."

"Trout?"

"What else? I heard what Marie did last night."

"I didn't," Evan said, "but I imagine I'll catch it on the five o'clock news."

"Yup." Pat nodded. "She's a terror that lady of yours."

Jenn frowned. "Marie? A terror?"

"It's what she does," Pat said. "I'm gathering you found everything you wanted Jenn?"

"A lot more than I wanted but not everything. There's one that my professor recommends…'Writing Down the Bones'?"

"That's a pretty popular book, unlike some we've discussed." She smiled at Evan. "You'd have to leave your name for it but it could be a while. People don't give that one up too easily."

"No that's okay. I'm going home at the end of the month."

Evan dropped the books into his canvas bag. "It's one of my bibles Jennifer. I have an extra copy you can have." He threw the bag over his shoulder. "Now step away from the dog and let's move on."

Chapter 19

"Now where?" Jenn asked as the light changed to 'walk'.

"A thrift shop, just a street up."

"Is that where you found Jenny?"

"You know about Jenny? No, she was from the hospital shop a few blocks back."

"Marie told me about her. I gather you buy a lot of stuff at thrift stores."

"And yard sales, flea markets…that sort of thing. I like finding collectibles…toys mostly, and I love rebuilding old stuff. Most of the smaller furniture pieces in the house are refinished cast-offs."

"When was the last time you bought anything new?"

He squinted, thinking. "1978."

"Really? And that was?"

"Underwear. You're really leaving that soon?"

"Uh huh, I have to get home. Why…ya gonna miss me?" She coyly purred.

"Yes, as a matter of fact."

"Oh…" She frowned. "That wasn't what I expected. I'll miss you too."

"The Spanish flag…red and yellow right?"

Jenn shook her head. "Right."

"You need a hat."

"What?"

"A hat. It's hot. You need a hat."

"Or a cat and a hat, fancy that," she sang.

"Pack it in." Evan smiled. "You really are becoming bearable company kid."

"You too old guy. Were you really looking forward to spending time with me or with Claire's daughter?"

"Honestly at first, the daughter. Now…" Once again he laid his arm across her shoulders.

This time she didn't flinch.

"Now?" she asked.

"I'd like to get to know Jennifer MacAvoy a bit better. What's your favorite colour?"

She giggled. "Taupe."

"Flower?"

"I know this sounds old-fashioned but daisies."

"There's nothing wrong with old-fashioned." He stopped short of commenting that they were Claire's favorite back then. It was important to separate the two of them now.

They strolled across the parking lot toward the thrift shop comparing movies, animals, and anything else that came to mind.

Chapter 20

Jenn shivered as they entered the store. "Geez why do they keep it so cold in here?"

"To keep we stale-dated customers fresh," Evan quipped. "So toys first, or hats?"

"How about ear muffs?" She looked around at the racks of clothing, books, records, and knick-knacks surrounding her. "Let's check out the toys."

She followed him down a clothing aisle to a pegboard stocked with clear plastic bags. This was the fastest he'd moved since they'd met. He was already sorting through the pegs when she caught up to him.

"Find a treasure?" She peered over his shoulder. "What the hell are you doing?"

He had a bagged doll in his hands and was slipping the dress up off her legs. "I'm checking to see if she has ball sockets or straight joints," he said.

"Does the word 'pervert' mean anything to you?"

He laughed. "I'm looking to see how her legs are attached. The rounded sockets break more readily but they're easier to fix and allow for better movement…simpler to dress and pose."

"Exactly how are you going to dress and pose this humiliated little beauty?"

"I'm not. Wrong sockets."

"Unwanted because of something she had no control over. Sad, really."

"Actually it is. I have a magic wardrobe with a couple of nice outfits from the late sixties that need filling. She has the look, the figure, the hair…just not the legs and she's a little too young, probably mid-to-late eighties."

"I really am growing concerned about you."

"Why?"

"Never mind."

"Ah, now this…" He held out a small bag of metal figures. "This is a find."

"Cowboys?"

"Not just any cowboys…Lone Star castings, and for ninety-nine cents. You can't beat that with a stick."

"You truly haven't grown up have you?"

"I tried it once, didn't much like it."

"So these cowboys are valuable?"

"Not really, probably about ten bucks but they're a part of my childhood. I've found the King Arthur series and a few of the toy guns I had but these cowboys have eluded me until now."

"You could probably buy them on-line."

"Yes but that would take away the thrill of the hunt wouldn't it?"

She watched as he sorted through every bag on the rack, occasionally pulling one down and adding it to the handful he was already holding against his stomach. He seemed younger now as he sang some old doo-wop song. Marie was right…there are a whole lot of people hiding inside that one body.

Evan reached down into the bottom row then quickly stood. "Now this is cool. A Bullitt Mustang." He held the bag in front of her. "It even has the right plate number. It's a little worn but certainly worth a couple of bucks."

"Wow that really is super cool! What is it exactly?"

"It's from a movie made in about '68. Steve McQueen played a rogue cop named Bullitt."

"And this was his car."

"Yup."

"You even know the license plate?"

"Yup, JJZ-109."

"What's your plate number?"

He shrugged his shoulders. "It really is a helluva film. From a research standpoint there are some great shots of the real San Francisco in the late sixties and a pretty cool soundtrack. We can watch it tonight, if you want."

"Sounds good. I'll bring the popcorn."

"And red licorice…we can't have a movie without red licorice. Now let's see if we can find you a hat."

Jenn nodded then followed him through the aisles. Suddenly everything seemed distant. She felt cold and light-headed. She hoped it was the air-conditioning but she knew it was the red licorice.

Her mum refuses to watch a movie without it.

Chapter 21

"Love the hat," Marie called as they climbed out of the Rover.

"Yeah," Jenn grumbled, "I had this really cool black 'L.A. County Coroners Office' ball cap but he talked me outa that one and into this one. Apparently it makes me look cute, like Annie Hall. Then guess which one he buys?"

"I don't have to, but it really does look cute and that brim will keep the sun off."

"That was one of his justifications too." In an exaggerated impression she shook her finger in the air and coarsely said, "'Oh, that one only keeps the sun off the front' and 'Oh, black attracts the heat' and 'Oh, it's just not feminine enough'…jerk."

Marie laughed. "I gather you're not scared of him anymore."

"I can't believe you've put up with him since the ice age," Jenn growled and then broke into a smile. "Actually I can see why you've put up with him. Life certainly isn't boring."

"That it's not, and I really do like the hat."

"Me too. Who's Annie Hall?"

"Oh dear child, so young. Diane Keaton is one of his all-time favorites." She put her hand beside her lips and whispered, "She still makes him frisky. We have the movie. You and I can watch it sometime."

"Not tonight, we're watching Bullitt."

"And I've got the snacks." Evan handed Marie the grocery bag. "Doesn't she look cute in that hat?"

Marie looked at Jenn then back at Evan. "Yes but she'd look even cuter in the one you're wearing."

Chapter 22

Marie and Jenn sat in the old couch on the porch. "So what did you think of the movie?" Marie asked.

"I really enjoyed it. I didn't think I would but I did. Steve McQueen was pretty hot and Evan's right about the scenery. All I've seen of San Francisco are the touristy shots like Alcatraz, Fisherman's Wharf and the Golden Gate but the side streets and old houses really look cool."

"I imagine it brings back some memories for him and probably your mum if she's seen it."

"So you know about that trip?"

"Sure. He's told me all about the Haight-Ashbury experience. Andy and I have had a few chats about it too. I was pretty jealous of Claire for a while."

"I can understand that. He makes light of their relationship but it seems like there's a lot more to it." Jenn looked at the porch floor. "I'm sorry, I shouldn't be saying this."

"No, you should be," Marie said. "From everything he and Andy have told me about your mum she's a really beautiful, caring, and giving person. I can see how they'd really get along."

"Yeah, she's all that. I'm just hearing some things about her that are a little surprising."

"We all have closets and some of them are leased to skeletons."

"Oh these aren't bad skeletons, just unexpected. I'm seeing her in a whole new light. She was always Mum…take me to my soccer games, buy me shoes, bandage my knees Mum. But now she's a whole other person."

Marie giggled. "I do see what you mean."

"I knew she was pretty liberal but her mum and dad were so uptight about everything. I can't imagine what made her do some of this stuff."

"It's probably because her mum and dad were uptight. It's such a fine line between protecting and smothering our children. It's natural for them to want to break free of those apron strings and explore the things that their parents wouldn't have thought of them doing."

"Even if the parents themselves had done it?"

"Especially if they had. Kids have to make their own mistakes. You can tell them what's right and wrong or good and bad but sometimes the only way they can understand how far they can go is to go too far."

Jenn smiled. "There's more than one philosopher under this roof."

"No, it's the voice of experience. My parents were strict, dad especially. He really frightened me whenever I even approached the line let alone crossed it. This was back when it was still okay to spank your children and believe me, I got a few."

"For what?"

"Coming home late, not doing dishes…whatever. It didn't take much."

"That's awful. I can't imagine my dad doing anything like that."

"They were different times Jenn. When I was fifteen I ran away from home and got myself into all kinds of scrapes for about a year. After a rough night of booze and some kind of pills I woke up in a blizzard cuddled up with a dead guy behind a dumpster."

"God! A friend?"

"No, I didn't know him but he was wearing my jacket. I'm not sure why."

Jenn grimaced. "How do you get past something like that?"

"You don't. You try to hide it but it never goes away. I still have nightmares every so often."

"Then what did you do?"

"I wandered around in the snow for hours working up the courage to go home. I decided I'd rather have my ass whipped than spend another night like that. When I finally tapped on the front door my dad pulled me into his arms and cried louder than I did. I never felt safer than at that moment and he never raised his hand to me after that. My warm old bed meant more to me that night than ever."

"I'll bet. Does Evan know about this?"

"Of course. I'd a few bad relationships before he came along. I figured all guys were the same but then this weirdo checks into my life and my perceptions suddenly changed. He wasn't a party animal and was so quiet and gentle. He has his faults but nothing that can't be overlooked."

"I can think of a few," Jenn muttered.

"He's just giving you a bad time. You haven't seen the darker side and I think he'll do everything to prevent you from doing so. He likes you and I can see why."

"I thought it was just because of my mum at first."

"Maybe at first but he's comfortable with having you here. If he wasn't you'd be gone."

"With a wolf attached to my butt. You were really jealous of Mum?"

"Not because of Evan or their relationship but because of what she did. She lived the way that I wanted to live but I didn't have the courage to take that first step. Hopping in a van and running off to California, living the free life…I was jealous. I still am to a degree. I keep thinking I missed out on something."

"Me too." Jenn turned and looked into the doorway. "So where is Evan? I figured he'd be right behind us."

"Andy phoned while you two were out buying hats and asked if he would call her tonight."

"How's she doing?"

Marie shrugged her shoulders. "She sounds okay but you never know."

"He's been talking a long time although I guess that's none of my business."

"Or mine. They're old friends in the middle of a trying situation. They'll be fine."

"I feel guilty interrupting him with this interview thing. It suddenly seems so petty."

"Don't feel guilty, it's the distraction he needs right now. If anything it'll help him get through this."

Jenn sank down in the couch and rested her feet on the porch railing. "Honestly Marie, it doesn't seem to be bothering him at all."

"It is...he's just not showing it. That's one of the faults I mentioned. On the surface he doesn't get too emotional one way or the other. It's sometimes pretty hard to know what he's feeling."

"Except when he finds little cowboys at a thrift shop."

"Oh yes, then he's just like a kid with an old toy."

They both looked over their shoulders as the back door opened.

"Claire says 'hi' to all." Evan reached the phone to Marie. "And Andy would like to talk with you."

Marie stood and took the phone into the house as he sat beside Jenn.

"Nice night," he whispered.

"You talked to Mum?"

"Carl tracked her down and got her to call Andy. I guess she's been there for a couple of days. She answered the phone...."

"You okay?"

"I don't know. Oh here," He handed her the ball cap. "She told me to stop picking on you."

Jenn pulled the cap on and down over her eyes then smirked. "Such a good mum."

"Yes she is. It was nice to talk to her. Just the sound of her voice...it really hasn't changed."

He stared out at the river, barely breathing. Jenn fidgeted, trying to decide whether or not to get up and leave him to his thoughts.

"It really is a nice night," she said, "and it's so peaceful here. I see why you like watching the sunset."

"I'm trapped in twilight. As a kid I escaped to the movie theater every chance I got. The most magical of moments was the time before the trailers hit the screen. The curtains were lit with red lamps along the bottom and blue across the top, blending at the center. They reminded me of a sunset. They were the portal from the everyday world into the realms of mystery and fantasy like the setting sun is the doorway between day and night...reality and dreams."

"I never thought of it that way."

"You can't think about it Jenn. That's the problem. People think too much."

"You really think so?"

"Well done," Evan said, "now stop thinking."

"How possible is that?"

"Everything is fleeting, like the sunset. To truly appreciate this moment you can't think about it. You have to let your senses experience it…to just let it happen."

"That's not easy."

"No, because we are taught to think things through. At birth we survive by instinct but later on we learn to think and over-think situations."

"I'm still not sure I understand the point."

"Don't think about it." He looked along the porch then out into the yard. "Where's the mutt?"

Jenn shrugged. "I haven't seen her since we came outside."

He snapped his fingers twice and a mass of white crawled out from under the porch, ran up the steps and dropped at his feet. He chuckled. "If only I could train Marie to do that. I assume you have your little machine handy?"

"Do you really want to do this?"

"More than ever."

"Sometimes it's good to talk feelings through."

"I've spent the last twenty minutes doing just that. That's enough for tonight. Do you want a drink or something before we start?"

"No, I'm good." She clicked on the recorder.

Chapter 23

"When we last left Claire and Evan they were crossing the bridge into San Francisco," Jenn said with the dramatics of a bad soap opera announcer.

Evan leaned back on the couch and rested his feet on the railing beside Jenn's. "Charlie seemed to know where he was going so I let him guide us through. I think it was Market Street that we came in on. We turned off Market and he took us on a tour through a couple of older neighborhoods pointing out houses where their friends lived or where they'd crashed after a 'pretty groovy' party. Then we turned onto Haight. You could sense the excitement in the van but it was quiet on the street. We were expecting to see more people. We found Ashbury, let our passengers off, and then sat there wondering what was next. We'd passed a park a few blocks earlier so we turned down Ashbury, hung a left and made our way back to stretch our legs and figure out what we were going to do."

"So it wasn't the mass of humanity it was cracked up to be?"

"We saw that later. Some kids in the park told us that the Monterey Pop Festival was on the next day and a lot of the usual hang-abouts had made the pilgrimage."

"That was a pretty big event wasn't it?"

"Yeah, Joplin…the Dead…Jefferson Airplane."

"Did you go?"

"One of our big regrets. It would've about a two hundred and fifty mile round trip and we just didn't have the money. But other than getting in on the collective party atmosphere of a festival you could catch any of those groups almost any time in those days. About a week later Airplane and Hendrix were at the Fillmore."

"Did you see any of them?"

"No. We ended up leaving the park after we bailed Jack out of jail."

"Jack was arrested? Dare I ask why?"

"It all started with Andy and your mum going into this corner grocery store and coming back with cans of beans, stews, and peaches tucked inside their shirts, under their skirts…wherever."

"They stole them?"

"You didn't hear it from me. It'd cost us more than we figured to get there and all we had left was what we'd allowed for gas. Jack and I were talking about going home but neither of the girls wanted to do that. They decided they'd try to get some food so we could stay at least a few more days. When they got back to the van and spread the tins on the floor we figured we had enough meals for about four days. Of course then we realized that we didn't have a can-opener. Jack volunteered and hit the same shop. The next thing we know he's running past the van, can-opener in hand with this tiny Oriental woman swinging a long stick in hot pursuit. Lord that little lady could run. He decided to lose her in the park and ran smack-damn into a cop who was trying to convince some dopers to go home."

"If you had to steal food how did you get the money to bail him out?"

"Your mother and Andy cooked up a scheme to sell body art…stampings of body parts blended into flowers."

"I'm not sure I want to hear this."

"It's not what you're thinking. Without telling me they took some of our gas money and picked up an art pad and poster paints. Then they hit the same grocery store and bought some apricots, peaches…anything they found that resembled or could easily be cut or formed to resemble body-bits. They sat in the back of the van making lady-parts flowers by painting the altered fruit then stamping it onto the paper."

"Lady-parts?" Jenn laughed. "Always the gentleman."

"The van was disgusting…blue half-apples, melons, squashed purple peaches and red apricots…and the smell was awful, although not half as bad as Charlie and Beth as I recall."

"Yuch."

"With practice and some judicious shaping the blooms became surprisingly realistic. They joined all the 'flowers' with green lines and leaves, a few love and peace words then set up a display in the park and sold them for one or two bucks each."

"People actually bought this stuff?"

"Big time…we sold out the first day. The girls had to buy more paint and paper and expanded into nipple flowers which were pretty great art and actually nipples."

"Whoa…they used the real thing?"

"Yup, but most of them were mine and Jack's. His were more aesthetically pleasing."

"You're making this up."

"Nope, I still have a couple of the paintings in my closet. I often wonder if any of those things are still hanging on walls somewhere. We made nearly a hundred dollars in a couple of days. The tourists loved them. 'True San Francisco Hippie-Nippie Art' is what Claire wrote on the poster. Old men especially got into it. 'You're sure these are yours?' they'd ask. Andy would show them the paint she'd strategically soaked into her shirt and they'd buy it lock, stock, and nipple. If they only knew they were mine."

"I can't believe you said all that with a straight face. So the money went to bailing Jack out?"

"We sprung him the second day. It cost us twenty-five with a promise to appear. We rationed the rest for meals and gas…just enough to get us home without any undue stress. There really wasn't much left for entertainment so we spent a few days bumming around, doing the sights and beaches."

"And shopping."

"Yeah I did a bit of that. Mostly books, especially the little mimeographed poetry books the kids wrote and sold on the street for a dime or a quarter. There was some really great work there."

"I'm gathering Jack didn't appear."

"No and that's why he never went back to the States. He figured there'd be a nation-wide manhunt or at least a warrant out for him."

"I'm sure there's a statute of limitations on Grand Theft can-opener."

"Actually I don't know whether it was the threat of court or the chance of running into that little woman again that kept him on this side of the border."

"Snarly huh?"

"Oh yeah. She stick-whupped a couple of hippies just on principle on her way back to the store."

"You're lucky you were there back then. That's something not a lot of people can say."

"I don't say it too often either. I'm glad we did the trip although I'd like to have seen the Haight before the summer of love destroyed it. The whole area was an example of incredible Victorian architecture, the sort of old houses you see in movies and on postcards. In earlier years it had ended up being a blue-collar, low rent district and one by one the houses began to fall apart. Rents fell with them and as a result a lot of artists ended up there. In the early to mid-sixties it turned into a kind of west coast Greenwich Village with beat poets, coffee clubs, and jazz bars…the whole experience. Then the tide turned and the hippies emerged. A lot of them were middle class kids who'd left the suburbs looking for their freedom. They discovered the beat lifestyle and grew their hair, smoked pot, and made love not war. The publicity attracted thousands of kids who wanted to be a part of the scene. The housing, welfare, and support programs couldn't handle the onslaught and basic mayhem ensued. The original peace-guys eventually moved on and left the wannabes trying to survive in dream rubble."

"Way to burst my bubble." Jenn sighed. "It sounds pretty sad to me."

"In the end it was. I hear they've rebuilt the area now. I should go back…."

Jenn stood and stretched her arms. "That's all for tonight folks," she announced into the recorder before turning it off.

"You're doing okay Jennifer."

She looked at him curiously. "Okay?"

"With the interview. You're starting to get on track, mapping out the story from the starting point?"

"I've learned to look for all the little things that create the big picture. It's not always how it appears."

"Ah, first-year journalism?"

Jenn shook her head. "Thirteenth-year Mum. It was part of the 'boy' talk…look for the little things and don't be distracted by the pretty picture."

"You like pretty boys?"

"Only those who don't know they are."

"I would have thought your taste would have been a tad more cerebral."

"I guess it is now." Jenn smiled. "Pretty is in the eye of the beholder."

"Bad experiences?"

"Mostly no, but I'd better get some sleep. Thanks for this Evan, although there's a lot here that I won't use."

"You said you wanted to understand."

"I do…hell I've almost got enough information to do your biography. Is it okay if I play this for Mum?"

"Sure, she might get a kick out of it."

"I know she will. Goodnight."

Chapter 24

As Evan heard the door close behind him Ginn crawled up on the couch and laid her head across his knees. The sky was a deepening purple; the air was calm and the subtle yet distinct fragrance of unseen twilight flowers wafted across the yard. But not all was right with this evening.

If Jennifer had started the thoughts tumbling then Claire's voice had sent them spinning totally out of control. She echoed yesterday's dreams, full of promise and laughter. Then there was Andy. She told him that she had it together and her voice bore witness but he couldn't believe it. And Marie…stuck in the middle of two emotional fronts that were colliding within him. He sensed the gathering storm.

Ginn whined and arched her neck. He looked into her eyes and rested his hand on her shoulders, gently kneading the firm flesh.

Those eyes, reflecting the glare of the porch light. Glowing…liquid…understanding.

"Wanna run away girl?" he asked softly.

Again she dropped her head across his knees.

"Me neither."

The door quietly opened. "You two okay out here?" Marie whispered.

"We're not sure." He felt her hand on his shoulder and set his upon hers. "I don't know what to think Marie, how to act…I don't really know anything right now."

She tapped his shoulder. "Listen to the wolf."

He looked up at Marie then back at Ginn. "What the hell does that mean?"

"This morning you said she was digging for her peace of mind. It looks like she found it."

"She's oblivious."

"Maybe, but she does know that right now she's the happiest hound in the valley. Whatever happens later on tonight or tomorrow or the next day, she'll deal with it as it comes. You're always the one preaching the 'now' and how that's the important thing, right?"

"Yes'm."

"Fretting over tomorrow isn't the Evan Morris I've let live with me for all these years...since the ice age I'm told."

"You've 'let live' with you?" He half-smiled. "And I don't have to ask where the 'ice-age' comment came from."

"She's a beautiful girl. A lot like Claire I assume?"

"Too much so. It's like a roller coaster ride into the past. I didn't realize the kind of turmoil she'd put me through."

"She's not doing it, you are. She was quite concerned about how you'd react to her so I told her to let it all unfold and see what happens. That's what she's done, that's what Ginn does, and that's what you should be doing. You're always the calm at the center of any storm...you have to handle it the way you usually do, with patience and understanding."

"Where have I heard that before?"

"Practice what you preach Evan. Andy tells me she's driving down tomorrow but she's not sure about Saturday?"

"Yeah I'm meeting her in the restaurant at the hotel tomorrow night. She wants to talk some more."

"You'd be the obvious one. She also mentioned that Steve and Barb had parted ways."

"Feigned surprise," he mumbled. "Really Marie? Gosh...what happened?"

"She didn't say. Apparently it was years ago."

"Ah, that damned time difference again. Anything else you care to share?"

"Nothing else, really." She sighed softly. "It's so strange thinking of Andy without Jack. How's Claire dealing with all of this?"

"She says she's okay."

"You believe her?"

"No reason not to. It doesn't sound like she's changed at all."

"Is this good or bad?"

"Neither." Evan shrugged his shoulders. "It just is."

"Exactly."

"What's this about you stirring up the book club last night?"

"It's what I do." She leaned and kissed him. "I'm off to bed. Goodnight."

"Night."

Ginn lifted her head as the door closed.

"You were listening?" he asked.

Whine.

"You agree with her?"

Whine.

"Women…."

Chapter 25

Jenn tossed and turned. Her mouth was dry, her head filled with rambling thoughts and questions. She was still trying to get around his 'don't think about it' advice. Don't think about what? She imagined Evan with her mother. It was far easier than it should be. They were so much alike. Then she thought about her father and guilt crept over her. Sleep was going to be difficult tonight. She glanced through the window at the moon. Not quite full but satisfied, as grandma used to say.

She quietly rose from the bed, pulled on her robe, and tiptoed to the kitchen.

Evan stood in the glow of the refrigerator light pouring milk into a bowl.

"Christ, geez," Jenn stammered, looking back down the hallway. "I'm sorry Evan."

"For what?"

"You're...um, never mind."

He let the door swing shut and shrugged then held out the bowl. "Can I get you some?"

She turned and looked up at the kitchen ceiling. "No...thank you. Just a drink of water."

"There's the tap." He nodded toward the sink. "Help yourself."

"Yes, no...that's fine. I can wait...over here."

"There are some bottles in the fridge." He started across the kitchen.

"No, really I'm fine. You can go back...over there." She leaned in the doorway, her arms crossed and her eyes still fixed on the ceiling fan. "I'm not all that thirsty anyway."

"Okay." Evan walked over to the dinette and sat. "I hope I didn't upset you. I figured you'd be asleep by now."

"Shocked me maybe."

"I guess the sight of a bare-assed old guy could do that."

"Yeah, but you're so casual about it."

"I'm used to it."

"I'm not." She giggled then shook her head. "I should get back to bed."

"Suit yourself." He smiled as he dipped the spoon into the cereal. "Goodnight, sleep warm."

She started to turn then saw the grin on his face. "You're actually enjoying this aren't you?"

"As a matter of fact yes, but I'd enjoy it more if you visited for a few minutes."

"I'll bet." She glanced down the darkened hall then back at Evan. "You promise to keep it under the table?"

"Of course. I really am sorry Jennifer...I tend to be a bit of a closet nudist."

As she walked toward him Jenn dramatically looked around the kitchen. "It doesn't look like we're in the closet anymore Toto." Cautiously she pulled a chair from under the dinette. "Okay, for a few minutes. But if this table starts lifting I'm leaving."

"Agreed...although if I could do that I'd take it on the road."

"You wouldn't need an equipment manager." Jenn clasped her hands and rested them in front of her. "So here I am."

"And here am I," he said.

"I noticed. Wanna play some checkers?"

"I'd get the wine..." Evan winked at her. "But then you've already won haven't you?"

She glanced around the kitchen again, searching for an adequate response.

None came.

She looked back at him. She was feeling more at ease now than ever before. This in itself was troubling. "You couldn't have picked a new moon to streak?" she asked.

"I don't have the energy to streak anymore, I can barely waddle." He glanced quickly about the room. "You're right; it is pretty bright in here. There's nothing like lunar lighting…or reflection, to be more accurate. Quite calming, don't you think?"

"Uh huh."

"Saturday night it'll be full. A white-wolf moon."

"Which is?"

"It is said that those witnessing the howl of the great white wolf when the moon is full and high shall be blessed with an abundance of love and harvest."

"Old legend?"

"I think I just made it up. Ginn sometimes goes a little nutty at full moon though."

"Oh…she runs around in a state of not dressedness too?"

"Not dressedness? Interesting."

Jenn leaned back, conscious of keeping her feet underneath the chair. "Mum didn't want to talk to me tonight?"

"I offered but she figured you were in good hands."

"If she could see me now I expect she'd think otherwise."

"You're okay Jennifer."

"I know. At the book shop today you called her your girlfriend."

"She was."

Jenn stared at him but her thoughts were somewhere else. Evan let her drift, allowing her to sort through whatever she was thinking.

"Jennifer?" he asked quietly.

"Sorry, I was…I'm still getting used to all of this. At first I got the impression you were just friends but now I see there's so much of her life that I don't know about. It's always been her and Dad. I've never thought about her being anybody's 'girlfriend' before and to hear you say it…I don't know…it's pretty weird. I'm definitely learning more about her than you."

"This is a good thing, isn't it?"

"It won't get me through university but, yes. Actually I've been giving your age theory some thought too."

"Based on the current situation?"

"No," Jenn said. "While I was trying to sleep."

"And?"

"It's not all that revolutionary. It's like the old saying 'You're as young as you feel'."

"Exactly."

She raised her eyebrows. "So what age are you now?"

He smiled warmly. "I feel like…a sixteen-year-old."

"Too bad there isn't one around."

"Have you started writing your interview?"

"What do you mean by that?"

Evan shrugged his shoulders then frowned. "That it's time you started?"

Jenn shook her head. "No…about you feeling sixteen."

"Oh…well, just that when you're around I feel like a kid again, that's all."

She squinted at him. "Even when you're not naked?"

"Sure, I guess."

"Boy you certainly know how to make a girl feel at ease."

"It's a curse, what can I say?"

"On that note I think I really should get back to bed." Jenn stood and slid the chair back under the table. She watched as he spooned the last of the milk out of the bowl. She wanted to tell him that he really had made her feel at ease but decided to keep that confusing little secret to herself. She stopped at the refrigerator and pulled out a bottle of water. "And yes," she said, "I've started putting it together. Goodnight Evan." She turned and walked quietly from the kitchen.

Evan wondered what she was thinking as she disappeared into the darkness. She seemed calm…calmer than he was. Only when he heard her door close did he push the chair back, put the bowl in the sink and head to his bedroom.

"Not dressedness," he mumbled as he stepped lightly down the hallway.

Marie heard him come back into the room and flicked on the bedside lamp.

"Can't sleep again?" She peered out through sleepy eyes. "My…what have we here?"

Evan grinned sheepishly. "Has it been that long?"

"Not in recent memory."

"I bumped into Jennifer in the kitchen." He slipped between the covers. "She walked in while I was getting cereal and…never mind."

Marie laughed. "Man, when you extend your hospitality…."

He put his hands over his face and rubbed his eyes. "Christ, and she thinks I'm the dirty one."

"Did she say anything about it?"

"Not really."

"You disappointed?"

He shrugged. "A little."

"Embarrassed?"

"A lot. There are times when a table is a man's best friend."

Marie surveyed the unnatural lie of the blankets and giggled a girlish giggle. "I think I might enjoy having that little catalyst around for a few days." She reached to the nightstand and turned out the light. "You know when I was young I used to love going to the circus."

"Okay."

"Know why?"

"No, why?"

She slid her hand across his thigh. "Because I never knew what I'd find under the Big-Top."

Chapter 26

As Jenn struggled into the kitchen Marie peered over the newspaper. "Sleep well?" she grinned.

Jenn shuffled to the counter and poured a cup of coffee. "Um, not really."

"I'm surprised. Most people that stay here usually have a pretty good night."

"Yeah well, the bed is great, I just…" She made her way to the dinette. "I don't know."

"Maybe you were just excited. This is a big opportunity for you…getting to uncover the real Evan Morris."

She tried to hide her smile. "I suppose. It's not going to be an easy job though."

"I imagine it'll be pretty hard on him too." Marie grinned again.

Jenn took a deep breath and looked out the window. "Maybe."

"I think he really enjoys hanging out with you."

"Uh…" She tensed to contain her laughter. "Yes, me too."

"So I guess this is another thing you and your mum have in common."

"What?"

"You've both seen him naked?"

Jenn let out a large sigh. "You bitch! He told you?"

"In a manner of speaking."

Her laughter spilled out. "I'm sorry Marie."

"It's not your fault dear, he really should have thought about you being in the house."

"No, about the 'bitch', I'm sorry."

"You tells it like it is child. That was fun!"

"Does he do that often?"

"Not as much as he used to but yes. Although I imagine after this he'll keep a lid on it."

"I couldn't believe how unaffected he was."

"Oh, I wouldn't say that." Marie grinned. "He must have thought you were asleep. I do know him Jenn, it was unintentional."

"I'm sure it was but I still lay there half the night thinking about it."

"I'm sure he'd love to hear that."

"No, not 'it'…the situation." She closed her eyes. "And now this situation. I'm sitting here talking to a woman about her naked husband. God!"

Marie was bordering on hysterics. "You wanted the bare facts right?"

"That's not funny."

"It's a little bit funny. Relax Jenn, I'm sure the memory will soon fade and you won't be psychologically scarred for life."

"Don't bet on it." Jenn's attention was drawn to a knock on the wall behind her.

"Am I interrupting something?" Evan called from the doorway.

Marie lifted the paper in front of her. "No dear, we were just discussing your shortcomings."

Jenn rested her elbows on the table and covered her face with her hands, her trembling body revealing restrained giggles. "Hey Evan, what's up?" she blurted.

As the two women collapsed in fits of laughter Evan silently poured his morning brew then meandered out onto the porch to watch Ginn sniff out something in the back garden. The laughter from the kitchen came in waves, between the waves he detected whispers.

He smiled. This was good.

Jenn sipped her coffee then peered out the window. "You think he's mad?"

"In which sense?" Marie asked.

"Is he upset about us laughing at him?"

"I doubt it. He's probably on the porch laughing along with us."

"How could he be so comfortable with me seeing him…y'know?"

"He's always been like that. When he was eighteen or nineteen he worked as a model for art classes at the university. Then he got into the photography on both sides of the camera. That's where the comfort comes from. He's got an old album with photos of the gang at a cabin in Alberta somewhere. None of them ever gave it a second thought."

"I've always thought that the nudism thing was just an exhibitionist's excuse; the 'feeling free' and 'it's natural' were justifications."

"If Evan frequented the camps or beaches I might think that too but, believe it or not, he's really pretty modest and not all that outgoing."

"Are you sure he wouldn't be upset about you telling me all this?"

"I'm not saying anything he wouldn't. He's pretty open Jenn…remember that with your questions."

"I will. If you don't mind me asking, were you ever into that kind of thing?"

"Lord no. The rest of them were, except Barb. She was Steve's wife. A year after Evan and I got together the whole bunch of them came out to meet me. About midnight they all stripped and headed for the river. Barb and I unbuttoned, looked at each other, giggled, and re-buttoned. We just sat, drank wine, and watched the frivolity. I'm not sure I've ever laughed that much."

"I could never do that with the crowd I hang with. We did a beach party last summer and just the sight of a bikini…I swear if you even smile it's taken as an invitation."

"It's all about trust Jenn. These guys have a pretty decent respect for each other and the wives. As for the nudity, Evan had said that after a while I wouldn't notice and he was right. The first few minutes were an eyeful but after that it didn't seem all that important. Nobody paid much attention other than when Evan stood up and did a drunken hula around the camp-fire."

"Oh God, the imagery! He never grew out of it?"

"In most ways but he still has no problem hitting the wilderness and becoming as one with nature. I'll do trips with him but I can't get into it. I keep thinking that a hundred people on a jet to Hawaii will get a message from the Captain…'If those people on the left side of the plane will look out their windows, we're passing over a naked old broad'."

"Oh I don't know…you don't look like you have anything to be embarrassed about."

"Thank you but that really has nothing to do with it."

"He doesn't mind that you're not part of that lifestyle?"

"Evan doesn't force his ideals on anyone and he expects the same in return." She stood and pushed the chair back under the table. "I do have to get this place cleaned up. Why don't you try to get some of your interview done?"

"Actually I've been recording since I got here. I'm having some trouble separating the stuff that I need for the assignment and the personal stuff."

"You'll do fine, now go."

"You're sure I can't help?"

"Maybe later."

Chapter 27

Jenn walked out the back door to find Evan sitting on the top step watching Ginn watching him from the bottom step. Their eyes were fixed on each other, each moving their head from side to side in curious fashion.

She quietly sat beside him. "What are you two talking about?" she whispered.

"We're not talking, we're thinking," he whispered back.

"Oh." She looked at Ginn then Evan then back to Ginn. "What are you two thinking about?"

"We're wondering if people actually end up looking like their pets or if the pets end up looking like their people."

"I think Ginn's got more to be concerned about."

"Thanks."

"Hey, it could be worse…" she said, pulling the recorder from her shirt pocket. "You could have rescued a Pekinese."

"True. About last night," he said sheepishly. "I'm sorry."

"You have nothing to apologize for Evan."

He raised his eyebrows and grinned an evil grin. "Why thank you Jennifer."

"Not what I meant…perhaps I should wear a little bell around my neck?"

"It'd help."

"You're not angry are you?"

"About?"

"Marie and I," she said, "in the kitchen?"

"It's always good to hear laughter."

"But it was at your expense."

"That's okay Jennifer, I'm fine with it." He pointed to the recorder. "I assume you have some more questions?"

"First, off the record…tell me about this cabin in Alberta."

Evan sighed. "Jack's dad owned some land near Winfield. We went out there on week-ends."

"I was hoping for more than a headline."

"There's not much to tell. It was off an old dirt track, in a small meadow surrounded by trees. There was the cabin and a couple of outbuildings, a stream and a pond at the edge of the woods…some rabbits and deer."

"Sounds like a perfect place to get naked."

"Sometimes."

"You were with Mum at the time?"

"Yes."

"So she was part of that lifestyle?"

"Yes she was." He saw her expression turn pensive. "Having some trouble with that?"

"I don't know. From what you've told me so far I can imagine it but God, she is my mother."

"She was Claire a long time before she was your mother. Don't get too obsessed with that part of her life. She was the total package in those days."

"Yeah but it sounds like she spent most of them unwrapped."

Evan laughed like she hadn't heard him laugh. "Not most of them," he said. "They weren't drunken orgies Jenn. They were just singsongs around the campfire, skinny-dipping, and the occasional rousing game of touch football."

"Too much information. You called me 'Jenn'?"

"I thought you needed it."

"Oddly enough you're right, thanks."

"You're welcome. Now put your naked mum out of your mind and let's do an interview."

"Have you?" she asked.

"What?"

"Put my, uh…mum out of your mind?"

"Interview?"

"Okay…" She started the recorder. "You said you were influenced by John Lennon?"

"I loved his books but I loved so many authors around that time, still do. Edna St. Vincent Millay was the first, and Edgar Allen Poe. Then Leonard Cohen, Michael McClure, Irving Layton, Richard Brautigan…Rod McKuen. One of the highlights of our trip was discovering that if you kept going on Haight you ended up on Stanyan Street."

"I know this, 'Stanyan Street and Other Sorrows'. Mum has that book on her desk."

"I gave it to her. She used to get a little teary when she read 'Sloopy'. We were so hooked on McKuen back then that every footstep we took we wondered if he had stepped there. We even got a local to take our picture leaning against a Stanyan Street sign."

Jenn furrowed her brow. "That's you? She uses the photo as a bookmark."

Evan nodded. "She still has it? I thought I'd be the only one hanging on."

"Are you hanging on?"

"I don't let go easily."

"I'm beginning to see that. Mum mentioned that she'd met Leonard Cohen?"

"That was winter, 1966 I think. He was in Edmonton for a month or so. He was so accessible though. I'm not sure there were too many people into the art scene at that time that didn't meet him. A girl Claire knew from the U of A introduced her to him. He invited us to his hotel room. There had to twenty people there but it was such a personal and comfortable experience. I was so impressed, class all the way…even remembered my name when we said goodnight." He looked to the sky. "The next morning was so friggin' cold that the van wouldn't turn over so I caught a bus downtown and walked blocks to a pawn shop. I bought an old Suzuki guitar for five dollars then stopped at Eaton's and picked up an easy chord book. All the way home I'm playing this fantasy guitar and practicing the chords in the air. I was going to be the next Leonard Cohen."

"So he would be the one that influenced you most?"

"I suppose."

"But Bogwump was before all of this right?"

"Long before. How did you uncover that?"

"Marie. You didn't play guitar back then?"

"I really didn't play anything but I played everything. I was the singer with the tambourine, sticks, bells, or bucket…anything that made noise that I could keep the beat with."

"Ala Mick Jagger."

"Pretty much but without the moves."

"I don't know…I heard you had some pretty good moves."

"Pardon?"

Jenn winked at him. "Hula by the camp-fire?"

"I don't think you should be talking to Marie anymore."

"So really did you guys ever do anything?"

"Bogwump? Sure we played High School dances, did some road trips to Dapp and Clyde and a few other towns where everybody drank beer and drove pickups with a deer on the fender and a hound named Bufus in the bed."

"Wow, big timers. So people actually heard you?"

"What, you're surprised?"

"No, yes…I don't know. Did they like you?"

"Sure…our fan club met every second Tuesday in the phone booth outside the Cecil Hotel."

She looked down at her feet. "I got tossed from there once."

"The hotel or the phone booth?" He laughed. "Nobody gets tossed from the Cecil, what on earth did you do?"

"I was born too late. Who named the cat?"

"What cat?"

"Mum has pictures of her and this big black cat called Lenny."

"I'd forgotten about him. That poor feline went from being Sloopy to Lenny overnight…total identity crisis. His little bowl had 'Sloopy' in blue but it was crossed out and 'Lenny' was written above it in red. I wanted to rename him Suze, short for Suzanne, but Claire would have none of it."

"Well it was a boy cat after all."

"Kinda, I guess. I think he was a tad gender confused but it was the sixties, he would've been accepted."

"Of course he would have. 'Suzanne' was your favorite Cohen song?"

"It was the anthem for young poets everywhere. I'm not sure there's any other song that so clearly struck a chord with Canada's flower children. It came on the radio and you could picture yourself down by the river…tea, oranges, and all. What a marvelous piece of writing."

"Mum plays his music a lot…on the old stereo I guess you guys had?"

Evan closed his eyes. That small apartment overlooking the river came into clear focus…the laughter and the cat. Claire telling him how well he was doing on the guitar when even Lenny retreated to the bedroom as soon as he hit that first chord. He remembered the frost on the windows and the warmth in the room, candles and white wine, soft music and….

"Yoo hoo?"

"Sorry. I'm drifting to another time and place."

"Better place?"

"Different time. This old record player, brown and tan with a fold-out speaker?"

"That'd be it." She laughed. "Gawd it's so beaten but I'm told it sounds as good as ever. You guys really were deprived in those days. I bought her a Cohen CD for Christmas one year. I don't think she played it more than once."

"It's not the same. All these digitally re-mastered oldies are technically better but they don't have the feel that you get from vinyl. Plus there's nothing like the harmonic hum of a worn vacuum tube between scratchy cuts."

"I have no idea what that means."

"Don't worry about it. She really still has that old stereo?"

"Oh yeah…and all the records. She's about as much of a pack rat as you are. I'm seeing so many similarities and it's so obvious that you really cared about each other. I'd really like to know what happened."

"Me too. There was always something holding us back, I'm not sure what exactly. We always said we'd wait until it felt right for both of us. I guess it never did." Evan lowered his head and closed his eyes. The feelings continued to awaken. After all this time mere thoughts could still fan the embers.

Jenn bit her lip. "Call it quits for now?" she asked.

"No, I'm okay." He cleared his throat and looked across at her. "You've been unlocking doors from the moment I met you. There's so much I'm remembering now that I haven't thought of for years. I thank you for that. It's good. Perhaps time is the true eye of critical distance."

"Which is?"

"Stepping back from a situation to view it as someone else would; free of emotion and involvement. Artists are supposed to be able to do this although I fear most can't."

"I'm not sure how that applies here."

"I think this is the first time I've looked back at those days with Claire without thinking about the fact we grew apart. To be able to see all that we were then and to really appreciate what it was, what we had…is pretty special."

"She's a pretty special lady."

"That she is." He took her hands in his. "And you have inherited that from her."

"Thank you." She shivered at his touch, soft…gentle.

He studied her from toes to hair and leered. "That's not all you got from your mama."

"Okay, now you're freaking me out."

"I'm sorry kid."

"Don't call me 'kid' old man."

"Last I heard you had a fourteen day going?"

Jenn hesitated. "That was yesterday."

"And yesterday's gone…today?"

"Twenty?"

Evan quickly pulled back his hand and stood. "Alas still too young but you really are something special. You make me wish I was fifty years younger."

"Fifty? You'd be what…ten?"

"Yeah and I wouldn't give a damn."

"I think I should be flattered."

"You're not?"

"I am."

Chapter 28

Ginn set out to break up a gang of gabbing gulls at the river's edge while Evan and Jenn sat on a massive tree trunk placed on the beach by the high waters of some summer past.

Jenn studied his profile as he stared at the opposite shore. She was beyond trying to figure out what he was thinking. She felt her frustration growing. She was thoroughly enjoying her time here but things just weren't going the way she wanted.

"Evan?" she asked quietly.

"Jennifer?"

"What are you thinking about?"

"Sometimes you can damn near walk across this river."

"Oh. Have you?"

"No."

Ginn crouched as she drew nearer to the flock of ranting gulls, trying to get as low on the sand as she could. A quick wiggle of her haunches then she leapt. The gulls became a screaming cloud of confusion above her.

Jenn looked back at Evan. "What's your favorite colour?" she asked.

"I'm sorry. I guess I'm not great company am I?"

"Not really."

Ginn howled at the seagulls that now settled back down a hundred yards from where she had chased them.

"South," Evan commented. "The seagulls flew south."

"Gee and it's not anywhere near winter."

"But it will storm tonight."

"Tell me about her…Ginn?"

"What about her?"

"The taming part, in the shed. You said she was pretty wild. How did you change that?"

"I didn't…she did. I'd borrowed one of those padded suits that dog trainers use. I spent as much time with her in that shed as I could, saying her name over and over, talking about world events, reading to her and singing. At first she was always on the offensive. All I had to do was walk through the door and she was at me. I'd slide her food across the floor, each day sliding it not quite as far. Eventually she was eating a few feet from me. Then she assumed a defensive role…only attacking when she felt I was threatening. One day I went in with a brush to try and clear her matted fur." Evan shook his head. "She didn't like that at all so I let it be. She sat in the corner with her head on one side just looking at me like she was wondering what I was going to do next. We stared at each other for a while and she began edging closer. I took off my head protector and began brushing my own hair. When I started singing she came and sat beside me."

"You remember the song?"

"Bridge Over Troubled Water. By the time I got to the second verse she had her head on my legs and I was brushing the bad out of her."

"You'd been accepted."

"That's all anyone really wants Jennifer. That evening I went out to feed her and she was sitting by the door, tail flailing back and forth…no growls. I took off the suit and we spent the night comparing philosophies. The next morning I opened the door and waited outside. It must have taken her ten minutes to crawl out into the sunshine but when she realized she was free she ran like nothing I've never seen. That unleashed spirit. She was unbelievable."

"So are you," Jenn said. "I'm not sure how many people would have gone to all that trouble."

"It really wasn't all that much trouble considering how it all turned out." Evan clapped his hands. "Start your little machine, let's get serious."

Jenn turned on the recorder. "We still haven't really discussed why you dropped out of sight just when it looked like you were on your way."

"As I said, I don't really know. I just know I wasn't happy driving the van across the country doing the same thing night after night. After a while the highways, towns, and gas stations all looked the same. Different faces sat in the darkness but the people were all alike. I was physically and mentally exhausted. When I started out I thought that the road would be a great life. I figured it'd be like your mum and I taking off and exploring the backwoods but it wasn't like that at all. It was lonely, cold, and tiring."

"Be careful what you wish for?"

"Yup. Back then it didn't really matter where I was or what I was doing I'd find myself thinking that I'd rather be somewhere else. People are like that. We're never satisfied with the cards we're dealt. Still nestled in that deck hides that one card…that ace or king that will make us happier; that will make our life perfect. Over the years I've come to realize that there's no such card. We have to play the hand we've got and if we do it right we'll win more times than we lose or at least break even. That's all we can hope for. That's life."

"Some of your philosophies are pretty interesting. You could write a book."

"I have, binders full…and I've read them many times. That's why this stuff just trickles off my tongue. They're all in my bookcase."

"Ever thought of publishing them?"

Evan chuckled. "I'm sure nobody would take my ramblings too seriously."

"You might be surprised. I'd like to read some if I may?"

"Be my guest. I'll show you where they are when we get your book."

They stood and began the slow walk back to the house. Ginn walked beside them, head down and tongue dragging. Evan bent and gave her a rough rub. "Don't worry girl, seagulls get the better of every dog."

Jenn giggled. "Positive reinforcement?"

"We all need it once in a while."

"Yeah, I think I'm due for some."

"I'm not working out the way you'd hoped?"

"Me mostly, I'm too scattered. I seem to be getting so much information I can't use."

"I'm to blame for a lot of it," he said. "I promise to stay on task. Perhaps you should rethink your leaning on this."

"How do you mean?"

"You've done a lot of digging into my story but maybe there isn't enough there to do what you need to do."

"Maybe. There's just so much stuff coming at me that I wasn't expecting."

"But you are learning about your mum throughout all this. That's a good thing."

"Oh sure and I'm really positive that she'd like me to publish some of the stuff I've found out about her."

"But it is important to keep all that you discover. You can always edit right?"

"Right."

Evan pushed his hands into his pockets and kicked at the sand as they walked. "I look back on my writings and read those thoughts from before. Some I don't remember writing and some are as familiar now as the day I wrote them. I often wonder why some of them hang around forever while others end up in the grey mush in some little-used part of my brain. Mostly I wonder what the hell I was thinking. They must have meant something at the time so they should mean something now. I just can't figure out what. It's all about perception. What was important then isn't as important now and what seems to be unimportant now may someday be something on which your whole life hinges, you never know. That's why you should keep everything you discover on this assignment, even if you don't use it right away."

"That does make sense. But I do need something I can use now."

"Fire away."

"It must be pretty satisfying to play in front of an appreciative audience."

"First of all the audience was generally small, the majority of the clubs held 50 or so people and most of them were there for the drinks. The few that were close enough to hear me generally reacted positively so I guess there was a certain amount of appreciation."

"I suppose groupies were out of the question?" Jenn winked.

"Not really, although the frenzy wasn't there."

"Just a second…you're saying that you had groupies?"

"Young girls made out with the rockers but they made love to the poets."

"Care to talk about that for a while?"

"Is it an integral part of the plot?"

"I don't know, is it?"

He shrugged. "Probably not. If anything it would have been a reason to continue with a fledgling career."

"I somehow get the feeling that you wouldn't be a big fan of that sort of thing."

"What sort of thing?"

"A quickie back stage?"

He raised his eyebrows. "Jennifer?"

"Evan?" She laughed. "I'm sorry but wasn't that a part of the lifestyle?"

"Not as much as you might think. You're right though, I was never really into it."

"But it happened…."

"You've got me there." He hung his head and smiled. "I'm still not sure it's all that relevant Jennifer. Yes I had a few sleepovers but it wasn't a lifestyle, as you put it."

She sensed his growing discomfort. "Let's get back to the on-stage performing."

"To be blunt I wasn't that good at what I was doing, I was just lucky. There were so many young artists that were in the right place at the right time but only a few survived more than a year. I knew from the writing standpoint that I wasn't going to be the next Cohen and that I'd never be knock-knock-knockin' on Dylan's door. I guess I fooled a few people for a while but I never fooled me."

"I think you're being a little tough on yourself."

"I'm being honest with myself. I'm an okay writer and I can take a decent photograph. There are a few things I'm good at but I'm not great at any of them."

"I don't agree."

"And I thank you for that Jenn, but I'm happy with the way it all turned out."

"Jenn again?"

"Am I getting too familiar?"

"After last night I'm not sure that could happen. How did it all start, the book I mean."

"That was actually the simple part. Poetry had become cool at that time and it was easy to get published. I'd been writing for a few years and I had enough material that Lindeman felt was worthy to print, like they knew what was worthy. They were one of countless small production houses that expanded into publishing. Most of them really didn't know what they were doing…they just wanted to cash in on the market. Some made money but most didn't and they all shut down pretty quickly when the craze subsided. There were a lot of underground publishers that did the folded and stapled photocopied books and in their own way were actually more successful. They lasted longer but eventually they too disappeared into the void."

"Did you ever consider a second book?"

"Lindeman wanted one but I'd spent most of my life writing the material for the first one and I'd have three months to come up with stuff for the second. I didn't want to do that."

They climbed the worn wooden steps leading to the yard then sat on the bench overlooking the river.

"The record?" Jenn asked.

"Right place again. I was fortunate in that a lot of what I had done could be adapted to a melody with few changes. I guess that's an advantage of rhyming poetry instead of free verse."

"You didn't do much free verse."

"No. The scheme may be buried sometimes but I really do like rhyme. There are quite a few writers that have a knack with free verse but there are also a lot like me that don't have a clue. It's just prose by another name."

"I've played your record a few times lately…I think it's pretty good."

"So kind, you get that from your mum. She always gave me a hug while I was trying to put words and music together. The album itself was studio trickery. It's the product of double tracking, frequency equalization, and a large band with some girls doing backgrounds. The wizardry of a super sound engineer completed the deception. When Claire first heard it her reaction was 'it doesn't sound like you' and she was right. I couldn't carry off the illusion in person."

"I still think you could have done it. Most poets from those days weren't the strongest singers."

"Marie has said that over the years, although she wasn't quite as polite. Her description was 'sounding like a cat in a washing machine'."

"I believe I said 'dryer'." Marie interrupted. "How's the project going?"

Jenn slid across the bench letting Marie sit by Evan. "I'm finally getting some material I can use. This is a pretty wise man you have."

Marie nodded. "Sometimes."

Jenn furrowed her brow. "I'm still confused about the seagulls though."

Evan started to laugh. "What about them?"

"They flew south then you said it was going to storm tonight. How do you know?"

"The weather channel."

"You jerk!" She shut off the recorder. "I kept telling myself not to buy into it but would I listen to me?" She moved her head dramatically from side to side. "He's all yours Marie."

"I don't want him. I've got dead bird for supper and I still need to do up some potatoes."

"Oh, double-yummers." Jenn stood. "I'm surprised anyone ever eats here after you tell them what's on the menu. I'll take care of the spuds…you just relax for a while."

Chapter 29

Jenn knocked gingerly on the door jam. "Okay if I come in?" she asked quietly.

Evan was again tapping on the keys of his laptop. "Of course, and it's not a library Jennifer…you don't have to whisper."

The soothing ticking of the old railroad clock followed her as Jenn made her way around the shelves in his study. As she moved closer to his desk she heard music playing softly from the shelf behind him.

"Can you actually hear that?" she asked.

"Only when it's quiet," he said.

"Sorry…."

"No, that's okay. I like music to be unobtrusive. If I'm talking to someone or reading I can't really hear it but when I want to listen I just sit back and close my eyes."

"Donovan? Mum still listens to him quite a bit," she said. "She thinks 'Wear Your Love like Heaven' is one of the few true flower children songs."

"She thinks right," he mumbled. "As usual."

"You seem to be writing every time I come in here. Mind if I ask what?"

"Those philosophies we discussed earlier, random thoughts and feelings…pretty much anything that occurs to me throughout the day."

"A journal?"

"I guess. When I really got into the photography I studied everything I could about Edward Weston. He used daybooks to record the nuances in nature…the scene as it felt while he took the photograph. His thoughts both technically and personally say so much about the man and the image. I started doing the same thing about thirty years ago. That's where I came up with a lot of the verse that I use for my photos."

"Any philosophical wisdom from today?"

"Not really. Today was a day for just being."

"Yet inexplicably you still type."

He smiled and shook his head. "Between you and me, I've always wanted to write a novel."

"I think everyone would secretly like to do that. I'd like to write children's books."

"And so you shall, if you really want to."

"Same goes for your novel. Any ideas?"

"Too many, although I'm thinking that the story of an old coot being interviewed by a hip young journalism student might make for some entertaining reading."

"Art imitating life? Maybe. Are you thinking mystery, romance, horror, fantasy?"

"All of the above and with horses, pirates, intergalactic cruisers…I'm not genre-phobic."

Jenn giggled. "Seriously."

"I don't know. Most fiction writers create a character they can live vicariously through, an alter ego as such. I can't think of anyone I'd rather be than me, especially now."

"Did Marie tell you about the fan sites?"

"The what?"

"You have a couple of fan sites on line. You've never searched your name?"

"I've never thought about it." He moved the mouse then typed on the keyboard. A few seconds and clicks later his eyes widened and he smiled. "I'll be damned," he said.

Jenn giggled. "Pretty cool huh?"

"God I look so young."

"Yeah well, you should send them some new pictures."

"Actually I think I might. I can't believe anyone would go to the trouble to do this."

"There are people out there who care Evan. You should know that."

"Once again I don't know what to say. Do you intimidate men your age?"

"Where the hell did that come from?"

"You've got it all together Jennifer. You have a mature confidence about you. You're sensitive, intelligent, and quick. You've got more than a casual knowledge about a lot of things and can speak with an authority not found in many of your age. You intimidate me at times…I would imagine a less-seasoned male would feel threatened by you."

"I intimidate you?" She stopped and leaned against a shelf of books. "How?"

"Take the scene at the restaurant, when you reclaimed your border. That's the kind of psychological reading that few would appreciate let alone feel comfortable with. The real concern would be how much more is hidden beneath the surface…what else lies behind those eyes."

"Are you concerned?"

"No, I'm comfortable with myself and honestly I'm not trying to impress you…but if I were I'd have a helluva time figuring out how to do it."

"But I still intimidate you?"

"A little at times. It sounds like you expect a lot from Jennifer MacAvoy, which is great, but you've also set high standards for those around you whether you realize it or not. I occasionally have this nagging doubt as to whether or not I measure up to your expectations."

"Oh you measure up."

"Don't go there," he said with a sigh. "What I mean is that you defy your age. You're not what you appear. I imagine the typical twenty-year-old male would have some trouble with that."

"Dad said something along those lines once. I don't see it but if you two do maybe I should look again." She continued moving about the room, studying each collection. A framed black and white photograph caught her attention. Three young boys in white Ts, jeans, and leather jackets leaned against an old car, arms crossed, and a glare of open defiance on their faces. "This is interesting," she said. "It looks like something out of 'Grease'."

Evan nodded. "The rock-dawgs. That's Danny, Jack, and I in front of the old Merc we shared. Forty-seven heaven we called her."

"Oh my God, the hair!"

"Stylin' at the time…ducktails and motor oil."

"When was it taken?"

"Late sixty-three. That's why we were the confused part of the generation. Our roots were in the attitudes of the back half of the fifties and the front half of the sixties…burger joints with carhops, drive-ins, rock and roll, rat-tail combs, and hot rods. The American Graffiti stuff."

"That could be a whole other story."

"Could be. Hot summer nights cruisin' Jasper Avenue; three jerks hanging out the windows screaming and whistling, trying to pick up chicks." He grinned. "God we were idiots."

Jenn shrugged her shoulders. "It's a guy thing. Then came the back half of the sixties?"

"Yeah, and when that kicked in we were closer to being adults than kids. Messed with the old rockers' heads a might."

"Ah, but you adapted."

"I guess but it was probably good timing. We'd torn it up pretty good back then so when the laid-back days hit we were ready for a rest."

"I'd like to hear more about that sometime." She looked closely at the photograph. "So you'd be what age?"

"Sixteen, seventeen."

"You've still got it."

"What?"

"The bad boy glint in your eyes."

He grinned. "I really have no response to that Jennifer."

"You don't need one." Jenn leaned back against the shelf and let her eyes take in every wall, every shelf. "I can't believe all this stuff," she said.

Evan pulled off his glasses and rested his chin on his hands. "Every so often I feel like cleaning house but I can't. I'm hopelessly addicted to adding to the jumble. Dusting has become a major chore so I'm thinking it's time to pack some of it away."

She saw the fatigue in his eyes and heard his slow deliberate speech. "Are you okay?"

He nodded. "Tired, I guess."

"I don't think so." She moved to the shelf beside his desk. "You sound different, your patterns have changed. Even the way you're sitting, the body language...."

"Add observant to your résumé."

"I don't really have to be, it's obvious. You seem nervous...not in control."

"A little nervous maybe and I'm never in control. Only fools ever think they're in control."

"You're meeting Andy tonight?"

He glanced at the clock. "Yeah, I've got a while."

"Maybe that's why the nerves?"

"No, I don't know what I'll be walking into so there's no sense worrying about it." He reached behind him and sorted through a shelf of record albums, selected one and held it toward Jenn. "It was sixty years ago today...Sergeant Pepper taught the band to play," he sang.

"I believe that was 'twenty' years?"

"But I've had this LP for forty years therefore...." He stared at the cover. "Magic was the only word that could describe the feeling when I first listened to it all. I played it over and over with the headphones on, long into the night. They've been going in and out of style..."

"But they're guaranteed to raise a smile. Maybe I should get my book and leave?"

"No, please stay." He opened the upper right hand drawer of his desk and pulled out an eight-by-ten black and white photograph then stared at it intently. "She was wearing a full skirt that she'd made with fabric bought at a bazaar in a church parking lot. It had these huge yellow and orange flowers tied together with garish emerald leaves on a brown background. It was such an ugly pattern but she made it work. I remember the loose-knit beige shawl across her shoulders and that thick, blonde hair cascading nearly to her waist. We'd stopped at a hot dog cart on the way to the beach. As we walked along the sand she'd toss a piece of the bun into the air and laugh as the seagulls fought over it. I got this Donovan song stuck in my head, 'Colours'...I kept singing it as we walked. Every time I listen to it now it all comes back. Her hair and shawl riding the cool sea breeze, the sound of the gulls, the ocean, the smells...her smile."

Evan leaned back in his chair and breathed deeply. "To fly on the wings of a young girl's dream and see the world through a young girl's eyes. To be wrapped in the love of a young girl's heart and be the warmth in a young girl's smile." He looked at the photograph. "That's all I ever wanted."

Jenn studied the distance in his eyes. "When are you going to admit it?"

"What?"

"That you loved her, that you still love her?"

"Perception…another of her gifts to you."

"It doesn't take a genius Evan. This is what you're having trouble with isn't it?"

"Partly." He slid the photograph across the desk. "Not only do I proudly brag that this is one of my best, it's also a favorite."

Jenn studied the image and felt tears fill her eyes. "It's beautiful and she's beautiful. I don't know what to say."

"A simple thank-you will be sufficient."

"I can't take this, really."

"You have no choice. You've found out a lot about her over the last few days, some of it has shocked you but she really is a one-of-a-kind, your mum. If anything I think this photograph captured her better than any words could."

"No kidding. I can't even begin to describe how I feel right now Evan."

"What you can't describe is love," he said then leaned back in his chair and closed his eyes.

"Is this the real you?" Jenn asked quietly.

"I'm not sure what you mean."

"Marie said there were many people living inside you. This is one I haven't met. Is this the real you?"

"They all are but this is the one I'm most comfortable with." He opened his eyes and glanced at the clock again. "I went with the wolf."

"I'm sorry?"

"That first day instead of tossing you out…I listened to Ginn."

"And I appreciate that. Ever wished you hadn't?"

"Hell no, you're the nicest thing that's happened to me in quite some time. You're not the problem, I am. I look at you and more and more I see your mother. I look at that picture and realize that it was taken forty years ago and I wonder where it all went. I hadn't given it much thought until you stepped on Ginn at the restaurant."

"I never apologized to her for that did I?"

"It's okay...you've still got your nether cheeks. She must have forgiven you."

"That seems like such a long time ago. We've covered so much since Ginn let me stay."

He forced a smile. "That we have. You've really opened up my thoughts and emotions Jennifer. There are times when I wish you hadn't but there are more times that I love you for doing it."

Jenn held up the Beatles album. "Your generation is lucky to have something like this. You mentioned Donovan...there's Dylan, John Sebastian...I mean the lyrics and the feelings of the time were so memorable and poetic."

"Yes, 'Yummy Yummy Yummy I've Got Love in My Tummy' was sheer poetic genius."

She laughed. "No, but it fit didn't it?"

"I suppose."

"See? That's another thing I'm going to miss out on. The fifties, sixties, seventies...pretty much every generation up until mine has had a clearly defined musical style. I have nothing."

"Oh I don't know, you'll make a pretty cool hip-hop granny," he said. "There's some good music out there but I suppose you're right, nothing defined with the exception of perhaps rap."

"I somehow can't see myself getting misty-eyed over that. The feeling just isn't there."

"You make a good point and I'm impressed...but I'd better be going." He pointed to the bookcase behind her. "Your book should be up on that shelf to the left of Kong. You're welcome to stay and look around if you want, I don't mind. You might even come up with some more material for your interview."

"I think I've given up on that."

"No you haven't. I'm not sure what time I'll be back so...goodnight Jennifer."

"Goodnight Evan," she said then looked at the photograph. Her mother gazed out through time at the child who would not be born for twenty years. The light in her eyes was so familiar yet so foreign.

Again Jenn felt a shiver.

She placed the photograph back on his desk then glanced around the den. He'd said it was okay to look around but it didn't feel okay. She looked up at King Kong. She'd watched the new version and while she knew he had been computer-generated she still wept when the bullets tore into him and he fell from the Empire State Building. She remembered being embarrassed when her dad saw the tears and teased her about being so emotional over something that wasn't real.

Jenn stood and began her tour of his world, beginning with the shelves behind the desk.

The top shelf held figures of different alien and dragon characters, beneath them stacks of old magazines and newspapers. The rest of the unit was filled with records. She ran her fingers along the edges, reading the artists. Joan Baez, The Lovin' Spoonful, Chris deBurgh, Dave Brubeck, The Beatles and Beach Boys, Gordon Lightfoot, Waylon Jennings, Bob Dylan, and many she didn't recognize. Rock, country, classical, jazz…it was all there. Stacks of CDs sat on the floor in front of them. Some newer names she knew, some older she didn't.

A row of white binders dominated the top shelf of the next unit, each labeled as to content: Poetry, Photo-Words, and Random Thoughts. Beneath his writings were three shelves jammed with books by authors from Stephen King to Emily Bronte, Michael Connelly to Edgar Allen Poe. Books on body language, forensic science, photography, astrology, and women's erotica…a selection as diverse as the music collection.

She started toward the shelf where Kong ruled, passing a large collection of small cars, knights in armor, space ships, dinosaurs, and some familiar cowboys.

She stood on her toes to check the books the great ape was guarding. These were the authors that he'd talked about: Edward Weston, Millay, Brautigan, John Lennon, Leonard Cohen, and a few self-help writing books. 'Writing Down The Bones' was under Kong's right arm. As she pulled it free he roared. She jumped back and shook her head.

"Stupid monkey," she said sheepishly.

On a shelf below the ape, between a fuzzy white rabbit and a stack of old cameras, she saw a face. A pale, smiling face surrounded by carefully brushed long blond hair.

She listened as the music continued from somewhere behind her. Still Donovan but now it was 'Colours'. She no longer believed in coincidence. 'This is all somehow meant to be,' she thought as she sang along softly, surprised that she remembered the lyrics.

Jenn reached behind the rabbit and cautiously pulled the doll into view. She seemed so light and delicate, so fragile. She gently pushed an errant strand of hair from those turquoise eyes and smiled back at her with the same half-smile.

"Hi Jenny," she whispered, adjusting the tiny beige knit shawl.

Chapter 30

Jenn sat down beside Marie in the couch on the porch. She watched Ginn navigate the underbrush along the riverbank. Ghost-like she slipped silently into the yard then moved along the path beside the garden. She started climbing the steps then suddenly stopped. She lowered her head and glared at the newcomer in her house.

"What's she doing Marie?" Jenn asked.

"Just a little staring contest…ignore her."

Jenn returned the fierce stare. Eyes locked and barely breathing, the two of them seemed frozen in time.

Marie leaned towards her and whispered, "Give it up girl, you'll never win. Evan hasn't and he's got a helluva lot more time to waste than you do."

"I'm going to try," Jenn replied, barely moving her lips.

"Okay, but remember I warned you."

"About what?"

"If it goes on too long she'll run you, glaring and growling all the way. That's when most sane folks blink."

"That's cheating."

"Tell her that."

Jenn looked skyward. "Okay Ginn, you win."

Ginn barked then bounced to the bottom of the steps and lay down, her tail whipping from side to side.

Jenn shook her head. "She knows it too doesn't she…that she won?"

"Yup. Damn near human that critter."

"I suppose Evan taught her that?"

"Actually she figured it out herself, at least that's the way he tells it."

"I can't believe where she came from and where she is now. It's amazing what a little love can do."

"A lot of love." Marie looked at Ginn. "There's an affinity between she and Evan that's almost unnatural. I honestly thought she'd have to be put down at the start; vicious would have been an understatement. He spent days and nights with her. He ate and slept with her…it was a mission. He saw the beauty and would do anything to keep it from being destroyed."

"He says she's still wild underneath?"

"Aren't we all?"

"I'll tell you Marie when she showed me her mad face I was really scared."

"She certainly has the look down but that's a game too. The pair of them spent a lot of time wrestling and chasing sticks out here. Ginn would growl and shake her head when he tried to take the stick away. He kept saying 'mad face' over and over. Now all he has to do is say it."

"No kidding. She's never attacked anyone?"

"If she had she probably wouldn't still be here. Why do you ask?"

"I guess I was wondering what would happen if someone threatened you or Evan."

"I'm not sure, but it wouldn't be pleasant. We're her people, especially Evan. If anyone tried anything she'd probably tear them apart. That special bond again."

"It's a good thing I'm not doing a gossip article. There's not too much bad about this guy."

"How about his temper, pig-headedness, lack of focus, possessiveness, his distance…want more? There's a lot he won't show you."

"I can imagine some of it but the temper?"

"Oh yes, pretty mean when he loses it. He avoids confrontation at all costs." Marie pointed to the dark clouds gathering over the mountain. "There's that storm the seagulls warned you about."

"I knew it had nothing to do with the gulls but he said it so matter-of-factly."

"Actually he says you can read nature to predict the weather. Something about how high the birds or butterflies fly and high or low pressure systems…I can't remember."

Jenn rested her head on the back of the couch. "I've seen this many men in one body you mentioned. Sometimes he's so glib and quick then other times he's like some of my teachers over the years."

"How so?"

"When we talk about those old days or life in general he almost sounds like he's giving a lecture. It all seems so well-rehearsed and thought out."

"I'm not sure about the 'rehearsed' part but the 'thought out' is accurate. He doesn't get into those types of conversations easily but he's well-versed when it comes to things he's passionate about. Just check the books around this place. I'm not sure you can name a subject that isn't represented."

"Yeah, I noticed."

Suddenly Ginn howled.

Jenn sat up straight. "What the hell!!"

"She's just reminding all the woodland creatures that she's in charge."

"I'll bet there are a lot of wet sheets in the neighborhood about now. Does she do that often?"

"Only when she hears other wolves in the hills…and sometimes around the full moon, maintaining the legend and all that."

"The white-wolf moon…Evan told me about her going a little squirrelly."

"I haven't heard that one before, it's kind of nice. When did he come up with it?"

"In the kitchen when he was…" Jenn smiled. "Ah, you know."

"He comes up with a lot of things when he's…ah, you know."

"I'll bet but I don't want to hear them. Do you buy into his not growing up philosophy?"

"I don't know but I do see how it works for him. He figures he's done all the growing up he needs to do so it's easy for him to preach. Honestly I think it's more of an escape from reality but unfortunately reality has a nasty habit of finding him every now and then."

"She's really scared of cats?"

"Who?"

Jenn nodded towards Ginn. "The Queen of the forest. Evan says she's afraid of them."

"There's only one that I know of but most cats tend to skip our place. Marion took in this twenty-five pound feline with torn ears, one eye, and a crapload of cattitude. Her Majesty was stretched out in the shade when this clumsy black thing fell off the top of the fence and onto her back. The cat dug in her claws and rode Ginn all over the yard. What a racket! The wolf was howling, the cat was spitting…finally Ginn did the drop and roll and the cat took off. He still wanders through the yard now and then but she retreats under the step."

Jenn glanced at her watch. "I wonder how Evan's doing?"

"Normally I would say he's fine, but tonight…I don't know."

"He seemed awfully nervous to me before he left."

"Me too. This has been an overwhelming week for him."

"I haven't done anything to make it easier."

"No you haven't, but it was something that had to be done. I've seen more life in him lately than I've seen in years. You've been good for him."

Jenn leaned forward and rested her elbows on her knees. "I'm thinking of dropping the interview."

"He won't let you."

"He's already told me that. Why?"

"Because he believes in you Jenn."

"Again, why?"

"Matters of the heart are pretty tough for him to get around. For all he pretends to understand he really doesn't."

"Matters of the heart?"

"He loves you. It's that simple."

"Okay that's not something I wanted to hear Mrs. Morris, wife of Evan."

"Me either but that's the way it is. He doesn't allow himself to get too familiar with people, even friends." Marie put her hand on Jenn's shoulder. "You've become closer to him in the last few days than anyone has since I've known him. In a different time and place I imagine he'd be losing a lot of sleep over you."

"I've never understood that. Wouldn't the feelings have to be strong enough here and now in order to use this different place and time justification?"

"You're right and they probably are. The question is would he do anything about it? I might be a little worried if you were older and not Claire's daughter but even then I know him too well. It'd also help if you weren't blonde. He does have a thing for blondes."

"Yeah, I noticed." She lowered her gaze from the rising moon to the porch beneath her feet.

"Spill it Jenn," Marie said, "what's on your mind?"

"You suggest that he has these feelings and I really should be uncomfortable with that but I'm not. I'm totally relaxed and free when I'm around him and I should be concerned about that, but I'm not." She looked across the couch at Marie. "And I should be uncomfortable talking with you about this but I'm not. I don't understand what's happening here."

"What's happening is a normal reaction even though it may seem wrong. You can't stop feelings. They're going to happen even if you try to deny them. He'll tell you that it's what you do with them or about them that's important. I can see that look in Evan's eyes when he looks at you. It's a truly caring look. Those comforts you're feeling are honest and believe me when you find someone who makes you feel that secure it's pretty special and rare. You're safe Jenn…appreciate it and don't be concerned."

"Last night…in the kitchen?"

"Can't get past that can you?"

"I never will but not because of the obvious. If someone had told me I'd end up in a situation like that I'd have been terrified but when it happened I was so, I don't know…at ease?"

"I guess it all depends on who you're with in that situation. You could have left at any time."

"But the problem is that I didn't."

"That's not a problem, that's the comfort factor. Perhaps you sensed it?"

"Maybe. I wonder how he's doing."

"Pretty much the same as ten minutes ago when you asked."

"Would it be okay if I went for a soak in the tub?"

"Of course, you can light the candles…matches are in the medicine cabinet. Might I suggest a small glass of wine to complete the mood?"

"Actually that does sound nice." She stood. "I won't be long."

"Take all the time you want Jenn, just relax. I'm thinking tomorrow could be a bit stressful."

Chapter 31

After filling the tub Jenn set the glass of wine on the edge, found the matches and lit the candles…one at each corner of the bath and one on either side of the sink. She turned out the light, slipped out of her clothing, and gazed into the mirror. In the warm candle-glow her reflection seemed older. She looked deeply into her own eyes then winked.

'Child,' she thought. 'Unlike any child you've ever met Mister Morris.'

She stepped into the warm foamy water and let her body slide down until the bubbles kissed her chin. She looked around the room. Shadows stood motionless against the sand-colored walls like stoic guards protecting their charge. She blew gently toward the flame, setting the troops in chattered motion…scurrying within their confined spaces, seeking out those who would dare disturb this serene moment.

Closing her eyes she relaxed, catching the faint mandarin perfume of the candles beside her.

Mandarin.

Oranges…that come all the way from China.

The photograph, that soft-grained black and white image of a woman as old then as her daughter is now. Pastels. She would colour the portrait in pastel gentleness. Her white blouse delicately blurred, her shawl the shades of amber, her eyes of vibrant aqua. Eyes they shared. Eyes that now taunted her, inviting her to accept the love she has to offer. Jenn smiled, concentrating on the image. Colour in sky

Prussian blue. Soft hair of wheat dancing with the wind, water-wash clouds and butterflies of many colours so light on wing. Alizarin crimson. Flowing ribbons, twists of pink and blue drifting through white-blossomed trees while the sun rains gold, bathing with love the woman she felt she was seeing for the first time.

Grainy and faded like an old home movie, she laughed silently…dancing childlike by the ocean. Textured dreams of rainbow hues, that's what little Claire was made of.

Jenn smiled to herself. Little Claire. She'd love to hear that.

"Mum," she whispered. For the first time since she'd left home she missed her, really missed her. There was so much she needed to say; so much she wanted to know.

Her thoughts started to drift, gently blending. She thought of Evan. Everything to hide yet hiding nothing…checkers. Marie…his rock…yet soft. Last night an endless dream began…last night with Marie. Ginn…unquestioned love…free. Jenny…hidden in plain sight…soft music. Cowboys and dragons…colours…yellow is the colour…sunset and movies…another place. California…beaches and seagulls…lightning…silver rain…another time…

A noise.

She jumped.

Then another knock on the door, Marie's muffled voice…"Are you okay Jenn?"

"Oh, yes…" The water was cold. "How long have I been in here?"

"About a half-hour. You're sure you're okay?"

"Uh, I don't know, yes. I guess I drifted off."

"Okay. I have tea ready if you're interested."

"Yes, I am. Thank-you. I'll be right out."

Chapter 32

Evan stood at the entrance to the restaurant searching through the sea of dimly lit faces. In the far corner at a table for two she posed rather than sat. Her Mediterranean good looks and quiet yet commanding demeanor were still there. Her flowing jet-black hair with streaks of grey, vibrant sea-green eyes and statuesque frame gave no hint as to what simmered below the surface. Classic and sexy yet ruthless to no end, she was the tough one of the old gang…a role she had relished.

You didn't mess with Andrea.

He wound his way through the tables all the time staring at her. Her face though bearing small signs of the burdens of age was light, her eyes distant, and her lips set in a curious Mona Lisa-like smile. She wore white, bright and plenty. It glowed against her olive flesh. She was as attractive now as ever, perhaps even more.

He slid into the chair across from her.

"Hi," was all he could think to say.

"God, you're old," she responded.

"But you're looking good."

"You shaved your beard?"

"A few years ago."

"Have I ever seen you without it?"

"Probably not." He shrugged. "Can I try 'hi' again?"

"I'm sorry Evan…I'm just so damned confused right now. Hi, it really is good to see you. I wasn't sure I wanted to come to this though."

"I'm a little shocked that you did."

"Part of me needs to." She played with the wine glass between her hands, running her fingers along the stem. "The rest of them don't know I'm here. I'd appreciate it if they didn't find out unless I show up."

"I understand."

"You always did. That's why I wanted to talk to you."

The waitress arrived at the table and took his order. As the girl walked away Andy raised her eyebrows. "A double Caesar? I remember you being a beer and naughty wine kind of guy."

"It feels like a Caesar night." He leaned back against the booth. "You really do look terrific Andy. I'm sorry, but so soon after…I didn't expect this."

"Ceejay says the same thing. There's nothing to mourn Evan, in recent memory anyway. I grieved the loss of the man I knew about ten years ago when he turned bastard and I walked. It's funny…I always thought mid-life crisis was some kind of joke on stupid birthday cards."

"I'm sorry."

"Suicide." Her voice wavered. "There…finally. That's the first time I've dared to say it out loud. But heart attack sounds so much better don't you think?"

Evan wanted to ask how but it really didn't matter. Instead he nodded then looked through the window into the parking lot. A young couple was hot and heavy over the hood of a bright metallic blue import not twenty feet away from a discussion on death. Ignorance was indeed bliss.

Finally Andy spoke. "You don't seem surprised."

"I suppose nothing really surprises me anymore."

The waitress slid the Caesar in front of him. He smiled a thank-you then looked back at Andy. "I'm sorry…I guess that wasn't the right thing to say."

"There isn't a right thing to say." She glanced out the window. "He brought a bike home one night, big sucker, black and loud. Said it was time for him to live again but the bike didn't do it so he started teeny-bopping. I came back from a weekend at my mum's and found him passed out on the couch. It was pretty clear what he'd been up to. The little bitch had pulled a Britney and left her panties under my coffee table. I wanted to smack him down but he was already there so I packed another suitcase and went back to Mum's."

"Can't blame you for that."

"He did though, for everything. What a waste of my life."

"Not always." He gently stirred the celery in the Caesar. "There was a lot of good."

"I don't feel anything Evan. I should, shouldn't I? The books say I should…."

Her face was expressionless, her eyes filled with fear. He had never heard her sound vulnerable.

"You will," he whispered, "it's not your fault Andy."

"But I'm supposed to be angry because the bastard quit on me, left me alone. If anything I quit on him so I should feel guilty but I don't feel that either. When they called and told me about his death there was an instant sense of emptiness but when I went to the house and saw him I felt a weight disappear. That can't be right."

He pulled the celery from the glass and let it drip into the deep red. "Everybody deals with things in their own way. I don't know what happened in the last ten years but I do know what went before and so do you. It may take time Andy but you'll deal with it somehow and it'll be the right way for you. You know I'm always here, at least as a listener."

She reached across the table and took his hand. "You were always the voice of reason. You and Ceejay were the perfect couple yet you went separate ways. You're both happy and neither of you have changed really. The rest of us held onto each other and gradually lost all that we were."

"It's never lost, just misplaced."

She forced a smile. "Like the TV remote?"

He chuckled. "Yeah."

"I found the remote but I never found me again."

"You're buried in there somewhere…it just takes a little digging sometimes."

"Aren't you the one that always said to forget the past, there's no future in it?"

"Something like that. How are the kids with all of this?"

"A little shook about his death of course but not about the last ten years. Collin has been my biggest supporter. He'd always been so close to his dad that I expected that he'd be a problem but neither of them were." She sipped her wine. "Claire tells me she sent you a house-guest?"

"Jennifer, she's quite the girl."

"So I hear. I saw her when she was about twelve…spitting image of her mum back then."

"Not quite as spitting now but there's no mistaking whose daughter she is."

"Cutie?"

Evan nodded.

"Do I detect a smirk?" Andy asked. "And a bit of a blush?"

"A bit," he conceded, sipping his drink.

She tapped her fingers on the table and stared at him. "Got a little personal growth happening have we?"

"Could be but alas, could never be. She is spring fashion and I am winter long-johns."

"How Evanly poetic…besides Ceejay would cripple you."

"She'd have to stand in line."

"Ah yes…and how is Marie?"

"Good, as always…and anxious to see you."

"I want to see her too. You lucked out with that one Evan."

"Hey, so did she. How did you keep all of this from the rest of the gang?"

"The few times anyone called the house Jack told them I was out of town, shopping or something. Anything to keep them from knowing we'd failed, not that they had anything to brag about. When was the last time you saw any of them?"

"Other than you and Jack, I guess the time you were all here. Danny and Carol used to stop by on their way to the coast but it's been years."

"God you're in for a shock. I'd like to be there tomorrow just to catch your reaction, especially to Steve."

"I hear he and Barb split?"

"A long time ago, just after her smart attack. That jerk was no good from day one."

"There never was any love-loss between you two."

"Nope, not since the day he cornered me in Danny's studio. Ceejay and I were the flower children. We were born to put out, doncha know?"

"Claire?"

"Not my place, sorry. Has Jenn told you about Devon?"

Evan tried to ignore the tension building inside him. "Devon?"

"Her father."

"I didn't know his name…retired lawyer is all she said. What kind of guy is he?"

"You'd like him, I think. I do, a lot. She lucked out with that one, same as you." Andy tipped the glass, draining the last drops. "Anyway, the wine has had the desired effect…I'm sleepy. Walk me to my room?"

"Of course."

He downed the Caesar with an involuntary shiver, dropped a twenty on the table then followed her through the restaurant. When they got to the elevator she pressed the button and leaned against the doorframe.

"I fear I've had a wee bit too much," she whispered. She reached and gripped Evan's arm and pulled him to her. "Wanna fool around?"

"That's the wine talking."

"Yup, and I'm the translator. Don't worry Evan, I'm only kidding. It's just so damn good to see you again."

The elevator door opened and they stepped inside. On the way up she held onto him like it was the last slow dance at the Prom. When they stepped out on the fifth floor she pointed across the hall. "This is mine," she said, reaching into her purse.

"You sure you want to be alone tonight?" he asked as she swiped the keycard.

"And that's the Caesar talking." She laughed, pushing on the door. "Besides, who said I was alone?"

Claire sat on the end of the bed. She looked up from her book as the door swung open.

Then she winked. "Hey Wolfman!"

Chapter 33

"Wolfman?" Marie asked.

"We used to sit around until midnight so we could listen to Wolfman Jack on the radio. There was another station in Montana or somewhere that was almost on the same frequency so we couldn't pick him up until they changed pattern. All of us tried to do Wolfman impressions and apparently I was the best so it became my nickname for a while."

"Actually it's even more fitting now." She nodded at Ginn sitting in the middle of the yard watching them, her head to one side. "Ever wonder what she's thinking when she does that?"

Evan looked at the white mass glowing almost blue in the moonlight. He couldn't begin to figure out his thoughts let alone hers. "I'll never get over how beautiful she is…such a peaceful soul. I'm sure whatever she's thinking it must be good."

"You made her that way."

"She always had it…it just took someone to help her find it." He stared up at the dark clouds that now dominated the sky. "Looks like the gulls were right. But it's supposed to clear by morning."

"The beavers tell you that?"

"No, the short weather guy with the brush cut, mustache, and bad suit. Come to think of it he does kinda look like a beaver. You ready for tomorrow?"

She shrugged her shoulders. "I guess. Are you ever going to tell me where you hid them?"

"Nope."

"Never?"

"Never."

"Come on Evan, what's a backyard party without Japanese lanterns?"

"Tasteful?"

"They add to the ambiance."

He pointed out at the yard. "We live on a riverbank across from a mountain. Big trees, pretty flowers, and fresh air surround us...hell we even have a wolf. How much more ambiance do we really need?"

"But they're cute."

"But they're plastic."

"I'll find them you know."

"You've got a better shot at finding Hoffa."

Marie sighed. "So Claire's coming tomorrow?"

"She'd like to meet you plus get in a visit with Jennifer while she's here."

"I'm a little nervous about this."

"Not half as nervous as she is." He reached across the couch and pulled her close. "On the other hand a good old knock 'em down cat fight around the campfire would be entertaining."

"Over you? Hardly. If she's that bent on reclamation she can have you."

"She's more than happy with how her life turned out. So am I."

"Good. I was starting to get concerned."

"No need, but I can understand why. Jennifer has made me realize that in some ways I'm hanging on to what Claire and I had back then and that I still have feelings. I'm just not sure it's as much about Claire as it is about the memories."

"You don't have to tell me you loved her Evan, it's obvious. I just have to think of who you spent your life with. But out of curiosity...could I take her?"

"You don't have to."

She snuggled against him. "I'm sure I could take her daughter."

"Why would you want to?"

"I've seen the way you look at her dear."

"Hell I'm old enough to be her big brother."

"Right, like that makes a difference. Seriously Evan, Jenn's a pretty appealing young lady. I can see how she could stir an old guy up."

"She has…no question."

"She talked to me earlier about your feelings. I told her she was safe."

"Of course she is. I've told her that."

She looked up into his eyes. "Tell me that."

"She's safe Marie."

"I must admit I was curious about your reaction after the kitchen incident."

"God Marie I'm old not cold. I had no more control over that than I did the situation. I won't harbor needless guilt for an unintentional leaning."

"Funny…I don't recall much of a leaning."

Evan looked skyward. "I'm going to hear about this for the rest of my life, right?"

"Probably." Marie smiled. "Come on, it's not all that often you get caught with your pants down…by someone else anyway. I'm sorry Evan…I guess I'm just getting wrapped up in all this emotional crap too. Our little Evermore has been turned completely upside down and there doesn't seem to be a damn thing I can do about it. Throughout everything that's happening I'm the odd man out and I'll have to admit I don't like it."

He held her tighter. "I understand and I'm sorry but it'll all be over tomorrow night. I know it's difficult but honestly it isn't easy on me either."

"I know it isn't and there's no need to apologize, it's just me. I really do enjoy Jenn's company and I know I'll miss her but it's also going to be nice to get the kingdom back to ourselves."

Chapter 34

Jenn felt herself falling, brambles scratching her arms. She tried to stand but tree roots spiraled through the earth clutching her feet. She couldn't move. Behind her the panting drew closer and when she thought it couldn't get any louder, it stopped.

She knew.

She could feel the warm breath on her neck. She turned to face her pursuer. The white wolf stood motionless within feet of her, teeth bared.

Then it howled.

Not like those at the Wildlife Park, the edge had gone from their voices. This one still held the terror of the wild.

She tried to run but her feet remained imprisoned.

The wolf closed in. Panting, eyes cold, breath hot…closer.

She tried to talk, to beg, but she had no voice.

Her mother called from somewhere in the darkness.

Lightning struck, thunder shook the ground, and the wolf lunged.

Jenn sat upright, waking herself as she always did when the dreams became too real. She moved to the edge of the bed and looked into the mirror. Pale, her eyes wide open. She took a deep breath, stood, and walked to the window. The grass glistened as raindrops fell gently, silver-like in the eerie light. The moon had found space between the scattering storm clouds and cast a peaceful glow over the mountain. Jenn shivered as she pulled her robe around her.

She walked to the bedroom door and listened, managing to silently open it. Slowly she stepped along the hall to the kitchen, stopped at the doorway and hesitantly peeked in.

All was quiet, the kitchen deserted. She tiptoed to the sink, found a clean glass on the washboard, and filled it with a gentle trickle from the tap.

As she sipped the water she turned and came face to face with her nightmare.

Ginn barked…the glass crashed to the floor.

Jenn jumped onto the counter and pulled her feet up, her heart pounding heavily.

"Don't move Jennifer," Evan said as he turned on the light. "You okay?"

"So far." She shielded her eyes to the brightness. "But I ain't moving for nothing. Is she really mad?"

"Ginn? No, she's fine. She's probably wondering why you're on the counter. She won't hurt you…you're one of the family."

"Then why can't I move?"

"Glass, it's all over the floor. I'll get the broom and pan, you just stay there."

Jenn started to giggle. "Cool PJs."

"Yeah, well…" He pulled the dustpan from the closet. "I decided I should save myself any further embarrassment."

"Funny, you seem more embarrassed tonight than you did then. Love the blue though, and the tag on the collar…so very chic and tight. Didn't have your size?"

"I could just as easily put this stuff away and leave you up there for the night."

"Sorry…and I really am sorry I woke you. I was thirsty."

Evan knelt before her and carefully brushed the broken glass into the pan. "Not a problem. The hound woke us when she heard someone moving about in the house."

"Good girl. I dreamt about her, a nightmare actually. That's what woke me. Then when I turned and she was sitting right behind me…."

Ginn whined then looked back as Marie leaned against the fridge. "Come now Jenn, don't make him beg. And what is it with you two and the kitchen? I prepare meals in here for crying out loud…get your ass off my counter."

"Sorry." Jenn laughed and lowered herself to the floor. "I was just admiring the Emperor's new clothes. Oh wait…that was last time wasn't it?"

Evan stood and handed her the broom and dustpan. "Okay Missy, you made it…you clean it up. I'm going back to bed. You know I'm getting just a tad tired of you two dragging out my little faux pas."

"I'm sure it wouldn't take two of us to drag it out," Marie muttered.

Evan shook his head and walked past her. "Goodnight," he grumbled then disappeared down the hall.

Jenn watched him then looked at Marie. "Think we maybe went too far?"

Marie nodded. "I think so. Let's get this mess cleaned up."

Chapter 35

The morning sun was particularly giving as Marie savored her coffee and quietly read the paper. This was her time, the brief respite before Evan staggered down the hallway and directed the rest of the day. She didn't look up as his bare feet squeaked a path across the freshly cleaned kitchen floor. He did this on purpose, she figured, but she wouldn't react this time.

"Good morning," she said, her eyes not leaving the paper.

"Hopefully." He poured the coffee from the carafe into an Edmonton Oilers mug then squeaked across to the counter and stood staring at an empty spot where the sugar jar once lived.

Still without looking up Marie pointed to the cupboard directly above where the jar was supposed to be. "Second shelf," she said. "Sleep well?"

"As well as expected." He reached and opened the door. "Why is the sugar in the cupboard?"

"Ants, remember? What does that mean exactly?"

"What?"

"As well as expected?"

"I went to bed expecting a certain quality of sleep and I got it."

"You still look tired."

"I have low expectations." He twisted the top then spooned a measure into his coffee. "Isn't that why we put it in a jar?"

"In retrospect it seemed like a good idea but someone keeps leaving the lid off."

"You're letting one of natures smallest creatures control our lives Marie."

"Its just sugar Evan..."

"Today yes, but soon ants will be running wild in the streets."

"They already are."

"We can't have antarchy...we must stop this in its tracks. Your heightened security may not be enough."

"Never is," she mumbled. "What critters eat ants?"

"Bigger ants, penguins...I don't know. Why?"

"Maybe it's like aphids. Marion said she went out and rounded up a jar of ladybugs and put them on her vines to eat the aphids."

"Yeah but one day the aphids will join forces with somebuggy that eats ladybugs. Before you know it we'll have an escalating entomological situation in the sweet peas."

"Of course we will." Marie watched as he twisted the lid on the sugar then put the jar back on the counter. "Good morning?" she asked.

He squeaked to the dinette and sat across from her.

"Good morning," he said. "Where's our houseguest?"

"She's still in her room organizing notes or something. You didn't tell her that her mum was going to be here?"

"Claire wanted it to be a surprise." He started reading the back of the paper. "Kilo bags of hamster nummers are forty percent off."

"We don't have a hamster."

"Ah yes but hamsters are 'buy one get the second one free'." He sipped his coffee and frowned. "How would you feel if you were the second hamster? That'd be something the first hamster would hold over you all your life." He squinted his eyes and wrinkled his nose. "They bought me 'cos they wanted me..." he said in a high, raspy voice. "You were free. That's the only reason you're here. They didn't ever want you but you were free so they shrugged their shoulders and said 'if we really have to take another one give us the funny-looking hairball in the corner...'."

"What the hell are you talking about?"

"Nothing." Evan looked at the back of the paper again. "Big box has ladies undergarments half-off. We should go take a peek."

She ignored him as he continued reading and squeaking his feet under the table. He studied the back of the newsprint intently. Other than an ad for bunk beds in the same column as an article on Planned Parenthood, there was nothing to hold his interest. He tapped his fingers on the table. Soon he found a rhythm and, tapping with increasing authority, started singing:

"My Peggy Soo hoo hoo…hoo, hoo hoo hoo…"

Marie flicked the newspaper at him. "Stoppit," she hissed.

Playing quieter drums on the tabletop Evan peered along the baseboards under the counter where the sugar lived. Then he looked above the paper. Her eyes moved back and forth as she read, like one of those annoying black cat wall clocks with the tail and eyes that move to and fro with every tick.

"Tick, tock," he whispered, staring at her. "Tick, tock, tick, tock."

Still she ignored him.

"Tick, tock, tick, tock, tick, tock, tick, tock, tick…"

She was glaring at him, brow furrowed. "What are you doing?"

"You have incredibly mobile eyes."

"Thank you." Marie looked down at the paper. "This is disgusting."

"What is?"

"There's a story about a man who committed suicide by locking himself in a freezer."

"The ultimate act of self-preservation."

"It's not funny Evan."

"How do they know it was suicide?"

"He wrote a note to his wife saying he was going to end it all by locking himself in the freezer?"

"A man of his word, you gotta respect that." He sipped his coffee and again looked at the baseboards under the counter where the sugar lived. "How did he lock the freezer? The lock's supposed to be on the outside isn't it?"

"Accept it Evan. The man's dead…frozen to death. Does anything else really matter?"

He shrugged. "I guess not. What else was in the freezer?"

"I don't know. Why?"

"Wifey will probably have to throw out a lot of good stuff, what with hubby being dead in there and all. It could get expensive."

Marie glared at him, silently stood, picked up her cup then squeaked across the kitchen floor to the back door. She let the screen door slam behind her as she stepped out onto the porch.

"Tick, tock, tick, tock..." Evan whispered as he sipped his coffee.

Marie made herself comfortable on the couch while Ginn climbed out from under the porch, shook her coat loose, stretched then climbed the stairs.

"Brekkies in your dish girl," Marie said.

Ginn looked at the dish beside the couch, yawned, and crawled up to rest her head on Marie's lap. They looked at each other until Marie settled her hand in the midst of the long softness behind the wolf's ears and scritched her neck.

"The old man's bent," she whispered.

Ginn whined, her tail drifting slowly back and forth.

"I know, but more so than usual," Marie said, leaning her head back on the couch. She closed her eyes and imagined the wife of the frozen man. How must she have felt finding the note then opening the freezer? What if she didn't find the note? Perhaps she just went to the freezer to get some mint chocolate chip ice cream or some grape juice concentrate. She pictured the woman's face as the light came on and amid the freezer fog, she found him. What amount of despair would lead a man to crawl into a freezer to end it all? Evan was right; they can't be locked from the inside...could be suspicious. What was he wearing? Perhaps he wore nothing, why would he? How big was the freezer? Did he have to curl up to fit inside? An image came to mind. Marie pictured a naked frigid man, his legs pulled up and resembling a huge frozen Christmas turkey packed between the ice cream and the homemade pies. Then she giggled.

"Oh crap," she said as more involuntary giggles rippled through her.

Ginn looked up and whined again.

Marie looked into her deep blue eyes. "Nothing," she said, catching her breath. "Go back to sleep."

Evan stepped out onto the porch, leaned back, and arched his neck. "Do your bones crack more now than they used to?"

"You okay?" she asked.

"I'm old," he replied, sounding extra-old.

"You're allowed to be both you know, okay and old."

"I hate multi-tasking."

"Spill it Evan, what's going on?"

"If I knew I'd make it go off. I'm just a little confused I guess. Yesterday I was kinda ready for today. Today I'm kinda not." The gate-lock clicked. He looked along the path. Dobson stepped onto the lawn and walked head-lowered with purpose across the yard. Evan watched him run down the bank and onto the beach. "Does he do that often?"

Marie nodded. "He started about a week ago."

"Why?"

"I'm not sure, really."

"In the old days we could shoot him."

"Yes, but would you?"

"Yeah." He shuffled across the porch and sat on the top step. He leaned back and arched his neck again, wincing at the sound. "Hear that?"

"You're getting on Evan, come to grips with it. You can hide behind your 'not growing up' flag forever but it won't change the fact that you're not as young as you used to be. Everyone gets old and there's nothing you can do about it…its life."

"A simple 'yes' or 'no' would've sufficed," he muttered. "Jenn's kicking about the kitchen."

"Okay." She gently moved Ginn aside and stood. "It'll be fine Evan," she said, opening the door. "It always is, isn't it?"

"Always." He gazed at Dobson's footprints on the still damp grass. He'd contemplated trying to nap before they arrived but he knew it wouldn't work. It had been a long, cold, and lonely night. When he did sleep it was peppered with rapid-fire unrelated images and rushing noises but most of the night was spent awake and thinking. He thought mostly of Claire and how she looked as that door opened. The years fell off his shoulders when she smiled. This wasn't good. It wouldn't take much to ignite those feelings that he now realized had been smoldering for decades. He had to keep it all in check.

Then there was Andy. It was probably better for her if she decided not to be here but he knew she would be.

He heard the gate open and looked along the path. Claire came around the corner of the house dressed semi-retro in a full floral skirt and puffy peach blouse with three strands of assorted colored and shaped beads around her neck.

"Now I wish I'd worn my jeans," she commented, walking warily past the gnomes. "Nosey little buggers aren't they?"

"They're just curious."

"And yellow," she added.

Evan met her at the bottom of the steps and gave her a welcoming hug. "I'm really glad you're here. I love the beads."

"I earned them in New Orleans."

"Wouldn't surprise me." He looked along the walk. "Where's Andy?"

"On her cell with Mitchie."

"Mitchie?"

"Michelle. She's Steve's little girl, one of his rentals."

"Starting early are we? Andy told me about the incident with him."

"Its history Evan…let it go." She pointed at Pokey. "Why is that one so damned forthcoming?"

"He's my homage to the young lads of today."

"Dare I ask why?"

"They're inclined to lead with their pants."

"Ah yes, that stupid alpha-male shit. Don't you know that we females are supposed to be like, really impressed?" She laughed. "But you're right…they do tend to put it all out there."

"Augmented assets mostly…must be akin to a push-up bra."

"I sense a certain disdain. Not too fussy about today's youth?"

"I find it interesting that the girls today seem to mature way too early and the boys are taking far longer to get out of that drooling idiot stage."

"Ouch, that's a bit harsh. Besides it's always been like that."

"I guess. Seriously…didn't you worry about some of the guys Jennifer brought home?"

"Of course, it's my job. And you're right, 'drooling idiots' would cover a few of them." She shook her head. "They'd follow her around like a hound in heat. I remember Devon's reaction when this Trevor kid played cock of the roost in the house. He was back out on the step and down the street on his skateboard in five seconds, never to return."

"I think I might like this man of yours."

"I think so too. I have to trust Jenn to make her own choices. It's the only way she'll be able to separate the bad from the good. She's a pretty smart young lady and lately her taste has definitely improved. I still play mama lion and she reprimands me every time I ask where she's been or who she's been with. It's hard to let go, especially with the girls."

"Lynn Carey."

"Pardon?"

"Mama Lion."

"Don't start that with me Evan Morris. I spent far too much of those two years trying to figure out what you meant with those cryptic songs and singers."

"Sorry."

She smiled an old Claire smile. "No you're not, you enjoy driving me nuts."

He winked and smiled back. "It's what I do best."

"It is. But you must have gone through the same thing with your daughter and the boys?"

"Yeah." He pointed to a huge rose bush at the back of the yard. "Drooling idiots make great compost. I don't know, maybe I've become old-fashioned as well as antique."

"According to those you're inclined to malign we all have."

"I'm not maligning anyone. It's statement of fact. I suppose I might have been like that back then, I don't really remember."

"I remember the boys in high school and generally they were loud, obnoxious, and juvenile but there were some good ones, just like today. You can't paint all guys with the same brush."

He dropped his head to one side and looked into her eyes. "You did." A mischievous smile formed. "Remember?"

"I do, and you were oh-so-pretty in pink." Claire looked around the yard. "So where is my little girl?"

"She's with Marie in the kitchen."

"Jenn and kitchen, now those are two words I've rarely heard in the same conversation."

"Mum!" Jenn yelled as she burst through the door and bolted towards her. "What are you doing here?"

"I rode down with Andy." Mother and daughter locked in a vigorous embrace.

"I can't believe this," Jenn said, "why didn't you tell me?"

"Actually I didn't decide until yesterday morning when she asked. It seemed like a good idea."

"You were here last night? Did the old hippie know?"

"Yes but I told him not to say anything, and you show some respect young lady."

"Sorry…elderly hippie."

"That's better." Claire laughed then looked to the top of the steps. "Marie? I'm Claire."

"I gathered," said Marie as she joined them on the path. "There's no mistaking the resemblance. It's good to finally meet you."

They fumbled a hug.

"I'm sorry," Claire said, "I was really nervous about this moment."

Marie nodded. "Me too, thankfully it's over. Now I'm afraid I'll have to put you to work."

"Whatever you need."

Evan watched the three women climb the steps and go into the house. While the introduction seemed to go well he couldn't help but feel that disaster was checking her look in the mirror.

"Good morning Evan." Andy smiled as she approached him. "You look exhausted."

"Better than 'old'," he said.

"Sorry about that." She dropped a cell phone into her purse. "The posse just left Jasper. They decided to party last night so some of them'll be sleeping all the way."

"I assume this Mitchie is driving then?"

"Hell no, Carl is the designated driver…liver problems. I don't think Mitchie's feet can reach the pedals yet."

Evan smiled. Based on preliminary dynamics this was going to be an interesting evening.

Andy squinted at Pokey. "What's with the horny dwarf?"

He frowned. "Gnome...I've learned a lot about the female animal since I made him. You're all turning into dirty old women. Not one of you can pass the little guy without noticing."

"Too hard not to...where's Ceejay?"

"In the kitchen with Marie and Jenn."

"She was really on edge about this Evan. She almost decided to stay at the hotel."

"I'm glad she didn't and so far everything seems okay. As it looks like we have seven or eight hours to prepare for the onslaught is there anything you girls want to do?"

"Girls?"

"You'll always be girls...."

"Actually I'd like to just relax and get reacquainted if that's okay?"

"Fine by me."

Chapter 36

Mother and daughter walked along the beach, Jenn tossing a stick for Ginn while Claire enjoyed the fresh air. "It's beautiful here," she said, "just the sort of place I would expect Evan to settle down. Marie seems nice?"

"She is," Jenn replied, "really nice. But she wasn't looking forward to meeting you."

"That went both ways. So what do you think of your mum's old flame?"

"Why didn't you tell me how involved you were?"

"I'm not sure, really. I did tell you a lot about my childhood."

"But you overlooked those two years. Bad memories?"

"A couple," said Claire, "but by and large they were pretty special times."

"That's what he says."

"You still haven't told me what you think."

"I really like him, but there's so much more I'd like to find out."

"I doubt you will. He doesn't believe in letting people see everything."

"Oh…" Jenn smirked. "I wouldn't say that."

Claire stopped walking and frowned at her daughter. "What's going on?"

Jenn recounted the events in the kitchen, giving only as much detail as she felt comfortable giving. By the time she was done

Claire had collapsed onto the sand in laughter. "I can just imagine the look on his face…and yours!"

Jenn shook her head. "Mum, this isn't funny."

"Oh yes it is. Did you tell Marie?"

"Apparently he did. All she said was that you and I had one more thing in common, we'd both seen him…you know."

Again Claire burst into giggles. "God Jenn it really is funny, and Marie's right. I wonder how many mums and daughters can say that?"

"At least two too many. You're not mad at him are you?"

"No Jenn, I think I still know him. He would never put you in that situation deliberately."

"Can I ask you something?"

"Always."

"Evan and I talked that lifestyle, the undressed part. He thinks I'm too hung up on it and I should let it go, but it's not easy. I just can't understand it, especially about you."

"Why not me?"

"Well…" Jenn shrugged. "The fact that you're my mother, a revered and respected role model for an impressionable young girl has a lot to do with it."

"Maybe we should step out of those roles for a minute and talk woman to woman?"

"Actually I'd like that."

Claire stood and they continued their walk down the beach. "I don't know how much he's told you but I do understand you getting hung up on it. You're probably a little shocked at your old mum."

"Depends on your definition of 'little'. How did you get into that sort of thing?"

"You say that with certain disgust Jenn, but it wasn't like that at all." She looked out over the river. "We'd been camping in a park in San Francisco with a bunch of kids. It was pretty much a twenty-four hour a day party. One morning Evan decided that he'd had enough of it so we crossed over the Golden Gate then cruised until we found a way down to a beach. The guys were stoked because there was this old military base where we turned off. Concrete bunkers, the whole works. It was a pretty steep hike down to the shore but it was worth it."

"This was after the hippie-nippie art?"

"He shared that did he?" Claire shook her head. "Yes, it was. This place was spectacular. There were these huge rocks, deep blue sky, high waves, and just enough sand. It was so isolated. We spent what was left of the afternoon just lying in the sun. That evening we lit a campfire and heated up something-or-other out of a can."

"That you stole."

"Damn, how much did he tell you? No wonder you're having problems with all of this."

"I'm sorry," said Jenn, "I'll be quiet now. So you heated up the hot food...then what?"

"It started to pour so we climbed back up to the van and listened to the rain on the roof. Andy lit a couple of candles and pulled out a deck of cards. We played rummy, or something. When it came back around for her to deal, she set the stack face down between the candles on the floor of the van and suggested we try something funner. She told Jack to guess whether the top card was red or black. He said red, and it was. She said he was safe then she took a card and called it black. It was red. She took off one of her shoes and tossed it behind her and then told Evan it was his turn and the funner game was on. It ended up with Jack and Evan in the buff watching Andy and I finish the game."

"So everybody was going to end up unclothed anyway."

"Nude isn't a bad word Jenn and yes, that was the point. Andy however, either through good luck or well-tuned ESP abilities, ended up spending twenty minutes playing the game by herself."

"And what did the rest of you do?"

"Watched and waited. It got pretty intense. When Andy finally dropped her drawers we had to send two very self-conscious men out into the rain to cool off."

"Waaaay too much!" Jenn waved her hands in the air. "This is just weird. I'm not sure I like this woman to woman stuff."

Claire put her arm across Jenn's shoulder. "That's the way it was. If you don't want to know..."

"...don't ask. I guess I wasn't expecting all the sordid details."

"Sorry but it doesn't sound like Evan spared you much either."

"I've got it all on my recorder."

"I think I'd like to hear that."

"I think I'd like you to. Marie said it was all innocent fun."

"I'm not sure I'd use the word 'innocent' but there wasn't any free love or swapping if that's what she means, although Andy would have leapt at the chance."

Jenn's eyes widened. "She wanted Evan?"

"Oh yeah, the look on her face when Evan bared all was pretty obvious. Although I'll have to admit that I was a more than a little curious when Jack peeled 'em off. I told her I wasn't interested but she could check with Evan if she wanted."

"That was a bit risky wasn't it?"

"Not really, I knew him too well. If she had asked him I knew what his answer would have been but she didn't. The fact that she talked to me first meant everything. That moment forged our friendship for all these years. It was simple, I was with Evan and she was with Jack. The only thing that changed was we'd seen each other naked. Everything else stayed the same."

"I'm still having trouble with that concept."

"Most people can't understand it. I didn't before that night and I'm not sure I do now but at the time it was okay. A lot of respect grew out of that naughty little game."

"That's another thing Marie talks about, the trust and respect for each other."

"You have to have it at times like that, at any time really. We'd spent a lot of time watching the real flower children jumping from guy to guy in the park. I guess I was a little old-fashioned but I thought it was disgusting. Evan's comment was that they had no respect for their bodies or their souls. I figured they were just too ripped to care. I think that was the real reason we moved to the beach. Andy and I couldn't go out without attracting half-naked young boys with more in the basement than the attic."

"Mum!"

"Sorry, but that was life for a lot of those people…smoking and making out. Even after Andy dropped a few of them they still didn't get the message."

"Dropped them?"

"Put 'em down. She was the fighter in the bunch; the farm girl who hauled sacks of grain, toted bales…the whole thing. Jack used to say that when he met her she was carrying a cow under each arm while she kicked the bull out of the barn."

"She was really that tough?"

Claire nodded. "I'd bet she still is."

"Okay, so these guys are after you?"

"The girls did the same with our guys. Andy was continually peeling some stoned flo-chi off of Jack. Evan finally got fed up with it and we left. Our time at that beach was pretty liberating both physically and emotionally. We spent two days running free and learning a lot about each other and not just the obvious." Claire chuckled. "The toughest lesson was to discover how quickly flesh that had never seen the light of day would fry up, especially the guys."

"Um, I'm afraid to comment on that."

"Good decision. So how did you really feel in the kitchen with the elderly hippie."

"Well…" Jenn took a deep breath. "At first I guess I was shocked. He was so casual about it and he chatted on as though nothing was wrong. Soon it didn't really matter to me either. He was on the other side of the table not three feet away but he was still just Evan and dressed or not he somehow manages to put me at ease."

"I know what you mean. You trusted him?"

"I must have, I stayed and talked to him. Tell me about the cabin?"

"Jack's dad had a deserted homestead property in the country and the four of us would go up on weekends. Evan named it the Bar-Ass Ranch."

"It figures."

"The first Saturday we went up for a picnic it was stinking hot. After too much wine Andy and I decided to head to the stream. We hadn't brought suits so we stripped to bras and panties and splashed around until Evan came down with a camera. He told us to smile on the count of three. We lost the underwear and smiled pretty for him."

"God Mum…really?"

"Everything was wet and see-through anyway so we figured what the hell. Besides we'd kind of gotten used to seeing each other on the trip and if it was okay in California why not Alberta?"

"I thought all you flower children went braless?"

"Guys liked to think so but not always. A lot of the time we wore this thin silky number, actually I think they even promoted it as the no-bra. That flimsy little thing didn't really do much of a job and wasn't held together by even a single stitch of modesty."

Jenn frowned. "Modesty?"

"Believe it or not we did have some. The first few trips out to the cabin were beautiful. We were totally relaxed and open and honest with each other. Sure we got into a few interesting activities but I guess they were pretty innocent, to use Marie's word."

"Yeah? I heard about the touch football. That doesn't sound all that innocent."

Claire smiled. "Okay, there were times…but really, it was all in fun. Ask your new buddy about it. I'm sure he still has the pictures."

"You wouldn't mind?"

"Hell no, they can't be any worse than what we've talked about can they?"

"I guess not. You said the first few trips were beautiful. What happened?"

"Simple. Steve and the rest of them got involved. At first everything seemed okay. The relationships were still sacred and so were the feelings…the respect thing we talked about. But in time the wine turned to dope, the crowd got bigger then bolder and the innocent fun wasn't enough for most of them. Things got carried away so Evan and I withdrew our membership."

"Yeah but wasn't that the whole hippie credo…sex and drugs, that sort of thing?"

"They called us hippies but it was based on the look and the gypsy-style life we lived for a while. I prefer to think of us as peripheral and not true hippies in the usual sense of the word and in all honesty I'd rather not be linked to the name period. We still had certain values. We didn't do the drugs and we couldn't be as indiscriminate as the rest of them. I sometimes wonder what those girls thought of themselves after they got straight and grew up a little. I know I'd have been pretty ashamed of myself. I even get a little embarrassed thinking about some of the stuff that we did and really, it was nothing. Evan's comment on self-respect hit it on the head."

"You still seem to be good friends with Andy though."

"And Jack up until he started playing around, then we drifted apart. When Carl called and asked me to phone her I just went over. It was a bad situation but it was clear that the friendship was still there. I love Andy, she's a little spinney but she's still a true friend."

"I think maybe I'd like to get back to the mother-daughter thing but thanks for being so up front with me."

"Always...but Evan's right. You really have to let this part go. There's so much more to the story."

"I know." Jenn smiled. "But this is the fun chapter."

"I suppose it is but you have to focus on what you started out to do. The story of Evan's brief career doesn't go back to the time you're insisting on talking about. It was after all that."

"But he became what he became because of all that, right?"

"To an extent but I'd be willing to bet he'd have followed the same course and been much the same person today even if we hadn't done that trip or the ranch."

"Maybe..." She gazed down at the sand beneath her. "Mum, I know we've had the 'just say no' talk but you've never told me about your experiences with drugs. You just said you didn't do them, Evan said you tried pot twice."

"We did try it a couple of times to see what the fuss was about but that was all. Evan saw what it did to otherwise sensible people and that pretty much ended it. It wasn't a big deal for either of us one way or the other. Jack and Andy got into it a bit though."

"They didn't pressure you guys?"

"Respect, remember? It was fine with us that they did and they were okay that we didn't."

"Do you mind me asking what attracted you to him?" Jenn asked.

"I don't really know. I was at a reading...he came and sat with me and we talked. I got a pretty comfortable feeling even then. All the boys I knew at the time were loud, pushy, and needy in every sense of the word. Along comes this quiet, unassuming guy who just wanted to talk. He was so shy it was sexy."

"Evan shy?"

Claire shook her head. "It was a week before I finally forced him to hold hands."

"He told me he was smitten instantly."

"He was and I knew it, but I wanted to be sure. The fact that he didn't rush me into anything was the capper. It was at least another week before he got up the nerve to kiss me."

"Sounds like you want to nominate him for Sainthood."

"Hell no," said Claire, "that's the last thing he is. He could be a real bad ass when he wanted to be. I somehow get the feeling that's still true. It certainly was back then."

"Care to expand on that?"

"I've expanded too much already. Besides we're out of the woman to woman thing."

"Did he ever call you 'Jenny'?"

"Interesting question. Did he say something?"

"No, I just wondered."

"Only when he was teasing me." Claire closed her eyes and smiled. "I'd forgotten that."

"He says he still cares for you. Do you feel the same way?"

"I always will. He's never given me any reason to feel otherwise."

"But isn't this like you're betraying dad?"

"Can I plead the Fifth?"

"This is Canada Mum, sorry."

Claire took Jenn's hand as they walked. "He really said that?"

"It took a while for him to admit it but it really is obvious."

"You're turning into a little tattle-tale Jenn. I don't think he'd appreciate you telling me this."

"I'm not sure he'd be bothered, plus you can't tell me you haven't noticed it yourself."

Claire thought of the look at the hotel when he realized she was there. The welcoming hug that was so gentle yet so firm and lasted far too long, the trembling in his arms, in her knees, and the feeling that she never wanted to let go of him again.

"I've noticed," she said quietly.

Chapter 37

Evan edged up to Marie as she shredded a lettuce and tossed it into a large salad bowl. "All these women here and you're stuck all alone in the kitchen?" he asked.

"I kicked them out. They were giggling and carrying on like schoolgirls."

"Sixty-year old schoolgirls?"

"I didn't say they were smart schoolgirls." Marie laughed. "They were just having a little fun although I do have to question the age of your other woman. I'd guess forty-five, tops. Think she's had a little nip and tuck here and there now and then?"

"Wife and ex-girlfriend 101. So where is everybody?"

"Jenn and her big sister took Ginn for a walk along the river and Andy's snestled out on the porch. I'm a little worried Evan…this doesn't seem to have hit her yet."

"I know but until it does there's not much we can do. Need a hand?"

"No, you can beat it too."

He leaned back against the counter and crossed his arms. "Out with it," he said.

"It's Claire, I'm sorry…."

He put his arm around her. "It's okay, I can imagine how I'd feel if you brought an old boyfriend home."

"Oh you'd handle it just fine. That's what pisses me off. Besides there aren't any boyfriends that I'd care to bring home to meet my husband."

"Tankboy?"

"Especially him." She turned and put her face against his shoulder. "I like her Evan."

He pulled back and looked into her eyes. "What?"

"I really wanted to not like her, I was prepared for that but dammit she's okay. I can see why you felt…why you feel the way you do about her."

"Uh huh, so what's the problem?"

"You three have such history. I know there was life before Marie but it sounds like such a good life. I really feel like an eavesdropper, like I'm peeping through a keyhole at all I missed. I don't have much to compare it with. We really don't have a lot in common."

"Okay, so why don't I finish up what you're doing and you go out there and find something to share with them."

"Don't patronize me old man. It's like you're sending me off to a new school and encouraging me to make friends."

"I suppose it does, but you all have at least one thing in common."

"What's that?"

"Me?"

"I'm sure we'll find something better dear."

"There is nothing better…dear."

She tossed another handful of lettuce into the wooden salad bowl. "I really am concerned about Andy. The last few years sound like they were pretty tough but sooner or later she has to let it out. The realization will hit her, I know it."

"It will and hopefully it'll be while she's here and has friends around her. Now, can I help you with anything?"

"Tell you what, just pour a coffee and park at the table. We can talk while I finish this up."

Chapter 38

Jenn and Claire quietly walked up the steps onto the porch. Andy was stretched out on the couch, her eyes closed and her left arm draped over her forehead.

"Should we wake her?" Jenn whispered.

"She's not asleep," Claire answered.

"How do you know?"

"She's not purring."

Jenn tried to giggle quietly. "Purring? She purrs?"

"Like a cougar."

"Not a kitten?"

"A few years ago maybe…no, she was a cougar back then too."

Andy raised her hand from her forehead, single digit prominent. "And another one for your llama," she muttered.

"She's not making any sense," Jenn said. "She must have been asleep."

Claire sat in the rocking chair across from the couch. "That's about the only time she does make sense. How are you doing Andy?"

"I don't know," she replied. "I'm pretty anxious about the crew coming by tonight. I'm thinking of going back to the hotel. Would you come with me?"

"Of course, if that's what you want."

Andy swung her legs off the couch and patted the cushion. "Here Jenn, sit."

Jenn sat and put her feet up on the railing.

Claire watched her daughter kick off her shoes. "You really have made yourself at home haven't you?"

"They make it easy. So Andy, I know what the term 'cougar' refers to these days…"

Claire stopped her. "Careful Jenn, our chat on the beach was nothing compared to what this lady could tell you."

Jenn looked at her mum then grinned at Andy. "Enlighten me," she said.

Andy smiled. "Remind me to tell you about Little Boy Blue in Boots at the motel in Oregon when the old prude isn't around."

"Old prude?" Claire leaned back in the rocking chair. "I've just spent a half-hour dispelling that rumor."

"Yeah…" Jenn lowered her gaze. "We had a woman-to-woman chat about the trip to San Francisco, hippie-art…the Bar-Ass ranch. All the nudes fit to print, y'know."

Andy raised her eyebrows. "You talked about that stuff?"

Claire nodded. "It sounds like Evan painted a one-sided view of our lives back then. I told her that it wasn't the whole picture."

Andy closed her eyes and rested her head on the back of the couch. "There really was so much more to it Jenn. We were a family in an almost perfect world. All of us were pretty much on our own. Our real families were in other countries or provinces, your grandparents were in Calgary. We were all we had. We lived in this beater house by the airport. It was so bad at the start that Evan hung a 'Squalor' sign over the door. He and Jack had made a deal to fix it up in exchange for rent but when the work was done the owner sold the place from under us. It was good while it lasted though." A gentle expression crossed her face. "I still think of those days as the best ever. No matter what happened on the outside you'd come home and everything was all right. There were smiles in every drawer. Everything was straight up. We were equal in every way and we were always there for each other. We had some rough times but they only helped build the bond, especially between the old prude and me."

"But you two are so different," Jenn said. "That had to be pretty tough."

"We all had different attitudes…different ways of doing things but small stuff like that didn't get in the way of the better picture and really, we're not so different."

Claire pulled her feet up on the chair and rested her chin on her knees. "It worked so well. The guys had jobs and we went to university. We all shared the chores and the painting and fix-up. Everybody pulled their weight."

Jenn looked across at Claire. "Sounds like an urban commune."

"I guess it was in a way, especially after Danny and Carol moved in."

"Always room for two more?"

"Those two especially. Jack and Evan knew nothing about rebuilding houses but Danny knew it all. He'd been augmenting his income from the music with under the table construction jobs so when it came to roofing the house or rebuilding the garage he took charge. Carol took things a little more seriously than the rest of us and she ended up being the grounding we all needed. They fit in really well. Like Andy said, everything was straight up."

Jenn frowned. "Sounds boring. You guys didn't party?"

"Probably no more than anybody else about that time. The guys were putting in long days with jobs and the house; the girls were studying pretty well every night. But when the week-end rolled around we partied tough."

"At the ranch?"

"No, the ranch was a different world altogether. It was a retreat from the rest of it. Sure, we brought along a little wine or whatever and we had some silly fun but there were no drunken bashes. Mostly they were quiet times…together times."

"But six people living in the same house…there had to be problems."

"I'll take this one," Andy said. "Other than only having one bathroom there weren't that many issues. If anything came up, we'd talk it through. It was simple because we were all pretty laid-back types. Then your mum came up with this candle-chat idea and it made it even easier."

"Candle-chat?"

"It's based on an old native custom, the talking stick or something…except we used a candle. We'd sit around the table with only the candle lit. It was passed around and when it was in front of you it was your opportunity say anything that was on your mind with no repercussion, just discussion."

Jenn smiled at her mum. "Man, does that sound familiar."

Claire nodded. "Devon and I did the same thing with the kids but without the candle."

Andy laughed. "Yeah, Jack and I tried the chats with ours. After the first confessional he decided he'd rather not know what they were up to."

"Devon felt much the same way once this little terror starting owning up." Claire reached and patted Jenn's knee. "You gave him more than a few grey hairs."

Andy sat up straight. "Really? Tell me more…."

Jenn shook her head. "Another time…when the old prude isn't around."

Chapter 39

"She's very much like her mum isn't she?" Marie asked as she sat beside Evan at the table.

"We've already covered that," he said.

"I know, I'm just trying to get a conversation going."

He leaned the chair back and put his hands behind his head. "Didn't you tell me that ants are repelled by walnuts?"

"It isn't going to work."

"What isn't?"

"Rambling rhetoric. I'm serious Evan, I really do like Claire."

"What every husband wants to hear."

"I would have thought so."

"Actually I suppose it is." He let the chair drop forward with a crash. "It's not really Claire although she's part of it. I'm just wondering what might have been."

"How very un-Evanish of you."

"It is isn't it?" He smiled, pushing the chair back again as he peered out the window at the three on the porch. "Maybe it's Peter speaking. It was so easy putting Evan Morris to rest but bringing him back…it's tough Marie."

"Do you really want him back?"

"I think so. I'm mostly wondering why I let him go in the first place. I'm not sure he wants to come back though. I think he's holding a grudge…playing hard to get."

"Small point here…same person?"

"That's what Ginn said."

"I'm sure she did. Even though you've been Peter for all these years you're still the person Evan was…or is." She shuddered.

"Okay, now I'm confused."

"You should check it out from this side." He set the chair down quietly on the floor. "It should be that simple shouldn't it?"

"It is that simple Evan."

"So why do I feel like a frog in a toilet?"

"All of this…Jack's death, Jenn, Claire, and Andy…it's a lot happening all at once."

"Welcome to the undulating universe of cosmic coincidence. Remember Monday?"

"Uh yes, why?"

"So do I…clearly. The rest of the week, not so much."

"A little emotional overload perhaps?"

"No question." He looked around the kitchen. "Maybe if we scattered a few walnuts about?"

"What, so they'll trip over them? It's not the nut; it's the oil in the walnut leaf they don't like."

"Done a little research have we?"

"We're at war Evan, we must know our enemy."

"Not much of a war…more of a spat. I've only seen a couple over the last few days and they were rapidly retreating toward the door waving teeny white flags."

"They'll be back when they figure out how to un-lid the sugar. Frog in a toilet?"

"Emotionally treading water in life's swirling sewage-bound torrent."

"Uh-huh." She patted his knee. "That one needs work."

Chapter 40

Marie turned when she heard the door open. "Enjoy your walk Jenn?"

"It was a learning experience." She leaned in the doorway to the kitchen. "Hey Evan, can we talk some more?"

"Anytime," he said. "What's up?"

"I've decided to expand my interview and I'd like to ask you a few more questions if I may."

"Expand?"

"You were right about rethinking my leanings. Based on everything we've talked about I've decided to turn it into an article on the sixties, more of a lifestyle approach."

"So I'm out?"

"No, the interview's still in but it really isn't all about you Evan."

"Of course it is," he said. "Last night you were ready to give up?"

"It didn't seem like anything was coming together but now I've got the angle. I felt guilty about crashing your little paradise and after thinking about it I realized I could do this without tearing apart the life that you've worked so hard to build. I've got most of your part down but I need some serious background to keep it honest. I really would like to explore it further?"

"Not a bad idea." He turned to Marie. "You okay with everything here?" he asked.

"Always am, you two go talk." She stood and walked toward the counter. "I'll just finish up the dressing then go commonize with Claire and Andy."

"Let's head to the study and get comfortable." Evan smiled at Jenn. "Only one request…please no more about the partying? I really am tired of dredging all that up."

"That's what Mum said…let it go, there's so much more to the story." She turned and followed him down the hallway. "That's what I'd like to talk about if it's okay?"

"That's more than okay and I promise to try and stay on task."

"Me too." She clicked on the recorder. "Let's do the whole trip again, leaving out what we've already discussed. First your overall take on the sixties…what do you think it all meant from a sociological standpoint?"

"Okay, now you're sounding like a journalist. That's a loaded question and the best one you've asked so far." He slipped into his chair behind the desk as Jenn sat down in front of him. She set the recorder beside the lamp waiting for his answer. His expression became one of curiosity. "My overall impression…" He closed his eyes. "That won't be easy to sum up in a few sentences."

"I've got extra batteries," she said.

"For me it was a personal experience and I tend only to reflect on my own thoughts but I suppose they would answer your question. Obviously there was a huge shift in the ideals and dreams from the generation before. The tragic part was all those people had fought the war then come home and busted their butts trying to provide for their families. Through the fifties they worked hard to build a future for their children, a future filled with promise…homes, cars, and happy babies…and we tossed it away. It was as if we had slapped their faces and told them that they'd wasted all that time and energy."

"I never thought of it from that aspect, the parents."

"There were fathers who'd worked a hell of a lot of overtime to get their kids into college then one bright sunny day the kid drops out and wanders the streets with a thousand other drop-outs harboring no motivations other than getting high and doing nothing."

"Okay, but the movement itself was founded on sound values, power to the people and stop the war…all those things, right?"

"Certainly the ideals were sound and the early energy was well-directed and motivated but the movement also attracted the less desirable in the same way that rock concerts and other gatherings do today. You have your core group, in this case the people who truly believed in something bigger than they were…the new values of love, peace and harmony…the real peace guys. Basically they practiced peaceful disobedience, preferring to be dragged to jail for sitting rather than fighting. Their lifestyle was such that it attracted many who didn't have the same ideals. They were just into the drugs and crap. Rock concert crowds or even today's peaceful protesters always have that element whose sole purpose is to party hardy and create a little shit. Same thing, basically."

"So did it accomplish anything?"

"Another loaded question. What started out as a peaceful awareness movement ended up being a rejection of everything that the establishment stood for. It wasn't as much about finding alternatives or trying to rebuild society as it was about damning the very society that allowed them this freedom of expression. What could have been a positive mass consciousness ended up being totally negative. I saw the whole thing as a contradiction. All this love and peace was happening on the west coast while Motor City madness, to quote Lightfoot, was running rampant and their 'brothers' were being gunned down in the streets. These kids were suffering sunstroke while cities burned on the other side of the country. The flower children got doped up and made out on the streets of San Francisco as tanks and troops took over the streets of Detroit. The irony of the situation was lost on everyone." He arched his back, stretching his arms over his head. "I think most people went through the sixties suffering from gross ignorance. They came out of 1967 assuming that all the daisies, peace, love, and brotherhood had accomplished something. Then came 1968…Bobby Kennedy, Martin Luther King…college protests, more civil unrest and an escalating war on the other side of the world. For a brief time a certain segment of the world came together in flowerful harmony but in the end it suffered a whimpering death."

Jenn leaned back in the chair. "Why did you go to San Francisco?"

"When Claire first suggested it we were all a little uncertain. But as we drove I felt the pull, the need to make the pilgrimage to the center of the culture. I couldn't explain it but there were thousands like me. It was like 'Close Encounters of the Third Kind'. I understand how Richard Dreyfuss felt being drawn to Devil's Tower without the slightest idea why. Overall I was disappointed in the San Francisco experience though. I expected something magical to happen but it didn't. It was a big let-down."

"But the four of you made your own magic."

"That's the best thing to come out of that trip. Claire, Andy, Jack, and I became a kind of alternative family. A lot of times there was very little conversation because we each knew what the others were thinking or feeling. There was a helluva lot of love there…and respect, trust, and understanding. Those tried and true values were reborn in that new age. I'm not sure you'll ever find four people that cared that much or were as emotionally bonded to each other."

"When did you get your first real feel for the culture?"

"I guess the park was really the beginning of the awareness for me. We drove through the city with the feeling we were on a tour bus going through one of those open wildlife preserves. We were safe inside while the animals roamed freely around the van begging for handouts. When we first arrived we felt a sort of alliance. They seemed so liberated and we identified with that but we'd never had the platform they had. As we got to know a few of them, studied the culture, and grew to understand the environment, we realized we didn't have anything in common with them. We really didn't fit in at all."

"How could you suddenly not fit in?" Jenn asked.

"The sixties were a cultural buffet. You'd belly up to the table and sample everything and if you liked it you went back for more. We chose what suited us…the liberation and love…and tossed a lot of stuff back, in particular the drugs. We figured the drugs clouded those things that we wanted to experience. When we witnessed the effect it had on others, particularly those in the park, we realized that for us anyway…we were right and they were wrong."

"All four of you chose to say no after that?"

"Claire and I especially. Andy and Jack played with it for a while."

"Mum thinks of you guys as peripheral hippie-types."

"That's a fair definition. I've never considered us hippies of any kind really. Like I said we took from their table like we were guests at their party. The people that saw us back then assumed that's what we were. I guess it's still true today."

"You'll have to admit that you do give that impression. Even Mum looks the part all of a sudden."

"She's just being Claire, that's all. I simply like being comfortable and this is how I'm most comfortable. But folks need to label everything. They see me and I have to be either street-people or old hippie. I'm never just me."

"So you weren't full-time hippies…you just took some of their lifestyle and played part-time hippies?"

"Unfortunately there's an underlying practicality involved. It's similar to some of the bikers that cruise the highways. A certain percentage of them ride weekends after spending five days as lawyers, accountants…whatever. Those five days give them the security to get leathered up and leave it all behind for two days…to fill that need that they have inside. They can experience the freedom because they know they have all the bases covered in the rest of their lives. Are they any less into the scene because it's only part time? I don't know but I do I give them credit for finding that balance in their lives. It's like the ranch…we had to have jobs to pay for that freedom. A few of the crowd figured we'd sold out but we didn't think of it that way. We had to eat and pay rent and the jobs also gave us the resources to buy the wine and cheese for our weekend romps in the country. It was a give and take thing. We had to give a part of our lives to someone for money in order to take back our lives on the weekends."

"But wouldn't you find yourself living for those weekends?"

"The key word is 'living' Jennifer."

"This selling out attitude is still around."

"It always will be, usually nurtured by people with no ambition or common sense."

"A friend of mine back home refuses to sell out to the capitalist web, as he calls it. He doesn't believe he needs a job to live."

"Ah," Evan said, "and how's he doing with that?"

"Good, I guess. He just moved in with another guy. He seems happy."

"A shot in the dark here…this other guy has a job?"

"Yeah, construction or something."

"So he's okay with not selling out as long as he can sponge off someone who did?"

Jenn shrugged her shoulders. "That's one way to look at it."

"It's the only way to look at it. Just look at some of the kids downtown. They'll freely tell you they're not trapped in this 'Capitalist Web' either, usually while they're asking for spare change from the sell-outs or adjusting the volume on the ipod. You can't be free without a little cash and sometimes you've got to work hard to get it."

"You're talking to someone who had to flip burgers to pay for university."

"With your dad being a lawyer I'm surprised your parents didn't front you."

"They did but I'm paying them back…it was my idea."

"I'm impressed," he said. "Feels good doesn't it?"

"I'll tell you when I make that final payment. You take a pretty hard stance on drugs yet you must have been surrounded by them in those days."

"I have and I was. To me it doesn't matter what the drug is there will be consequences. Anything that alters the natural chemistry will have an effect over time, it's just logical…but then logic never really played a big part in that culture. There was this excuse that you used drugs to get into your own body, to find yourself. Bottom line was once you got into the drugs you didn't give a damn about your body or yourself. Perhaps it worked for some but overall it resulted in a lot of nice people getting more lost than when they started. We were sitting by the van one night and watched this guy send his girl over to a tent to get dope. She said she didn't have any money, he told her to do whatever it took. We saw this naive little fourteen-year-old do whatever it took. Andy's comment was 'I know I'm easy but if I ever get that stupid shoot me'. Boys pimped the girls out for drugs and the girls were too stoned or too stupid to realize they were doing it. Miss Naiveté runs away from her bitchy mother and hooks up with this guy who warps her up, gets her good and high then auctions her off to the highest bidder, mostly to groups of guys who'd pooled their resources to get some fresh action. By the end of the night she's screaming for that bitchy mother. Haight wasn't the heaven of legend. It was the dirtiest of all worlds. When the guys weren't pounding the crap out of each other they were wandering around handing out pills to the girls. They'd suck 'em up not knowing what they were. Every day someone was hauled away in an ambulance for overdosing, heat stroke, a beating…one reason or another. One girl died and the few that missed her mourned the loss by doing the same old same old. Another girl nearly died at the wake. It was unbelievable."

"But you tried marijuana back then."

"Yeah. In my heightened relaxation I remember sitting and watching the park people and wondering what they were doing…what I was doing. The more I thought about it the more I came to the conclusion that drugs were either an escape from your interpretation of reality or a crutch to help you cope with that reality. Either way your reality got screwed."

"Interpretation of reality?"

"Reality is perception. There is no all-encompassing real world, just how we interpret our corner of it. The real world for a millionaire sipping wine on a beach in St. Tropez isn't the same real world of the starving child in Somalia. Reality can be manipulated and drugs go a long way in aiding that manipulation."

"None of you ever tried any other drugs?"

For the first time he paused, formulating an answer. "I never tried any other drugs Jennifer."

"That wasn't my question."

"That was my answer."

"Fair enough," Jenn whispered. "This freedom…it covered all aspects of life, especially relationships?"

"That's another interesting thing to come out of the summer of love, the breaking down of cultural barriers. It brought people of different races, religions, and backgrounds together. It became accepted within the culture to partner with someone outside of your own ethnicity. Not long before this I had a friend named Bobby who was black. We were watching television at his house one night and this news bulletin about a racial riot in New Jersey came on. The camera picked up the cops with their clubs beating on the people in the streets. Bobby turned to his dad and asked him why they were doing that to us. That moment I realized that I was 'they' and he was 'us'. It didn't change our friendship but it did open my eyes."

"I'm not sure we're on the same page. Wouldn't that be building a barrier?"

"Yes, the realization of differences can create barriers but accepting those differences can just as easily tear them down. It didn't affect our friendship but it did make me see the problem. I hadn't paid much attention to the unrest until that evening. It hadn't directly affected me so it didn't matter. I was suffering from that widespread blind-eye syndrome at the time. As I said this was in the early sixties…the late sixties brought a lot of people together for the first time to try and right the earlier wrongs."

"I was thinking more of the personal relationships, the love and the…you know."

"Sex. It always comes back to that."

"I'm sorry."

"No, in this context it's a fair topic. One nice thing to come out of the sixties was that people could hug and say 'I love you' without it being an invitation for sex. Having said that I'm not sure there has ever been or ever will be a time when sex was so rampant. Most girls had discovered the pill and that gave them the freedom to explore their sexuality without a pregnancy concern. They didn't stop to think about the other horrors this voyage of discovery could bring. Mostly it gave some girls the opportunity to act as primal and stupid as the boys. The main problem with relationships back then was that it was still always about the guy. He valued his needs more than the simple recognition that the vessel beneath him was a person with her own needs and feelings. To some extent it's always been like that though."

"Going back to the caveman."

"Ah, but then it was instinct. The survival of the species was uppermost. Caveman didn't think twice about…procreating with the closest available cavewoman. Monogamy wasn't one of the first words uttered around the watering hole."

"But what if there was this really hot cave-chick, wouldn't one cave-guy try to claim her?"

"He'd probably have died trying. I don't think the other cave-guys would have stood for exclusivity. Plus I've seen the drawings and none of them were all that hot."

"Ah, but to a hip cave-boy, you know?"

"I'm sorry but male or female, other than the dangly bits, they all looked pretty much alike."

"Dangly bits?" Jenn laughed. "Yes, I'm sure I read that term in one of the Darwin essays."

"He may not have written it that way but I'm sure he thought about it."

"But at some point even early man created a society as such."

"Sure they did, and family groups developed but I doubt they had rules covering the, uh, procreation aspect. Basic rules to govern a moral society came later and were established by churches or lawmakers. Then the guys had to try and curb their enthusiasm when it came to earthy activities."

Jenn smirked. "Betcha they were a little pissed about that."

"Probably although I'm not sure many of them cared anyway. But those rules are what took mankind above the animals. Without them it'd still be okay to kill and cook the guy that nicked your car door at the shopping center."

"Were cavemen cannibals?"

"I don't know but with the cost of meat these days...."

"I think I've forgotten the point you were making."

"I was just saying that most men have evolved even though some haven't. There are still males who seek out the youngest and healthiest of the herd."

"But they have a name for them now."

"Yeah."

"Women's Lib?" she asked.

"What about it?"

"You were there when it all happened. From your perspective how did it feel?"

"Actually I liked the whole idea until I found out that bra burning was merely symbolic."

"Seriously?"

"No, of course not." Evan grinned. "I was, and still am all for it. Women's Lib has been around in some form or other since the 1800's. A big part of the package for the new wave of feminists in the sixties was the pill. Women could take charge of their sexuality and there was empowerment in that. The true hard-line feminists had issues with this new-found freedom but I don't think many men had too much of a problem with it."

"But equal rights, pay…all that?"

"The rest of the package. Although women's lib did a lot to create equality it stopped short in a lot of areas, but it wasn't necessarily a flaw in the movement. A lot of males still maintain a superiority complex even though most of them really have nothing to feel superior about. It's refreshing to see equality in any relationship."

"Mum says that some women carried it to the extreme?"

"Yeah, the hard-liners again. That probably hurt the progress more than anything. In any movement you're going to have the radicals. The word 'liberation' sounds confrontational to begin with but when you throw in a few militant personalities seeking to turn it into a revolution of superiority rather than equality it's even tougher to get your point across."

"But along came the love generation. Surely that had some kind of impact?"

"Unfortunately the idealism that grew from that experience grows weaker as the sixties slip further back into history. We've become a pushy, screaming society where people press each other's buttons just to get reactions, couples argue more these days than at any other time I can recall. This primal aggression lives on television, in the streets, and in the music. Kids are generally pushier, louder, more profane, and violent than ever. I know the respect for family, authority, and themselves isn't as obvious as it used to be. Unless they wake up and take a good look inside, that lack of respect…especially for themselves, is what will eventually destroy these kids."

"I would think some of the parents back then said the same thing about their kids?"

"Of course they did. It's a recurring nightmare for every generation. Fortunately enough of the little buggers survive to have kids and appreciate what they put their parents through."

"Didn't a lot of the New Age philosophies and religions appear about that time?"

"Ah, the spirituality aspect of the sixties. I never did quite catch onto that part of it but your mum got a little hooked in San Francisco. She met this young lady who preached the teachings of a guru from some country I'd never heard of. I remember hearing about those spiritual roads winding and weaving through all existence and ending up at the same place…within you. You are the center of the universe…all life revolves around you and all that crap. The 'we' generation was evolving into the 'me' generation and I didn't think that was what it was all about."

"I don't know if I agree. A lot of the new-age philosophies tell us that we are all one, one energy, one soul…brothers and all that. Isn't this just another spin on an old philosophy?"

"I hadn't thought of it that way. Perhaps you're right. But it's that interpretation thing again isn't it? You read what you want into something in order to get what you want out of it. I'll give you that one."

"But you don't agree?"

"No."

"There are probably millions of people who don't see eye to eye with you."

"People are sheep. They follow far too willingly. They need to hear someone say 'I will take care of you, I am here for you…I will love you' and it really doesn't matter who promises these things…politicians, religious leaders or extremists…they will follow."

"But these people must identify with something or they wouldn't be the followers you say they are."

"Someone says 'let me show you the way' and a lot of people get in line without any clear idea of where they're going. They identify with something that they're told to identify with and overlook the truths that each one of us has within. You can believe all the abstract philosophies and teachings you want but it's all for naught unless you believe in yourself first."

"But isn't this what these philosophies are supposed to teach us?"

"If you believe in yourself then why do you need them?"

"To appreciate the person you believe in?"

"You're already doing that by believing."

"To find comfort in a higher power…maybe the philosophy of one?"

"Or the combined philosophies of the all that make up the one."

Jenn raised her arms. "Oh hell I don't know…this is starting to get confusing."

Evan laughed. "I'm playing with you here Jennifer, I don't read that stuff. I'm not sure what any of it means and honestly, I don't care. Claire would be the one to get into that discussion."

"For someone who says he's not sure you seem pretty certain."

"Not really. The biggest problem for me is the way some people throw themselves into these philosophies. They give one hundred percent without leaving room in their minds to consider the possibility that there may be something else out there, something better for them. I'm not knocking any beliefs or faiths…I'm just saying that it's important to keep your mind open. The bottom line when it comes to any form of spirituality is that if it works for you congratulations, that's all that matters. I simply believe in being true to yourself. Once you do that you can be true to anyone and truth trumps everything else."

"Even love?"

"There can be no real love without truth."

"And you have to love yourself before you can love anyone else."

"Yup. That's one old saying that bears a lot of weight. Not like 'the worm has turned'…that doesn't make any sense at all."

"I think it means that the bad side of a person is showing."

He stroked his chin. "It might simply mean that the worm changed his mind."

"Or he's decided to try an alternate lifestyle."

"Maybe it's something like the shoe is on the other foot?"

Jenn frowned. "Worms don't have feet."

"You've run out of questions haven't you?"

"Uh-huh."

Chapter 41

Marie sat down in Jenn's place. "The roving reporter has cornered Evan to get some more of her project done so I guess it's just us."

"All ready for tonight?" Claire asked.

Marie shook her head. "As far as the food goes but I'm not sure any of us are ready for tonight. So what are we chatting about?"

"Well…" Claire smirked. "It's a meeting of the Evan Morris Club for Wayward Girls."

"If they weren't before they joined…did Jenn tell you what happened in the kitchen?"

"Yes, I wish I could have seen it."

"You did forty-years ago, remember?"

They both laughed as Andy leaned forward, her elbows on her knees. "Excuse me, what did I miss?"

"Just a little moonlight cfnm," Claire said, "your favorite game, remember?"

"Jenn got Evan naked?"

"He already was." Marie laughed. "She walked in on him getting a late-night snack. No big deal."

"I wouldn't say that in front of him. As our newest member I think she should be out here telling us about it. I know I've got a few questions."

"It was accidental Andy…I've never seen him look quite that sheepish. Well, maybe once."

"Sounds interesting," Claire said. "Do tell?"

"It was right after we met." Marie looked behind her at the closed door and grinned. "My family ran this motel on the outskirts.

Unit 112 was tucked around the corner and was always the last one we'd book. When I worked late on the desk there were no buses running so I'd usually crash there. One day I told Evan about it and that night, just as I was getting into bed, he tapped on the window. I opened it and climbed out. We sat at a picnic bench and talked until dawn. I'm out there in an admittedly unsexy nightgown but still we just talked. The next night was the same thing. Four nights I'd crawl out the window and other than a goodnight kiss on the cheek when he pushed me back in nothing happened. The fifth night I left the nightgown in my bag and when the window opened…I pulled him in. It still took me twenty minutes to get him into bed. The next morning he was sauntering around in the buff while I was getting dressed and the door swings open. Tricia the weekend housekeeper walked in, saw him, and just stood there staring. She must have been sixteen at the time. Evan calmly introduced himself then offered her ten bucks if she'd forget what she had just seen. She took the money but I doubt she ever forgot."

Claire laughed along with the other two women then raised her hand. "I have a somewhat similar story," she said. "We'd just moved into this high-rise downtown, fifth floor. The second night he didn't come home until after two. We'd set up to do dinner and a movie with another couple so I was pretty upset. When he staggered through the door he told me he'd had some drinks with the guys in the band. The jerk could barely stand. I showed him the couch and went to bed. I just lay there fuming. About a half-hour later I heard him outside. 'Claire…Claire,' he screamed, just like Brando and the 'Stella' bit. I went out on the balcony and looked down…I just about died. He was holding this old guitar that he'd been trying to learn to play. Other than that he was buck-naked. In his drunken stupor he'd written a song to me. I can't remember all of it but the first lines were 'Sweet Claire, so fair, with your hair, everywhere…I love you'. When he was done he got a round of applause from all the apartments on our side of the building. I told him to come back up and I'd be waiting for him. Ten minutes later I'm still waiting when I heard him outside again. Stupid bugger had stripped before he went out and of course he didn't have his keys and couldn't remember the apartment number. I buzzed him in just as a couple of girls got home from a party. Details of that elevator ride were all over the building the next day. Every time he left the apartment people just smiled at him. He was pretty sheepish then as I recall."

Andy giggled. "Too bad they didn't have video in those days. Evan's right, you two are turning into dirty old women."

"Us?" Claire laughed. "What about you?"

"Hey, I've always been a dirty old woman but sweet Claire with your hair everywhere? I'm shocked."

"Give it a rest sweetie." Claire glowered.

Marie bordered on hysterics. "God this is fun, I've never talked about this sort of thing with anybody."

"Hey," Andy said, "half the fun of getting naughty is telling the girls about it the next day. I wish I had an Evan story to share but I respected our friendship way too much to cross that line."

"I know." Claire nodded. "Didn't stop you from trying get a rise out of him every chance you got though."

"Moi?"

"What did he call you…little Miss Gidditup? You were the biggest tease I've ever met."

"What can I say, it's an art. Besides what's this 'were'?"

They all turned as the door opened behind them and Evan stepped onto the porch. "What's all the giggling about?" he asked.

Marie shrugged her shoulders. "We're just telling naughty Evan stories."

He looked pointedly at all three women then pulled his hat down over his forehead. "I would expect nothing less from this crowd. Anybody need anything from the store?"

Andy raised her hand. "A healthy young cashier would be nice."

"Male or female?"

"Whichever looks freshest," Claire muttered.

He shook his head and started down the steps. "I have a few stories I could tell about you two. See you later."

"Actually I'll come with you," Marie said as she stood and followed him. "I haven't been out of the house for a few days."

Claire also stood. "And I'm going to track down Jenn and see what she's up to."

Andy quickly put her feet back up on the couch, stretched her arms above her head and closed her eyes.

Chapter 42

Claire carefully studied all the photographs on the way to the den. Most she hadn't seen but there were some scenics that she knew he'd taken on the California trip. She'd been standing beside him for a few of them. A black and white sunset defied all logic with its beauty…or was it simply the memories that it stirred. She moved along the wall stopping at each photograph, hearing his words and feeling his feelings each time he pressed the shutter. The last print was of an old castle wall. In perfect form a flock of white doves huddled in the ivy surrounding a dark stone gargoyle. She read the caption…'Just An Old Fashioned Dove Throng'…and laughed out loud. That touch of madness lived on, just not in her life anymore.

    Finally she reached the doorway and glanced inside. "God what a museum," she said.

    "Actually I thought it more a flea market," Jenn replied from the chair in front of his desk. "There's some pretty neat stuff here."

    "I can see that." She began her walk along the shelves, stopping first at King Kong. "He still likes this sort of stuff? I remember when we went to the St. Albert drive-in to see this guy."

    "Drive-in? Tell me more."

    "They were running a creature feature night. There was a movie about a dinosaur eating cowboys, then King Kong, then some beast from beneath the ocean that tore up New York."

    "You remember all that?"

    "As if it was yesterday."

    "I didn't think people went to drive-ins to watch the movie."

"Oh we used to fog up the windows pretty good but not that night. We watched those films from beginning to end although between the features a little mist would roll in. How are you coming with the interview?"

"I'm finished, pretty well. I just have to put it all in some kind of logical order."

"Finding logic in what you've uncovered may be a little difficult." She peered onto the shelf below Kong and pulled out the doll. "What's this? He's collecting dolls now?"

"Her name is…Jenny."

Claire looked closely at the doll in her hands. "I can see why." She slipped it back into place and continued her walk.

Jenn held up the photograph. "Is that all you can say?"

Claire turned, saw the picture and smiled. "Yes Jenn, that's all."

"He still loves you Mum, can't you see that?"

"I don't want to but I can, yes. Now if you don't mind I'd like to change the subject?"

"I'm sorry but I do mind. I'm finding out more about you than I ever thought possible. This whole part of your life has been a huge secret and it's such a big, beautiful part. I really want to know as much as there is to know."

"I understand Jenn but I'm not comfortable dealing with it here. There's too much that clouds my judgment."

"Like Evan?"

"Especially Evan. When you phoned me and I had you tell me about him…his looks and attitude, I was hoping he'd turned into a surly old fat bald man. Other than the grey hair, you described the Evan that I knew forty years ago. That's when it all started again. When Andy invited me along, I just had to come. It is good to see and be with him again but it's equally bad. It's dug up some memories and feelings that I'd buried many years ago."

"I'm sorry, I shouldn't be pushing this."

"No, you should…but I'm not ready to get into that discussion yet. I will Jenn, I promise, for now though let's move on?"

"Maybe this is something you don't want to talk about either but I just asked Evan a question that he didn't really answer."

"Maybe it was none of your concern. What was the question?"

"He admitted that you all smoked a little pot back then which is fine, we've already talked about that. I asked if any of you had done other drugs and he became pretty evasive. He said that he hadn't and that was the only answer he was willing to give. Is he protecting you?"

Claire slipped into the chair behind the desk. "Maybe you should let this one go Jenn."

"He is isn't he…protecting you?"

Jenn felt someone touch the back of her chair. She looked up and saw Andy.

"He's not protecting your mum Jenn," she said, "he's covering for me." She walked over to a bookshelf and absently started perusing the titles. "Tell her Ceejay, she should know. This little world she's been hearing about wasn't all idyllic and innocent."

Claire sat back in the chair. "You're sure?"

"Yes, I am. Besides we've never talked about it and you and Evan are the only ones that really know what happened. I certainly don't remember much."

Jenn swallowed. "It's okay Andy, Mum's right. It isn't my concern."

"Tell her…" Andy pulled a book of the shelf and nervously played with it between her fingers. "She does need to get the balance."

"Okay." Claire took a deep breath. "When we decided to leave the beach in Sausalito and head home Evan figured we should camp at the park one last time just to get a last look at the lifestyle. We settled in about four in the afternoon. Evan was happy just to sit beside the van while Andy, Jack, and I wandered and checked out the crafts and stuff the kids were selling on the sidewalks. I'd decided I'd had enough and went back and joined him. We talked about what we were and weren't going to miss about what we had seen. I'm not sure what happened to Jack but Andy kept coming by and asking us to get out and party with her but unfortunately we weren't really up for it."

"Don't carry that weight Ceejay, you couldn't have done anything," Andy said as she leafed through the book.

"Maybe not. It was probably about nine when we noticed a group of kids in a circle with their arms across each other's shoulders. They looked like a bunch of natives doing a ritual dance around a fire. There was a girl at the center of the circle gyrating and throwing off her clothes. Suddenly she collapsed and fell to the ground. You could hear her screaming all over the park. Evan realized it was Andy and he bolted across the grass. He had to knock a couple of kids down to break into the circle. Those 'peace-loving' folks started kicking and hitting him as he tried to get to her. I just stood there watching the whole thing happen." She put her hands to her head and leaned on the desk. "He finally got to his feet…the blood was streaming down his face."

Jenn reached and touched Claire's arm. "It's okay Mum, stop…"

"He was screaming…I couldn't understand a word. He grabbed the first kid he could get his hands on and pummeled the little bastard then threw him into a couple of other kids. There was a rage there that I never knew was in him. A girl came up, took a swing at him, and connected. He put her down her too. They all backed off at that point but they kept dancing at a safe distance while Evan knelt beside Andy. By the time I snapped out of it and went to help he had her sitting up and was holding her while she punched and clawed at him. She was crying, screaming, laughing…I was scared to death."

Jenn looked up at Andy. "What the hell!" she shouted.

Andy hung her head. "Jenn, I remember none of this. Every once in a while I have dreams that I think are probably parts of it but I'm really not sure."

Claire rubbed her eyes. "I just kept looking back and forth between the two of them. Andy's face was bright red, her eyes glaring wide open…her skin was burning and she was trembling and sweating. Evan was covered in blood, the tears were streaming and he was shaking as much as she was. This guy grabbed him by the shoulder. He jumped up and grabbed the guy's shirt. He was about to lace him when he saw the collar. It was a young priest named Michael who frequented the park and tried to help the kids wherever he could. He calmed Evan down a bit and told him to go for a walk then he looked at me and asked if I was all right. I was, I thought…then he told me that Andy was probably on a bad trip and that she'd probably be okay in a few hours. We had to just be there to make sure she didn't harm herself and let her come back on her own...we couldn't force it."

"LSD?" Jenn asked.

Claire nodded. "That's what he figured but there was so much shit and pills floating around at that time he couldn't be sure. We talked while he sat with Andy. He'd seen it all. The night before he'd had a kid die in his arms before the ambulance could get there. It was then I realized that I just wanted to get back home and leave all that hell behind us."

"Where was Jack while all this was happening?"

"He, uh...he..." She stared blankly at Andy. "He was part of the group that was still dancing and singing. When the priest told Evan to walk it off he stepped away but then he saw Jack. I thought he was going to kill him."

Andy interrupted. "Evan did that to him?"

Claire nodded. "Jack figured he'd gotten into a fight trying to help you...that was how he remembered it. Evan put everything he had left into the few blows it took to put Jack out. We didn't see him until around noon the next day. All night Evan and I took turns sitting with Andy in the van just talking and singing. Eventually she relaxed and fell asleep like Michael had said she would but we still watched her for the rest of the day. It was pretty intense."

Jenn looked at Andy. "You don't remember any of this?"

"What I remember were bright stars glittering in this red sky, a lot of movement...a lot of loud noises. Sirens, laughter, music, birds...my heartbeat. Some guy was pulling at me, trying to carry me away. I remember screaming for Evan to get him off of me." She stared at Claire. "I guess it was Evan all along. Why didn't you tell me?"

"Neither of you remembered what really happened so we figured it was best to leave it alone."

"I can see why you thought that. It would have destroyed everything we had back then."

"And everything we have now. I'm sorry Andy, we should have told you but..."

"It's okay, I wouldn't have told me either."

Jenn raised her hand. "I'm assuming that Evan was pretty beaten up too. How did you explain that to Andy? Surely she must have noticed."

Andy smiled. "They told me he'd fallen out of the van."

"And you bought it?"

"He was always falling out of the van, nothing new."

"Besides," Claire said, "it looked a lot worse than it was. He had a nosebleed and a bit of a bruised eye for a while. The major damage was a cut above the hairline. It bled a lot but it healed quickly. It's still noticeable though."

Jenn shook her head. "No wonder he didn't tell me about this. I can't imagine him being that angry. That would be scary."

"It was and I couldn't believe how long he held the anger. It took a couple of days before he sounded even close to normal. That's why we checked into the motel in Oregon, to give he and Andy a chance to rest a bit."

"Have you and Evan ever talked about this?"

"No, and we won't…and neither will you. He was pretty embarrassed about it. That was the only time I ever saw him really lose his temper and neither of us wanted to see it again."

Jenn nodded. "That was pretty heroic of him though."

"I thought so but he thought he'd been stupid. There were at least forty ripped kids there; they could easily have killed him."

Andy lifted a photo album from the top shelf. "I tend to agree with you on the hero bit but I can see where he wouldn't think so."

Jenn sighed deeply. "If I'd had any clue as to what it was all about I would have let it go, I'm sorry."

"It's okay." Andy opened the album and grinned. "On a lighter note kid, you wanna see some naked pictures of your dear old mum?"

Claire covered her face. "I was hoping those would remain hidden for at least another forty years!" She patted the desk. "Put it here so we can all have a laugh."

Jenn squinted at her. "You're not serious…we're really going to look at them?"

"You can leave if you want to Jenn but after that I need to relive some of the fun stuff."

Chapter 43

Evan followed Marie into the house and heard the laughter from down the hall.

"Schoolgirls again," he mumbled. "I wonder what they've found now."

"I'll put this stuff away…" Marie dropped the grocery bags on the counter. "You go see what they're up to."

He stood in the doorway watching the three women leaf through the pages of an old photograph album. "What's so funny?" he asked.

They all stopped laughing and turned to him. Claire spoke first, "I'm sorry Evan, we found this album and…I guess we shouldn't be snooping."

"No, that's fine…but the naughty ones are in the red book on the top shelf."

Jenn smiled knowingly at him. "Oh we've already covered those. This is just some stuff from other times."

"I'm aware of which one it is Jennifer." He walked slowly across the floor and dropped in the leather chair in front of the desk.

Andy frowned. "You're not angry are you? You sound angry."

"No, really I'm not. Have we heard from them yet?"

Claire shrugged. "I guess they'll be here when they get here. Andy's right, you do sound a little pissed. Is everything okay?"

"I'm fine. I've just got an uneasy feeling about tonight, that's all."

Claire nodded then turned the album towards him, pointing to a photograph. "Remember this guy?"

Evan surveyed a faded colour image of a frail man in torn denim shorts, his hair dirty, long, and knotted…an equally obscene beard to his chest. "Lobo. Wasn't that what he called himself?"

"Yes…wolf."

"I sense a recurring theme," he muttered.

Claire turned the album back and stared at the photograph. "Evan and I had thought it would be interesting to try getting back to the land. We thought of building our own cabin in the woods somewhere. We'd have a go at living off nature…growing our own veggies, eating nuts, berries, and the occasional stupid squirrel. On the way home we drove into this huge forest. We decided to take a break and go for a walk. I had just commented that it would be a perfect place to try the back to the earth thing when Lobo leapt out of the trees at us. He was carrying a long pointed branch. By the blood on the end we guessed he used it for hunting. He actually was a pretty nice guy once we gave him our sandwiches and cookies."

Even agreed. "We and our money were safe. He was a pretty peaceful sort and wanted nothing to do with the establishment. It looked like he'd been out there for years. He took us back to his house. It was pretty incredible. He'd woven the walls and roof out of thin branches and had an old tarp strapped over the top to rain-proof the place."

"But he was pretty bizarre," Claire continued. "He knew nothing of the world around him, not the music, news…anything. He kept talking to these invisible beings that were sitting beside him. He got into an argument with one of his friends while we sat and tried not to laugh. Then he started talking about his dog. He reached inside his house and pulled the carcass out to introduce us. I damn near threw up…it must have been dead for months. We got up and apologized for having to go and left him hugging the dog. God that was sad."

Evan looked at the photo again. "It cured me of wanting to become a hermit though."

Andy turned the album so she could see the picture. "I remember you telling us about him. I also remember that Jack and I were pretty cranky because we just wanted to get home and you two decided to go frolic in the woods."

Jenn turned to Evan. "From all I've heard getting back home must have been uppermost in all your minds?"

He nodded. "It was. While we were there we seemed to have this level of confusion. Mostly we had a good time but there was this underlying uncertainty or unrest, like we didn't belong. As soon as we hit the border and got our feet onto home soil the feeling lessened. We had a sense of security that we hadn't felt since we left."

"Isn't that the way a lot of people feel in another country?"

"Probably but most people view other cultures from the outside, as tourists. We tried to be a part of it. Once we accepted that we weren't and never would be we were fine, and homesick."

"How about the Bar-Ass ranch?" Jenn asked. "Wasn't that lifestyle a part of it in those days?"

"A part that I wish had remained in those days." Evan stretched his feet under the front of the desk. "It gets back to the buffet philosophy, take the good and leave the rest."

"Good?"

"It was good Jennifer."

"I don't know, I just saw some pictures…"

"Yes," Claire interrupted. "My daughter was particularly taken by the one of you standing beside the neighbor's horse."

Jenn glared at her mother. "I was not…although that is side of you I hadn't seen." She smiled at him coyly.

Andy walked around the chair and put her hands on Evan's shoulders. "There there, be nice to the old man…he had issues. He'd just discovered he wasn't half the stallion he thought he was, comparatively speaking."

He leaned back in the chair. "Agreed, but I make up for it in sensitivity."

"I hear you still come up short." Andy pulled his hair into a ponytail. "If you wore it like this you could at least present an outward impression of your internal stallionistic delusions."

He frowned. "My what?"

"You understood me."

"I've never understood you." Evan felt her hands grip his shoulders. "By the way, I didn't have issues."

"All men have issues."

"Not until some woman told us we did."

"Ignorance is bliss and men are so full of bliss."

"Bitch."

"Bastard. Have you got a dictionary in here somewhere?" she asked.

"Of course."

"Look up 'gelding' and don't sleep too soundly tonight."

"You win."

"Always do. Now shut up."

He closed his eyes and felt a tingle as Andy massaged his shoulders, the laughter in the room unimportant. For the first time today, he felt relaxed. His mind drifted through the photo albums as he listened to Claire telling Jenn about the other times that were more important than the fun days. The quiet walks, the searches for meaning and the simple pleasures derived from just being together. There really was so much good back then, totally unappreciated at the time.

He heard Claire's voice. "You're enjoying that way too much Evan."

He opened his eyes. Marie sat on the edge of the desk, smiling, with her arms crossed. "I agree," she said, "and you Missy can quit fondling my husband anytime you want to."

"Okay, I will." Andy kept rubbing his shoulders. "It's been so long since I've done this. You are so lucky Marie."

"In what way?"

"It's only Evan but you know where he is, what he's doing. He's loyal and dependable."

Marie chuckled. "So is Ginn but I don't see you massaging her back."

"You know what I mean."

"I think so."

Evan raised his arm. "I have a question?"

"Yes?" Andy stopped and rested her hands on his shoulders.

"This 'only' Evan that you speak of…care to elaborate?"

"You're just a man, that's all. No big deal, don't set your sights too high and you won't be disappointed. Marie's right…when I go home I'm getting a dog." Her voice trailed into silence.

He reached to his shoulder and closed his hand on hers.

"Where the hell are they?" she shouted. "Let's get this over with!"

Evan stood and turned. "Andy…" He watched her run down the hallway, Claire a few steps behind. He looked at Marie then Jenn.

"Reality sucks," he said quietly.

Jenn wiped her eyes then drew a deep breath. "I, uh…excuse me," she said as she passed him and walked quickly to the front door.

Marie rested her hand on his shoulder. "She's pretty tough Evan, she'll be okay."

"I know."

"How about you?"

"You don't think I'm tough?"

"Sensitive, remember? That old Pisces curse, soaking up the emotions of those around you?"

"You don't believe in that sort of thing do you?"

"No, but I am seeing it. You're so concerned about her, what about you?"

"It's been a long time Marie. When I first talked to Danny I felt the loss but when Andy told me about the last ten years I realized I didn't really know him all that well. I guess I feel the same way she does…the Jack I knew died a long time ago."

"I don't buy that and neither do you." She dropped her arm around his waist. "You've mastered the art of hiding your feelings but we both know that eventually they'll dig their way out from wherever you buried them. You will have to deal with it sooner or later."

"I know. I should steal her away for a walk. If we work it out together it might be easier on both of us."

"Andy's right, I am pretty lucky."

"Yes, you are." He leaned his head against hers.

Two quick beeps startled them. Marie glanced out the window.

"Great…now they decide to show," she said as a large white van pulled into the driveway.

Chapter 44

By the time Evan reached the back door Carl, Lauren, and Carol had made their way along the sidewalk and were being greeted by Marie and Ginn at the bottom of the steps. Carl seemed even shorter now, pale, and thinner…frail. His hair, as white as his beard, rubbed the collar of the denim shirt tucked into his jeans. Andy was right, the years had not been kind. Evan assumed the tall, overdressed woman beside him was his wife. Her look was one of polite disdain. She wore her dark brown hair long and perfectly placed…a beige leisure suit and red shirt accenting her height. It was still hard to picture Carl without Karen.

Carol glanced up at him, smiled politely then quickly turned away. Even after all this time.

Then Carl looked up and waved. "God Evan you taking in strays? And you've got a dog?"

Marie glared at him. "If I had a dollar for every time I've heard that one I'd hire a hit man and have your throat sliced and puréed," she said coldly.

Carl gave her a sheepish look. "Sorry, I was just trying to be funny."

"Practice boy, practice." Marie laughed. "Hi Carol, it's so good to see you again,"

"Me too." Carol smiled. "This is Carl's wife Lauren."

"Nice to meet you." The two women embraced as Carl hobbled slowly up the steps and shook hands with Evan. His grip was weak…limp.

"Hey Ev," he said, catching his breath. "It's been a long time. You shaved your beard?"

"It has, I did, and you didn't."

"Is that your daughter out front?"

"No, she's Claire's girl…Jennifer."

Carl searched the yard. "Claire's here?"

"Yup, somewhere."

"Oh. How's Marie with that?"

"She likes her."

"She knows about you two?"

"Of course."

Carl pulled a handkerchief from his pocket and wiped his forehead. "Christ, how do you handle this heat?"

"You get used to it. How are you doing Carl?"

"Not great. In medical terms most of my internal organs are fucked," he mumbled. "I'd really rather not talk about it."

"Okay," Evan said. "What have you been up to lately?"

"When I'm not at the hospital getting my guts drained I'm at home filling them up again."

"I'd really rather not talk about it."

Carl leaned on the railing and took a deep breath. "In a way I envy Jack…heart attack, quick and unannounced. Sure beats sitting around knowing ahead of time."

Evan shrugged. "I don't know…there's a lot to be said either way if you have to say it. At least you've got time for goodbyes, do a few things…you know?"

"I suppose. A year…that's what they told me I had. That was about a year ago."

"This really could be an interesting evening. Does Karen know?"

"I called her and got the predictable sympathy but it's been years Evan. We parted company with nothing left between us and nothing left is still what we have."

"I really am sorry Carl. How's Lauren with it?"

"A trooper. I had to beg her to come here though. She didn't want any part of it. She's really all I'm going to miss."

"I hear you don't miss anything," said Evan. "You just slip onto the next plane and don't even realize you've been anywhere else before."

"Next plane? Well I've got my reservation and boarding pass...I'll send you a postcard and let you know if all that's true."

"You won't remember me."

"That's one good thing about it then, isn't it?" Carl grinned. He looked to the bottom of the steps and moaned as Claire passed by. "Oh my, she hasn't changed much has she?"

"Nope, not really."

"Man I wouldn't want to be in your shoes right now. This has got to be a bitch."

Evan chuckled. "You don't know the half of it."

Claire joined the group of women. "Hi Carol. It's good to see you again," she said as she slipped in beside Marie.

"My God..." Carol said, "Claire?"

"And you must be Lauren?" Claire smiled and extended her hand. "Nice to meet you."

"And for me to meet you," Lauren said, a coolness in her voice. "Carl talks about you a lot."

"Oh?"

"Yes. When was the last time you saw him?"

Claire tensed. "I don't know, fifteen years ago maybe. Why?"

"Nothing, really. It's just that you're exactly as he described you."

Carol laughed. "Yeah, scary isn't it? She looks just like she did when...well, just when."

"Yes." Lauren raised her eyebrows. "We must talk about this 'when' sometime. I've heard so many stories."

Marie nudged Claire. "It's time to get the food out. I'll need some help?"

Claire nodded. "I'll be right there Marie. Where are the guys?"

Carol pointed to the porch as Marie headed toward the house. "Carl's up there with Evan but I have no idea where Danny got to. Where's Andy?"

"She'll be along soon."

"How's she doing?"

"I think it's starting to set in," Claire said, "although she was pretty much her old self when I left her. Honestly, I'm really not sure. But I'd better go give Marie a hand."

Chapter 45

Andy drew a deep breath, making her way along the side of the house. She hoped the front door would be open so she could slip in and gather her thoughts before meeting the crowd. A familiar face greeted her as she walked around the corner.

Like Evan, Danny hadn't changed much. His six-foot frame was slightly bent but it finally matched his personality. His arms were still large, his chest still broad but now it blended into a bit of an old guy gut. Slightly balding on top with shoulder length grey curly hair and thick beard he looked very much the part of the sixties rock star at a reunion concert, complete with jeans, white shirt, and leather vest. He turned and saw her approach and broke into a warm grin.

"You look a little raggedy Andy."

"And you still haven't hired a writer." She smiled as she hugged him. "Lordy is that cologne or did you do something indiscrete?"

"Aro-man Musk. Earthy isn't it?"

"If only. How are you Mule?"

He grinned. "I have acid reflux, post-nasal drip, and a growth on my butt."

Andy cupped a hand to her ear and frowned. "Stop children, what's that sound?"

Danny listened intently. "It sounds like extreme disinterest to me."

"Me too. So what's happening on the front forty?"

Jenn smiled awkwardly. "Danny here decided to check out the fox on the step."

Andy shook her head. "They don't call them 'foxes' these days Daniel, you're dating yourself."

"When you reach a certain age you have to. Nobody else will."

"Ahh yes, I can see it now. You take you out for a little candle-lit dinner and wine then you drive you back to your place. You invite you in for a nightcap on the premise of showing you your collection of rare Bolivian fungi. Does it work?"

"I got me to second base once."

"You are truly pathetic." She laughed and hugged him. "Christ it's great to see you."

"You too Andrea, I'm really sorry to hear about Jack."

"Thanks."

"Carol came out with me."

"Really? I thought you'd be stagging it."

"We talked, it's only right that we all try to be together."

Andy hugged a little harder. "I do appreciate that."

"We love you girl. If there's anything either of us can do?"

"Yeah, I know."

He put his hands on her shoulders and kissed her forehead. "I'd better get around back."

"Right."

Jenn stood and watched him go through the gate. "Interesting guy," she said. "Why did you call him 'Mule'?"

"You saw the group shot of the guys at the ranch?"

"Yeah?"

"Group shot…guys?"

"Yeah…oh." She felt a blush building. "But otherwise he seems nice."

"You don't think the otherwise is nice?"

"No comment."

"He is nice Jenn, he's wonderful. He's got the warmest soul and the biggest heart…probably the best of the bunch including Evan but he can double-talk you into insanity. The two of them together are certifiable. Once they get started you just sit back and enjoy the ride."

"I can see the similarity although I thought Jack was more like Evan."

"They were good friends but it was a completely different relationship, more like brothers really. The two of them could argue and often did but when the chips were down they were there for each other." She closed her eyes, smiled gently, and drew a staggered breath. "Evan and Danny though, they were the team. Evan still has the old hippie ways about him but Danny stayed the closest to the dreams they all had back then."

"How so?"

"When the bunch split and went into other areas Danny took on the wandering musician role and played with a few of the local groups. He bought into a studio and gave a lot of them their shot at fame. He's still well connected and books a few shows now and then. If you need any background on the musical scene in those days he'd probably be able to help you a lot more than Evan."

"Maybe I will try and talk to him. What about Carl?"

"He's pretty straight forward but the negative one of the bunch. He can get under your skin pretty easily if you let him. He tried to keep up with the rest of the crowd but he really has a butter knife wit. He was usually the odd one out. Nice guy but he definitely has the small man complex, wearing boots with high heels and driving big trucks, you know?"

"I do, I know a couple myself. What's the story on Steve?"

Andy held up her hand. "He's the only reason I questioned whether or not to be here tonight. Jerk, ass…you name it. He considers himself God's gift to women and the world in general. He was actually the cause of the ranch dying. The girls weren't as comfortable around him as we were with the other guys. One by one he gave each of us good reason."

"So how did he get to be part of that crowd? I can't see Evan or Danny putting up with too much."

"He was part of the original group long before your mum and I were involved. It was okay at first but once he crashed the private party he really changed. He managed to screw up everything that was good about what we'd built. The love and trust, family…it all died. When Evan and CeeJay dropped out things got pretty raunchy. Even I couldn't handle what was happening and Jack and I quit too. Have you met him yet?"

"No, he's supposed to be here in a bit."

"Steve is the true never grew up type of guy. He tried the music thing for a while but he couldn't cut it. He ended up doing anything he could do to get a little play-money. Barb was a legal for one of the big law firms back then so paying the bills wasn't too much of a problem. When they split she did great but nobody really knows what happened with Steve. He always had the sportiest cars and the youngest of women yet he never seemed to have a job, at least not one that he talked about."

"One can only guess…"

"One can." Andy reached her hand. "Come on, help me get myself together then I'll introduce you around."

Chapter 46

Claire looked out the window at Lauren. "Thanks Marie, I'm not sure where that was going."

"That's okay. Interesting woman but I can't see her with Carl. She's certainly not Karen."

"No but that's the problem with people who came along after. It's tough for them to understand the way it was."

"Tell me about it."

Claire rested her hand on Marie's shoulder. "I'm sorry, I wasn't thinking."

"No, you're right…it is tough. Evan spares me a lot of it but I know that something really special happened with all of you."

"It takes times like this to appreciate how special it was. How's he doing with everything?"

"He's had a little trouble," Marie said, "but he's managing to keep it all in perspective."

"He is Evan after all."

"That he is."

"How about you?"

"I'm Marie."

Claire laughed. "You're the exception Marie. You are so much a part of this crowd. What I meant was how are you doing with all of us being here?"

"Pretty good, although I must say you're really starting to piss me off."

"Me? What did I do?"

"It's what you didn't do. Grow old woman, you'll like it."

"You know what Evan says…."

"I know and I guess you're the living proof of it. But mark my words one day you'll be looking in the mirror and the last twenty years will fall from the ceiling and smother you in wrinkles and warts."

"And I'll send you a photograph."

"Make it an eight by ten. I'll frame it and hang it over the fireplace."

"You would too wouldn't you?"

Marie grinned. "You bet your sixty-year-old ass I would."

Chapter 47

Evan twisted the top off a bottle of beer and sat on the porch steps beside Danny.

"So what have you been up to lately Daniel?"

"I've been trying to free my inner sensitivities," Danny said.

"What?"

"My girly-bits…cut 'em loose."

"You have girly-bits?"

"You know what I mean…my feminine side."

"Yeah I got in touch with my feminine side a while back. She's a bit of a bitch."

"Mine's a bit of a slut." Danny grinned. "But I really like her. She's a redhead."

"Of course she is."

"Apparently we're all male and female emotionally; each within one and one within each…or something like that."

Evan frowned. "Okay."

"I read it some place."

"You read a lot of things?"

"Yeah." Danny tipped back his beer, swallowed then belched. "I really am sensitive."

"You're drunk."

"Yeah."

These were the moments Evan had missed, these slices of life that weren't healthy or heart-smart. They were just junk slices, mostly nonsense. "Do you believe it Danny?" he asked.

"What?"

"Each within one…that stuff?"

"I don't know. I have trouble believing a lot of things these days."

Evan placed his hand on Danny's shoulder. "You have to believe in believing before you can believe in anything else."

"You've taken deep to a whole new level."

"You think?"

"No." Danny tipped back his beer again then squinted into the back of the yard watching a white blur race through the trees. "I love your dog."

"She seems to like you."

"Remember Not Butte?"

"What's that got to do with my dog?"

"Nothing. Where was it?"

"Montana."

"I know Montana, what was the real name?"

"Shelby."

"Yeah, Shelby." He tipped his beer again then wiped his wrist across his lips. "Damn fine little town Shelby."

Evan nodded in agreement, eyes closed. "Damn fine." He pictured the small rail town and laughed a silent laugh. They had piled into Danny's 65 baby blue Fairlaine convertible and struck out for Butte although he couldn't remember why. He had fallen asleep in the back seat but was rudely awakened when the Ford flew over the railroad crossing. There in front of them was Shelby. He asked where they were and Not Butte was the collective response. Thereafter any place that wasn't their destination became 'Not' whatever.

Danny watched Ginn stalking something in the garden then shook his head. "Remember the biker road-house with the strippers?"

"That was Not Fargo."

"Right, Not Fargo…bloody trains kachunkin' past the hotel all night."

"That was Not Butte."

"You sure?"

"Sure as I'm not sitting here."

"Not Butte huh? Damn Evan, we lived it didn't we?"

Evan nodded again. "I had a girl from Not Fargo once," he said.

"Everybody's had a girl from Not Fargo."

"Not that one."

"Yeah, that one."

Evan furrowed his brow. "The blonde with the lasso tattoo and boots?"

"Yeah."

"Oh."

"They were good, those days."

"Yup. Our shaggy orange summer."

"Good bio title." Danny stretched, lifting his arms over his head. "The Rainbow wasn't it?"

"The hotel in Not Butte?"

"Yeah…fire escape, second floor. Psycho Sally-Dee?"

"You remember her but you don't remember Shelby?"

"Shelby never gave me toe cramps. Let's do it again Evan."

"Do what?"

"Write off a couple of weeks…be jerks, chase skirts…rock a little rough and tumble."

"I don't know…" Evan said, "I think the women may have something to say about that."

"They can come with us."

"Uh-huh. That's kind of like taking your cousin to the sock hop."

"Hey only once and I had her home before sun up. She's handling it pretty well?"

"Who and what?" Evan clumsily scraped his thumbnail on the beer bottle. He frowned and scraped harder. "When did they start painting the labels on these things?"

"The year the rock God died. Marie…the now-wife and the ex-girl?"

"Yeah, she is. Which rock God?"

"Pick one."

"You really wanna roll out?"

"Yeah, no." Danny peered down the neck of the clear bottle. "Yeah. I need more beer."

"So," Evan said, pulling a bottle from behind him and handing it off, "I understand you record the New Year's Celebration every year?"

"Thanks." Danny twisted off the top and took a short sip. "I don't talk about that too much. I don't want people to know, you know?"

"I think so."

"It's my idea. I don't want it stolen."

"It's safe with me."

"I know. It's art isn't it?"

Evan frowned. "Is it?"

"The same but different?"

"I see. No, I don't."

Danny held up two fingers. "In this many years I'll have enough drops to edit together."

"Okay."

"Then it'll be a forty-minute piece covering twenty years…with news and music clips."

"Ah, an audio-visual collage."

"I knew you'd understand."

"Not really."

Danny leaned forward and whispered, "I'm kidding you know."

"I know."

"I don't know crap about art."

"You never did…but you still record the ball drop, right?"

"Uh-huh."

"And you don't find this just a tad weird?"

"Yeah. What can I say, I'm eccentric."

"The first step is admitting it." Evan glanced across the yard. "Where are Steve and Mitchie?"

"They followed us in his Jaguar. Didn't want to cruise with the commoners I guess."

"Advance promotion on this duo doesn't entice me to catch the concert. What happened to him?"

Danny shrugged. "I see Barb occasionally, always a great lady."

"That's not what I asked."

"He gained a little weight and started throwing it around. Barb walked when she got tired of catching it."

"How bad?"

"She was smart enough to get out before it got too rough."

"This Mitchie girl, what's her story?"

"I don't know…I just met her the day before yesterday. Christ Evan, she can't be more than eighteen. Cute kid though. Remember little Tracy…served at the Sweet Spot?"

"I don't remember the Sweet Spot."

"Out on Seventh. The coffee place with the huge paintings."

"Barely."

"The young girl, about fifteen. Red hair to there, white shirt and black leotards?"

An image came to mind. "Sugar Shack?"

"That'd be the one. Mitchie could be her sister, or granddaughter now I guess."

Evan smiled. "She was pretty cute."

"She liked you."

"I was merely a big brother to the young lady."

"Yeah, right…all those artsy girls wanted to pork the poet."

"And some of the artsy boys too."

Claire passed in front of them and made her way across the yard. Danny let out a whispered whistle. "God she's still a gorgeous chunk of woman isn't she?"

"Yes she is." Evan sighed. "But there's another one." He pointed towards Carol.

Danny nodded. "Yeah, she is pretty special."

"She'd have to be…you've managed to hang onto her for forty years."

"Only when she lets me. Actually we haven't really been together for a couple of years."

"You're divorced?"

"No, still married. We're just not living together mostly. I sometimes stay over at her place, she sometimes at mine. We still love but we just can't seem to be able to live in the same house."

"Oh."

"And before you ask, yes we see other people casually. I'm kinda off and on with Charlotte…mostly off though. Rollie's been hanging with this nice guy. Ted…divorced, three kids. He's a little younger but nonetheless pretty cool."

"I wasn't going to ask but since you brought it up, he knows she's married?"

"Yeah, we go fishing once in a while and talk about it."

"You and Carol?"

"Ted. You know Carol doesn't like fishing. I think she must have had me in mind when she befriended him though, fisherman and all."

"Of course she did. So does Carol go…do things with your other people?"

"She and Charlotte bought Ted the boat for his birthday. That was a party."

"You went?"

"Sure, why not?"

Evan shook his head. "Right, why not. This Charlotte, what's she like?"

"Thirty-six…Sir Douglas Quintet."

"And you can handle that?"

"Macadamia magic, my man. It's a good relationship Evan…just a little quirky at times."

"A little? You've raised the quirky bar a notch and then some."

"We double-date every so often. It's pretty fun."

"And then some more. You are kidding, right?"

"No Evan, honestly. I know it sounds like a bad reality show but it's true."

"I'm still not sure if you're serious."

"Ask Carol, she'll tell you."

"I have to pee." Evan stood and walked up the steps into the house.

Chapter 48

Marie tossed a large bag of pretzels to Claire. "Dump these into the yellow bowl and tell me about Evan."

"Excuse me?"

"I'm wondering what it's like to meet the old boyfriend again after all this time."

"I don't really know. He hasn't changed as much as I thought he would have."

"The feelings, they're still there?"

Claire smiled. "To a certain extent, yes."

"He was your first serious relationship?"

"First relationship period. Maybe you never get over it. I haven't, really."

"I think that's going both ways. I appreciate your honesty Claire. He's talked about you over the years. I've always been curious about this woman who still haunts him and now can I see why she does. You're okay, although I really do wish you weighed another hundred pounds."

Claire laughed. "Actually I was hoping for the same with him, it would have made this whole thing easier."

Marie looked up from the table as Evan wandered into the kitchen. "So how's it going out there?" she asked.

"Weird." He pulled a beer from the fridge. "Danny just told me the most bizarre story."

"About Ted?"

"It's true? You knew?"

"Carol told me earlier. Sounds interesting doesn't it?"

"No. Well, yes…no. It's just weird."

"Apparently it's quite common these days. We really must get out more dear."

He twisted the cap off the bottle and leaned in the doorway. "Excuse me?"

"Think about it Evan, you and tankboy could go to hockey games together."

"Only if the Russians are in town," he said. "You're not serious?"

"About tankboy? I could be, under those new rules."

"No…about this sounding interesting."

"Yes I am serious, it does…but would I be interested?"

"This is what I'm asking."

"That would depend on who you're seeing at the time."

"What?"

"Seriously Evan, she and I would have to have more in common than just you. If I'm going to be hanging out with number two we'd better be able to come together and communicate on a higher, more meaningful level. That's all I'm saying."

He turned and walked towards the back door. "What makes you think she'd be number two?" he grumbled, stepping through the doorway onto the porch.

Marie and Claire were still chuckling as Andy and Jenn appeared out of the spare bedroom.

"What's with the old grouch?" Andy asked.

"He's just confused," Claire said.

"You'd think he'd be used to it by now." She held up her arms and displayed a black T-shirt with blue lettering. "What do you think Marie?"

"My God, where did you get that?"

"I had it made a few years ago when I was coming out to see you but didn't. See? 'Evan Morris Revival Tour' on the front and on the back…" She turned. "Twenty-six concert dates, all of them at your address. Way cool huh?"

"Way small huh?"

She pulled back her shoulders. "The better to flaunt 'em with my dear."

"Andy…"

"Go with it Marie. I know it's not the most politically correct thing I've ever done but hey, Jack would appreciate it."

Marie smiled. "You're right, he would…and so will Evan. I'm not sure the other guys will notice the shirt though."

"Where's the bad?" She turned to Jenn. "You've been pretty quiet. What do you think?"

"I think it'd fit me better," she muttered.

"Ah, but not as well my dear. You can have it when I'm done."

"Never mind. By then it'll be stretched beyond restoration."

"Lord girl you're getting as nasty as the rest of this crowd. Speaking of which, we'd best get out there."

"Wait," Marie said, "nobody goes empty-handed, grab a food tray."

Chapter 49

Evan and Ginn sat on the top step of the porch watching Danny and Carol move the picnic tables under the trees at the back of the yard. So far they were the life-blood of this gathering, joking and playing around like children…looking as much in love as they ever have. Their offbeat lifestyle obviously suited them although Evan couldn't understand it. Carl slipped a 'Best Of Sixties' CD in the portable player then sat back watching Lauren as she stood facing the river, arms crossed.

"Food coming through," Claire said, walking down the steps beside him.

He shifted to one side but still gazed out on the yard.

She stopped and turned at the bottom step. "Are you still feeling uneasy about tonight?"

"No question. What's with Lauren?"

"I'm not sure, but you're right about the air around here. Come on, help me start the party?"

"In a few minutes."

Evan watched her walk across the lawn to the tables, turning every few feet and smiling at him. He felt something brush against his hair.

"Eyes front sailor," Andy whispered in his ear, "she's way out of your league."

"Always has been," he said quietly. "I'm just wondering where she keeps her cell phone."

"What the hell does that mean?"

He heard Jenn's giggle behind him. "I'll explain later Andy," she said. "We'd better get the trays down there."

"Just a second..." Andy handed Jenn the tray. "Evan, close your eyes."

He chuckled. "I don't think so."

"Aw come on, you can look at her all night or at least until Marie catches you."

"It's not that, I just remember the last time you had me close my eyes."

"I promise this is different. Trust me."

He closed his eyes and smiled. "Okay, but as I recall you also said that the last time."

He felt her move down the stairs and sensed that she had stopped directly in front of him.

"Okay," she said, "you can look."

His smile quickly turned to laughter as he read the front of the T-shirt then watched her turn to show off the back.

"You like it?" she asked.

"I love it Andy, thanks. I really needed a giggle about now."

She turned and rested her elbows on his knees. "Anything else you need while I'm down here?" She winked.

"Ahem," Jenn said, "perhaps we should be moving on Andrea?"

"She's a nice kid but such a damned nuisance." Andy frowned and took back the tray. "You joining us?" she asked him.

"When I'm ready."

Evan stared into the crowd nursing his beer, planning on staying at least coherent this evening. He'd failed chemistry but he'd learned enough to know that the mix before him was unstable. Carl had joined them now, his arm around Andy. Lauren stood next to Claire. The conversation was obviously one sided...Lauren looking serious, Claire smiling that professional smile that he had taught her so many years ago. She kept looking over at him with the 'save me' expression that she had perfected out at the ranch. A movement at the gate caught his eye. Steve danced his way across the yard, a bottle of wine in his left hand and his right arm around Mitchie. Andy was right...he wouldn't have recognized him. He'd packed on the beef and not a hint of grey blemished his obviously enhanced black hair. With his white slacks and yellow shirt open to the navel he presented a caricature of a disco-king…thirty years behind the times. He then studied the girl, picturing those leotards and murder-red hair. She was definitely 'Sugar Shack', no mistake there. Danny was pretty accurate when he'd suggested that Tracy had been willing to serve up more than soda back then but she was just a child…as Mitchie is now. The innocence on her face argued with the tight white T-shirt and low-slung jeans. He tensed but told himself to let it be.

Then he felt a light touch on his shoulder. "Are you going to sit here all night?" Marie asked.

"Steve's here."

"I noticed."

"Michelle…she's just a baby."

"I noticed that too. You are going to keep calm about it though, aren't you?"

"I'll try."

"Evan, I know how you feel about this sort of thing but I'd think twice if I were you."

"I've thought thrice. It still feels like I should do something."

She patted his shoulder. "Might I remind you of another old man and young girl that have become pretty tight lately?"

He watched Steve caress Mitchie's hip. "It's not the same Marie," he whispered.

"Isn't it?"

"No." He stood and took the pretzel bowl from her. "Let's join the party."

As Marie and Evan approached the picnic table Carol stepped in front of them. "I'm borrowing your husband for a while, okay Marie?" she asked.

"I'm getting used to it," Marie said, "just hose him down when you're done."

Evan dropped the bowl on the edge of the table next to the CD player then wrapped his arms around Carol. "It's great to see you girl." He kissed her cheek and held her a little tighter. "It's been far too long."

She put her hands on his chest and pushed back. "You've never hugged me."

"You were with Danny…we had rules remember?"

She pointed to the end of the table. "See that guy?"

"The one that looks a lot like Danny?"

"Uh huh, I'm with him."

"How did you decide which one to bring…toss a coin?"

"I'm sorry I chose to mingle. I gather you don't approve of our living arrangement?"

"More the loving arrangement," Evan said. "I'm sorry Rollie, I just don't get it."

"Yes, well… you don't have to. It's really none of your business."

"I know but I thought I should get my feelings out there. Now that I have…"

"You know I never liked you."

"I know, but I liked you."

"You put up with me same way I put up with you."

"I still don't understand." He stepped back and spread his arms. "What's not to like?"

"Your arrogance has aged well."

"I wasn't arrogant."

"Right, you were always strutting around figuring you could charm the panties off any pretty little bit that crossed your path."

"I could, but I didn't."

"How noble of you," Carol said, "so few men would make that sacrifice."

"What can I say? I'm a Saint."

"Bulls hooves. I will give you credit for the rule thing though. You did have more than a few opportunities to bend it and you didn't."

Evan smiled. "So I wasn't all bad?"

"No, but if you had been I'm pretty sure that Claire would have built an interesting pair of book-ends. What the hell did she see in you anyway?"

Again he wrapped his arms around her. "She took the time to get to know the real Evan, the one who holds endless respect for those he truly cares for. The Evan that appreciates the woman who would allow him a few moments of her life; a brief interlude to simply caress her and lose himself in her delicate beauty…to unravel the mysteries hidden behind her intoxicating eyes, her moist, inviting lips."

She struggled but he held her tighter. "Sweet Carol..." he whispered coarsely, "we must set aside our differences and free those emotions imprisoning your denied yearnings. Share my desire and permit me to fan the smoldering savage fury within you so that together we might dance through the flames of unbridled passion."

"Piss off Evan." Carol freed herself from his arms and half-smiled. "I'm going to find a nice person to play with."

Evan watched her walk away, smiled then turned towards the table.

"She's still got her panties," Claire quipped as he stepped past her. "You're slipping old man."

"And you were eavesdropping. Doesn't much matter, she's hooked." He rubbed his hands together and winked. "I'll reel her in later."

"I doubt it. I think she upchucked the bait when you suggested you wanted to fan her smoldering whatever...but I could be wrong."

"Maybe I should have quit while I was ahead?"

"You were never ahead. I thought she hated you?"

"Not hate, just misunderstanding. But she's weakening."

"Cool. Give her another forty years and I betcha she'll letcha."

"That's the plan."

Claire closed her eyes and shivered. "God, that's a disgusting image...."

Chapter 50

Jenn sat beside Danny at the picnic table. "Andy tells me that you're an expert on the old music scene?"

"I am the old music scene kid." He grinned. "Not really an expert, I just stuck with it when the rest of them dropped out. I hear you're researching Evan. How's it going?"

"I don't know. You old guys can be confusing."

"It's a developed self-defense mechanism."

"Well developed." Jenn smiled. "Got a few minutes?"

"That all depends on what you've got in mind," he growled softly.

"I'd like to know a little bit about you for my files?" she smirked.

"Lordy you have been hanging around him. I'm all yours Foxy, what do you want to know?"

"Tell me about Bogwump? I figure it's a part of his life that must have had some impact on what he ended up doing."

"You're probably right. The whole band thing was a learning experience for Evan and I. The group was a study of everything that could go wrong in those days."

"How so?"

"Conflicting attitudes mostly. Three of us were into it, two weren't. Jack could play drums like a madman. He studied Gene Krupa and threw a lot of theatrics into the act."

"Gene who?"

"Krupa." Danny grimaced. "Let's see…picture Keith Moon with a suit and tie."

"Who?"

"Yeah."

"What?"

"Who."

Jenn grinned and shook her head. "Nope."

"Nope?"

"I've been warned about you Danny. You're not sucking me in."

"Okay." He grinned. "I was pretty good on bass and rhythm and Evan could almost carry a tune. Musically Carl was incredible but he and Steve were just along for the ride. We'd known each other for so long that we couldn't kick them out. They were usually drunk or high…never made rehearsal."

"So the chemistry wasn't there."

"At times it was but overall no. Evan, Jack, and I got along well but Evan and Steve always had this simmering dislike for each other. The tension between them was sometimes pretty severe. Carl just went with the flow or whoever had the booze, money or whatever."

"What kind of music did you guys play?"

"Mostly old stuff with a new beat." Danny tapped rhythmically on the table. "We had a version of Route 66 that rocked the rodents outa the rafters of those high school gyms. Evan and I wrote a few clunkers but generally we covered what was big at the time. The kids preferred that sort of stuff at the sock hops and what-nots."

"No screaming fans?"

"Only those who discovered we'd locked the exits."

"How long were you together?"

"I'm not sure we were ever really together but we played off and on for about five years."

"Evan said you did a couple of small towns?"

"Quite a few of them actually, usually overnighters. Nobody else wanted the hassle of the smaller centers but Evan booked us anywhere he could. He saw it as a captive audience as well as a great training ground for us. In those days we were the only group to play for the rural kids on their own turf so we always got a good reception. The raw emotion they put out for us was a helluva boost for our egos. The highlight I guess was the northern tour."

"You guys actually toured?"

"Once, such as it was. In '64 we played High Prairie, Peace River, and Dawson Creek on three consecutive nights. We even needed the Mounties to provide security on the way out of the hall in High Prairie."

"Bogwumpmania?" Jenn coyly grinned.

"Hardly." Danny laughed. "We'd stopped at this little roadside café to get supper before the dance. Jack put on a pretty decent British accent and told the waitress that we were the Rolling Stones and we only used Bogwump as a cover when we played small towns. I guess she believed him and spread the word. When we arrived at the hall there had to be two hundred kids yelling for us. That was a turn-on. It made us want more even if it was all a sham. The illusion was heightened when Evan did a Mick Jagger that I imagine they're still talking about up there."

"How could they not know you weren't the Stones?"

"They'd just released 'Not Fade Away'. Kids had heard it on the radio but obviously they hadn't seen them or we couldn't have gotten away with it. We'd all let the hair grow by then so it was pretty convincing."

"The name came from something Evan had written?"

"I think so. I never cared for it but it was no worse than a lot of the names back then." He glanced at Evan at the end of the table. "I often wondered what would have happened if he and I had stuck it through. When he took off on his own I tagged along for a while until I got a job with a band back home. Money won out over fun although I still often wish it hadn't."

"You were a part of that tour?" Jenn asked.

"I played back-up the first few weeks." Danny closed his eyes and took a deep breath. "Man that was fun while it lasted. He could have been good but it wasn't the life he wanted and being alone on the road for four months…that's tough. Most guys would thrive on the recognition, the wine and the women but it really wasn't Evan."

"We talked about the women but he said it wasn't a big deal."

"For him, no. I confess to a few indiscretions around that time but Evan was pretty much a straight up guy. He and your mum had drifted apart just before we hit the road and I think he always hoped they would sort things through."

"So the girls he mentioned weren't just a convenience?"

"Not at all. We were in Kelowna on the third or fourth night when these two girls approached us. They bought us drinks then we walked along a beach for a couple of hours. They hung on Evan's every word when he talked about life and love. Then we talked about their lives…how they wanted to get out and see the world. About two in the morning they went home and we went back to the motel."

"That was it?"

"It surprised me too," Danny said. "I figured the buying of the drinks was the warm-up to a little road lovin' but it ended up being a pretty special evening anyway. It wasn't like the rockers. Women who wanted to meet Evan wanted to meet the person. If it ended up an overnighter that was okay but mostly they just drank a little wine and got to know him better."

"Make love to the poets."

"And not necessarily in the physical sense. That was what made it so nice. I think Evan got as much out of it as they did. I remember getting back home and envying him."

"He said he didn't think he was good enough to go any further. How about you?"

Danny chuckled. "None of us were really. I still figure if he'd stuck with it he could have gone bigger. I did okay. Nothing major but I've been in the business for nearly fifty years so I must be good at something. Evan always had this self-doubt about him, a lack of confidence. He needed people to keep him going…to tell him he was doing okay. He draws from those close to him. That's why the tour was both good and bad. He sold some records and books but got mostly obligatory compliments from people…nothing of substance."

"How did you feel about him quitting?"

"When I heard that he'd disappeared I wasn't surprised. Evan was the kind of guy who'd try something and if he didn't like it he'd move on. He wasn't all that happy on the road. Like I said he didn't get the ego stroking that he needed. I can see how he lost interest."

"Tell me about your relationship?"

"Being here tonight reminds me of how close we were and I really miss it. I wish I'd come out more often. I can't begin to figure out what our relationship was or is." Danny shrugged and stood. "It's just good, that's all. I need a drink…can I get you something?"

"No thanks but I'd like to continue this discussion at a later date?"

"So would I." He pulled a card from his shirt pocket and handed it to her. "Call anytime."

"I will. By the way…'My Generation', 'Pictures of Lily', 'Pinball Wizard'?"

Danny smiled. "It appears I should have been warned about you too Foxy. Later…."

She watched him wind his way to the cooler of drinks at the far end of the table, stopping to hug both Andy and Claire on the way. They all had warm souls and big hearts. The ease she now felt with Evan had quickly extended to Danny. They were so much alike, each displaying the same gentle mannerism and both bearing a shameless caring that couldn't be denied. Jenn studied him intently as he picked a bottle from the cooler then sat down beside Marie.

She glanced at Carl and Steve as they laughed over the barbecue. She understood how they didn't fit with the others all those years ago. They didn't fit tonight either.

She looked along the table at Evan. He was smiling at Marie, his eyes saying so much.

Jenn took a deep breath and suddenly felt lonely.

Chapter 51

Claire grinned when Carol turned, walked back, and sat beside her. "You really think I'm the nice person?" she asked.

"You'll do." Carol smiled. "I'm sorry it took this to get us back together."

"Me too." Claire nodded towards Evan. "So that was quite a squeeze from Attila…you two thinking of making up?"

"No. I'd miss the bites and barbs."

"Yeah."

"Tonight, these people…I don't know. It's strange…scary. You wake up one morning and there it is gone. It really is gone isn't it?"

"Not if you don't want it to be."

Carol watched Evan rubbing Marie's shoulder. "He hasn't changed."

"Why should he? There wasn't too much wrong to begin with."

"I don't want it to be gone." She looked along the table at Danny. "When did everything get so frigging complicated?"

"September 30th, 1967."

"The day we said goodbye to the house? That was it wasn't it?"

"End of the dream. It shouldn't have been but it was."

Carol inhaled slowly, her breath unsteady. "I wish I'd appreciated it more."

"I think we all do. None of us realized it was anything special at the time. It was just what it was. Life was meant to be like that."

"Then we grew up and got smart."

Claire laughed. "Grew up maybe."

"Do you ever miss it?"

"Once in a while, especially now."

"I do…often. For years after I'd look back and think it was childish. That the long hair, jeans, flowers, and crap were just a waste of time. I'd put it all behind me until I found myself trying to explain those days to someone. The more I told her the more I realized that I really didn't know what it was about either." She held a clenched fist to her chest. "It was in here…I just couldn't put it into words."

"Everyone hangs too much on the sixties," Claire said. "People hear about our life back then and assume it was nothing but sex, drugs, and rock 'n roll. Look at the films on Woodstock and San Francisco. They certainly add credence to the motto."

"Yeah, I watch those and wonder where I was when all this was happening."

"Living in a house with five people spending weekends frolicking bare-assed in the country with the Doors and a jug of wine?"

Carol laughed. "God we had sweet times didn't we?"

"We did, but we weren't part of the cosmic awakening that made headlines. What we had, how we all came together, had nothing to do with the sixties. We were six people who found each other at a time when we needed to find something. It just happened to be 1967, just days on a calendar. We started out trying to believe in something bigger than us but we ended up believing in us. Maybe that's what it was all about."

Carol stared at the river and smiled. "The trip down here stuck in a van with them, with Danny. I laughed at every one of his stupid jokes. I can't believe how much I miss his insane jabbering. There was a point when it was quiet and I looked at him and realized that I felt really comfortable for the first time in years." She played with the glass in front of her, turning it slowly between her fingers. "I left because I thought I'd outgrown him, outgrown a life that belonged in the past…but I couldn't let him go. I guess that should have told me something."

Claire saw the distance in Carol's eyes, heard her voice empty. "You're right Carol," she said, "Evan really hasn't changed but neither has Danny. The caring is still there. Love and understanding, remember? They're the same guys they were a lifetime ago."

"Love and understanding…Evan's motto."

"One of them." Claire took her hand. "I can't do anything about Evan but you…"

"I intend to," she whispered, "tonight."

"I'm leaving her in your questionably capable hands Daniel." Evan stood as Danny slid along the bench next to Marie. "I'm thinking I should go make peace with Lauren."

"Pull that off and we're sending you to Iraq."

Evan patted Danny on the shoulder as he passed. "Might be safer," he mumbled.

As Danny took her hand Marie smiled up at him. "It's about time you got around to me."

He leaned and kissed her cheek. "Now now…you know there are always warm-up acts before the headliner."

"You're as full of it as ever. I heard about you and Carol. Interesting arrangement."

Danny shook his head. "Most people suggested a divorce."

"I've seen you naked. I wouldn't divorce you either."

"God women are so superficial. I'd love to be loved for my mind."

"Yeah, fat chance of that."

"Geez Marie, all I'm asking for is a little respect."

She tugged his beard. "You want respect…beg for it. I see you've met Jenn?"

"Yeah, neat kid. How's Evan doing with her?"

"In what way?"

Danny shrugged. "She's a lot Claire-ish. I imagine that's weighing heavily on him."

"It is…doubly-so now that her mum's here."

"Daughters lock up your mommas?"

"Lock 'em both up." She laughed. "No, it's really not a problem. I just haven't seen that look for a while, that's all."

Danny put his hand on her shoulder. "It is Evan we're talking about here Marie, not me."

"I know, and I am okay…but thanks for caring Danny." She winked. "You were always my favorite."

"Mrs. Morris! Are you trying to seduce me?"

"Would it do any good?"

"Not really," he said softly, "I'm intimidated by sexually-aggressive women."

"It's the new millennium Danny, we take what we want."

"Okay then." He sighed and held out his hand. "Take me."

"Anywhere in particular?"

"Let's hit the beach and watch the submarine races."

"Christ I haven't heard that one in years!"

"Was that a 'yes'?"

She moved closer to him. "Yes Danny," she whispered, "yes…yes…yes!"

He sat back and smiled. "You're serious?"

"I am," Marie whined, "I really, really am."

"Really?"

"Sure. If you truly want to try being loved for your mind there's nothing like a big walk with a little Plato under a full moon. I trust you've heard of Plato?"

"Mick's pup, right?"

"That'd be the one."

"I know you're just teasing Marie. Women are all alike. You get me alone with promises of cultural conversation and intellectual intercourse, lulling me into a false sense of equality. Then you have your way with me and after hours of degradation inflicted merely to satisfy your primal passions you simply toss me aside, leaving me alone and broken to wallow in heartache and humiliation…feeling all cheap, used and yuchy."

Marie patted his knee. "As romantic as it sounds I could never do that to you Danny."

"Screw it then, you can go by yourself." He laughed. "I'd better get back to my seat…hot stuff looks like she's getting jealous."

"In your dreams," Marie said. "But if you'd really settle for a quiet walk and talk on the beach later, I'm okay with it."

He stood and took her hand. "Me too."

Chapter 52

"Making the rounds?" Lauren asked as Evan approached her on the riverbank. She was guarded and distant, a challenge he wasn't sure he was up to tonight.

"Yup, I'm Evan."

"I know, and your reputation precedes you." She looked back towards the river. "Nice night."

"If it doesn't rain." He leaned against the tree beside her. "How about those Oilers?"

She quickly turned. "What exactly are you looking for Evan?"

"A little conversation?"

"And you chose me...I'm flattered."

Evan grinned. "Somebody had to and I was the only one drunk enough to volunteer."

"Thanks."

"You don't make it easy Lauren, y'know?"

"I know." She drew a deep breath. "None of this is easy. I shouldn't have come."

"Nope."

"Christ, you're just a big bundle of love aren't you?"

"Yup. Want some?"

She drew another deep breath and squinted into his eyes. "Do I look like I do?"

He stepped beside her. "You look like a woman who'd like someone to take her away from all of this confusion and lead her to a quiet place where she can figure it out…someone who'll listen without judgment, someone who'll understand."

Lauren raised her eyebrows and smiled nervously. "I suppose you're this someone?"

"Hell no, I just wanna get laid."

She laughed out loud. "I'm sorry," she said. "You must think I'm a real bitch."

"Yeah," Evan replied softly, spreading his arms. "But welcome to my world anyway."

Her expression lifted as they hugged. "I'm not sure I should be doing this. I've heard all kinds of stories about you."

"Lies," he said.

"All of them?"

"Most of them…some of them."

"I imagined you'd be taller."

"So did I…when I was shorter."

She laughed again. "What the hell am I doing here?"

"Reluctantly surrendering to the charms of a man you wish you'd met decades ago?"

"No." She pushed away from him. "I'm not part of any of this Evan, I really don't belong here."

"Right. You can't relate because you weren't there so you're an outsider. You're not Karen, you're over-dressed, you're scared, Carl's ignoring you…anything else?"

"Over-dressed?"

Evan shrugged. "Did I go too far?"

"No, you're right on all counts. But I'm a long way from surrendering."

He winked. "Give me time."

"Pretty confident aren't we?"

"No, I just know me." He leaned back against the tree and studied her empty eyes as she followed the laughter of children running along the beach. "He does love you Lauren."

"Damn, you are good." She turned and faced him. "You're especially right about the 'I'm not Karen' part. I feel it every day now. He's dragged out the old photos, talks about her, about you. A lot about Claire…how she and Karen…"

"They had a lot of years together."

"Yes, they did." She touched her eye. "Ever since he found out, y'know, things haven't been the same."

"Maybe that's normal, I don't know. We all think we're going to live forever even though we know we won't. Then one day somebody puts a date on forever and it's not forever anymore."

"I understand that. I just wish he'd realize that he's not the only one waiting."

"I'd like to think I'd live every minute to the fullest, let death chase me for as long as I have left…make it work damn hard to find me. I'm not in that situation so I really don't know how I'd react but I'm pretty sure I wouldn't sit around and wait. Waiting seems to be such a waste of precious time."

"Tell him that."

"I will." He put his arm across her shoulder and pulled her close. "You're good for him Lauren, I can see that. Karen was such a big part of his life but for all they once had, they don't have anything now. He has to be wondering what happened, why it happened. It doesn't mean he cares any less for you. He's just trying to tie up loose ends, to answer some of those unanswered questions, maybe make amends with himself and find a little peace. You do belong here, he needs you here."

"I'd like to hear that from him."

"Perhaps you're just not listening?" He rested his chin on the top of her head. "He's doing the dance tonight…enjoying himself. Maybe he is being a bit selfish but maybe he should be. He's going to relive and cherish those old days more than the rest of us because they're even more special to him now. The smallest details buried in the faintest memories, things the rest of us have forgotten or trivialized will loom large. He's reaching into the past to grab a piece of the magic we think those days were, even if they weren't. Tonight is all he has to do that. You have to be here for him, understanding how important this is to him. You're here because you are the biggest part of his life Lauren. That's why he insisted you come. You're the only one that really matters now." He felt her trembling as he pointed to the picnic table. "There's a space right next to the weird-beard in the jean shirt who's been staring at us for the last five minutes. It looks about your size."

Lauren slid her head out from under his chin and smiled up at him. "Thank-you for this Evan," she said softly, stepping back. "Carl certainly didn't exaggerate."

"Carl always exaggerates."

"Most times…sometimes." She turned and quickly walked away.

He watched her sit beside Carl, drape her arm over his shoulder and whisper in his ear. They kissed and laughed. As Claire walked behind them Lauren reached to her then awkwardly stood between the bench and the tabletop. Words were spoken, the two women hugged. Evan acknowledged Claire's wink and things grew silent. Yesterday vaulted across the lawn to gift him with memories of a smoke-filled coffee house infested with moaning pseudo-intellects who wore their cool like clip-on ties. She looked now as she did that night…classy and fresh, and with a spark that would glimmer forever. The guy beside her had sported a heavy-knit black turtleneck and jeans. A grey top hat crowned a thatch of truly unruly dark curly hair. He hid behind a sinister pair of sunglasses, holding a cigarette Nazi-style and stroking an indecisive beard. With feigned appreciation he'd nod knowingly throughout each reading then, at the end, he leaned towards Claire and whispered. She sat straight, shaking her head. He got up, walked out the door and disappeared into the cool Edmonton evening dragging his dashed intentions behind him. Evan was beginning to drown in the memory of that first night with Claire when a bark pulled him back. Ginn and Mitchie were playing fetch by the house, the girl giggling innocently as young girls should. He glanced along the table. Steve stood behind Marie, a drink in one hand rubbing her shoulder with the other. Evan felt his heart race as he walked quickly to his end of the table.

"You okay?" Claire asked as she slipped in beside Jenn. "You're looking a little lost."

"Yeah, I am a little lost." Jenn said, watching Danny make his way toward them. "I'm not sure what to think of all this. It's like a time-warp."

"That it is." Claire laughed. "Speaking of which…hey Danny."

"Ah chocolaty Claire, as lovely as lovely ever were." He sat and put his arm around her. "I see you've shared your wealth with the little one?"

"Little one?" Jenn scowled. "And it's 'as lovely as lovely ever was'."

"But 'was' doesn't rhyme with Claire."

"Neither does 'were'."

"Maybe not here."

"Maybe not anywhere?"

"Have ya ne'r been to Labrador lass?"

"No."

"Okay then."

"Okay what?"

Danny shrugged his shoulders. "I win."

"Pardon?"

"You have your mother's eyes…"

"Screw that, how did you win?"

He shrugged again. "Linguistic theorem."

"What?"

"A matrix of practical colloquialism as it applies to spatial and environmental diversity. It's simple really."

Jenn squinted at him. "The sixties really weren't all that nice to you were they?"

"Oh, they were lovin'…t'was the eighties what fried the grey. How are you doing Claire?"

"Tired, but really happy to see you again." She kissed his cheek. "Aro-man Musk?"

"A connoisseur to be sure."

"Devon uses it to keep cats out of the yard."

"Cheaper than a dog."

"Dog smells better. Carol looks good?"

"Yeah," Danny lowered his voice, "we're going to talk later."

"Uh huh." Claire put her arm around him. "And I couldn't be happier."

"Neither could I," he whispered. "Being with you guys tonight brought everything back, the memories, feelings…what we lost, y'know?"

"I know."

Chapter 53

With Ginn curled beneath his legs Evan sat quietly, preferring to listen to the many discussions blending before him. His mind drifted from subject to subject constructing his own thoughts should he ever be able to get a word in edgewise or otherwise. Daylight was fading, yielding to the subtle perfection of dusk. The peace he usually felt at this time was hidden beyond the shadowed trees lining the riverbank. Once again a gentle breeze carried the perfume of unseen blossoms across the yard, tempering the acrid lingering of over-broiled burgers and burnt sauce. The conversations fused into dull murmurings indistinguishable from each other. He assessed the group before him. The women were as beautiful as any man could wish for. Each bore a uniqueness of spirit, an essence beyond mere physical attraction. The men were, in the collective sense, men. Lauren and Carol exchanged secrets sprinkled with laughter while Carl nodded at him, giving the thumbs up. He looked better now, relaxed and happy. Claire and Andy were unbuttoning Danny's shirt while Jenn covered her eyes. Mitchie sat alone taking it all in, her eyes wide, a broad smile across her young face. He looked at Marie, her stare set above and beside him. Then he felt a poke in his ribs.

"Hey Morris, still slumming I see?"

"Present company included. How are you Steve?"

"Damn fine. You should have stuck with me Evan, there's a lot of nostalgia crap happening now…that garage shit. You might rustle up an old fan or two with the right marketing."

"I'm happy."

"Sure you are." He leaned over and nodded toward Jenn. "Who's the femme de la fresh?"

"You haven't been introduced? She's Claire's daughter, Jennifer."

"On closer inspection I guess it's obvious. She certainly has the goods."

Evan reached down and quieted Ginn as she growled. "Back off Steve," he said quietly.

"Tender spot?" Steve laughed. "So you and Claire are still friends?"

"Why wouldn't we be?"

"Old wives and girlfriends are beaten baggage Evan, best lost somewhere between flights."

"I see you avoided the baggage on this trip. Just a little carry-on?"

"Ah that notorious Morris wit." He rested his hand on Evan's shoulder. "I've really missed it not at all. You haven't changed have you?"

"Neither have you."

Steve leaned and whispered, "Except that I'm alive, not some broken down almost-was hiding out here in the backwoods."

"Obviously I must practice my hiding skills."

"Don't bother, nobody's looking." He pointed to Jenn. "You need a piece of stuff like that Morris…it keeps you young."

Evan gripped Steve's shirt and pulled him closer. "For Andy's benefit and in the interest of keeping peace I'll forgo any further comments if you'll do the same?"

Ginn moved out from under the table, sensing the tension above her. Steve heard the growl and looked into her eyes. "Yeah, sure…" He grinned then walked around the table and took his place beside Mitchie.

Evan was suddenly aware of how quiet the gathering had become. He looked up as one by one everyone diverted their attention from him and began subdued conversations. At the far end of the table Danny raised his hand and displayed the peace sign then slowly curled his index finger into hiding. Evan smiled in acknowledgement then stood. Once again all eyes were upon him, all voices stilled. He held up his beer bottle.

"As the host of this gathering I find it my responsibility to be the first to honor Jack. To be honest this isn't an easy thing for me to do. He was a dear friend and someone with whom I shared a lot during those informative years. Through the good and bad times he was there and even though we hadn't seen each other for far too long he was always in my thoughts, as he is now." He gazed skyward. "Jack, if you're listening in I know what you're thinking. Enough of this bullcrap, screw the tears and pass the beers!" He raised his bottle as he turned up the CD player. "This one's for you buddy...."

When the opening bars of 'Somebody To Love' cracked the evening air the tone changed and the tributes were launched.

Carl began by reminiscing about the night of the tattoo, explaining to Jenn that it was a young mans rite of passage. Jenn stared at him, shaking her head. "You've got to be kidding, having your butt tattooed is a rite of passage?"

"Sure," Carl said, "that giant leap into manhood."

"So you all got tattoos that night?"

"Hell no," Danny said, "our rite of passage was convincing Jack to go first then we slipped out the back door to the bar."

"That is so cruel! I can't believe you did that."

Evan sipped his beer slowly, listening yet not hearing. Stories of the band, road trips, and girls swirled around him but his thoughts rested in a San Francisco park in a time without time. A gentle smile crossed his face as he remembered the laughter and madness of youth in a care-less society. Small things, a look or gesture, a joke at the right time, quiet talks over cheap wine...an arm across a shoulder at his father's funeral. The bond he and Jack had formed back then, buried for so many years, now propelled its way to the surface dragging in its wake all the emotions that Marie had warned him about. He glanced down the table and realized what Carl must be going through. When all is said and done, it really is the little things that are special. Mostly it's the people, the loved ones and the lovers. What value is the rest without having someone to share it with, to care for? He looked across at Marie. She was polite, bearing with all of this for him. Tomorrow he would dig out those Japanese lanterns. Claire smiled, contributing where she could but appearing more uncomfortable than he'd ever seen her. He looked at

Andy…expressionless, forcibly smiling when acknowledged. He felt his muscles tighten as the stories droned on.

Chapter 54

Jenn stood and whispered to her mum then moved toward the riverbank, Ginn at her heels. Andy and Claire stood and slowly walked toward the side of the house, arms over each other's shoulders, heads down.

Evan watched their every step until they disappeared around the corner into the shadows. He checked his watch. If Jack had attended in spirit he would probably have left two hours ago when the lightness turned to mockery and backbiting…just like the good old days.

He looked at Carol and Danny. She had her arm around his shoulder and her face buried in his neck. This was the good thing to come out of the evening, they belonged together. Then he looked at Steve and saw the display of self-serving arrogance he'd managed to forget over forty years. His date sat cuddled with him, her hand in his lap.

Mitchie. Every instinct pushed him to take her aside and find out what she was doing. Then he thought of Jennifer. It really wasn't the same. Or was it?

Evan stood and stretched as Carl and Lauren made their way toward him. Carl steadied himself on the table as he walked, Lauren supporting him.

"You okay?" Evan asked, realizing quickly it was a stupid question.

"Call me a cab," Carl said, "but don't call me a 'cab'?" He laughed weakly. "Actually Ev I feel better tonight than I have in months. I owe you one buddy. Just tired, that's all."

The look on Laurens face told a different story but she mustered a smile. "It's been good, for both of us. But I think we should get back to the hotel and have a little quiet time."

Evan nodded and looked at Marie as she shut down her cell phone. "Cab will be about twenty minutes," she said reaching for Carl. "I'm so glad you came tonight Carl. It was so wonderful seeing you again." She moved toward Lauren. "And it was nice to meet you Lauren, although I imagine this was a little overwhelming for you."

"It was but mostly my doing. I'm sorry about earlier. I really did enjoy myself…hopefully we can get together again?"

"You know where we live, you're always welcome."

"Thank you. We'll go wait on the front step if that's okay? It's a little calmer out there."

"Sure." Marie stood. "I'll walk you around."

Evan hugged Carl. "Take care my friend," he said quietly then he held Lauren. "You take care of him for us, okay?"

She nodded. "I will, thanks Evan. You were right…I do wish I'd met you decades ago." She turned and walked with Carl and Marie to the pathway that led to the front yard.

He walked to the same path but turned the other way to search for Claire and Andy. As the scrambled sound of music and voices disappeared behind him he found the two women in an embrace in the darkness at the side of the house.

"Hi guys," he whispered. "Need another pair of arms?"

Andy looked up at him, tears in her eyes. "This isn't right Evan. This isn't what he would have wanted. Other than Danny and Carol he wouldn't have anything to do with any of them, you know?"

"I know." Evan nodded and put an arm on each of their shoulders.

She rested her head on his chest. "They never knew him, not the Jack that we knew. He wasn't the clown they're making him out to be. He had his faults and I couldn't overlook them but he doesn't deserve this. Evan please…make them go away?"

He felt relieved. "Whatever you want Andy."

Chapter 55

Jenn sat near the bottom of the steps staring at the moon. She'd seen how the stories about Jack were affecting Andy, why hadn't anyone else seen it? Why didn't they back off? She felt someone coming down the steps beside her. Steve stepped past as she looked up.

"Needed a little quiet?" he asked as he knelt on one knee in the sand in front of her.

"Yes, I guess. You sound like you're having a good time?"

"I always do." He smiled. "You're not?"

"I don't know…yes." She started to get up. "I'd better get back up there."

He reached and took her hand. "No, let's talk for a while."

"About?" She sat back down, a step further away from him.

"Anything. You live in Kamloops?"

"Temporarily, I'm just finishing up at the university."

"So you have your own place in town?"

"Uh, yes. And a roommate."

"I heard you were staying here with Evan."

"I'm writing an article for school, the sixties aspect of his life. Marie suggested I stay here while I was working on it."

"You picked the most interesting one of the bunch, except maybe for Andy." He moved up a step, almost touching her. "Have you talked to her about those days?"

"A little but it's really Evan I'm interested in."

"You look a lot like your mum."

"Yes, I've heard that."

"You are as beautiful now as she was back then. She was pretty good at breaking hearts. I bet you've broken a few yourself."

Jenn felt her stomach tighten. "I don't know what you mean."

"Just that you've probably had a few boyfriends?"

"I suppose."

"Anything serious?"

"How do you mean?"

"You know what I mean."

"I'd better go…"

"No." He put a hand of each of her knees. "We should talk some more. You fascinate me Jenn. We'll be good friends when we find that common ground."

"Common ground?" She felt a trembling build. "We don't have a common ground Steve."

"Ah, but you do with Evan, right?"

"My writing, yes." His grip firmed as she tried to pull her legs free. "That's what we have in common."

"I don't think so. He has this knack, probably just like with your mother."

"No, not just like." She grabbed his hands and tried to push him away. "Please let go?"

"Relax Jenn…I'm not going to do anything you don't want me to."

Jenn felt pain as he tightened his grip again. "You're hurting me, I don't want you to."

"Don't talk down to me child," he growled, his expression turning to anger. "Like mother like daughter, isn't that the old saying?"

"I'm not…sure…" She stared into his eyes. She needed time. "No…not really," she whispered.

"What do you mean?"

"I don't know…" She felt his hands relax. "I guess I'm a little upset when people assume I'm like her. I'm not. I'm my own person."

"You're right of course, I'm sorry." He gently rubbed her knees.

Tears filled her eyes, she shook uncontrollably now, staring out at the beach, trying to scream the scream that was trapped somewhere inside.

He slid one hand along her thigh and against the leg of her denim cut-offs. "I think we're close to finding that common ground Jenn," he said.

"Maybe..." Her mind raced. "Maybe we should get back to the party and we could, you know...later, get together?"

"Not a bad idea but let's test the waters first."

She shuddered at the coldness of his touch. Through tears she saw a flash of white on the sand behind him.

"I think you'd better stop," she whispered, grabbing his hand.

"Say it like you mean it."

Jenn took a deep breath and kicked at his stomach. "Get your fucking hands off me!"

He fell back and stood glaring at her. "You little bitch!" Steve raised his arm then heard the growl. He turned as the wolf leapt, pinning him against the riverbank, her face within inches of his. He gripped the collar and flesh around her neck, trying to push her back. She was growing more savage, twisting, trying to free herself...snapping at his face, catching his shirt...tearing.

"Call her off!" he shouted, barely heard above the growling.

"Ginn!" Jenn screamed. "Stop!!"

With Claire close behind, Evan quickly bounded down the steps. He grabbed Ginn by the collar.

"Good girl," he said as tugged at her. She wasn't listening. "Ginn!" he shouted, pulling her back with all his strength. "Enough!"

Ginn relaxed and let him guide her away but when Steve tried to stand she leapt again. Evan fought to hold her back as she stood on her hind feet, lunging at her target.

"What the hell's going on?" Claire shouted as she got to the sand. Jenn threw arms around her and held on tighter than she'd ever done, sobbing. Claire glared at Steve. "You son of a bitch!" she screamed.

Evan knelt beside Ginn. "Quiet now." He stroked her. "Good girl..." He looked across at Jenn. "What happened?"

"Nothing," she sobbed.

Claire pulled back and looked into her daughter's eyes. "What happened Jenn?"

"Nothing...Ginn...." she sobbed.

Evan stood and had Ginn sit beside him. "Claire, take Jenn up to the house."

Jenn turned to him. "No Evan…I'm okay, really. Just please boot his ass outa here."

He looked at her then turned to Steve. "You heard her."

Steve moved cautiously toward the steps then smiled. "Hey, she didn't say no."

Claire pushed away from Jenn and marched quickly to him. "But I did and it didn't make a bit of difference did it?"

"That was a long time ago sweetie."

"Then this has been a long time coming!" Her closed fist smashed into his cheek. "Never get anywhere near my daughter again!" As she stepped back he moved toward her.

Instantly Ginn growled.

"I'd think about that if I were you Steve." Evan warned.

"Yeah, right. Big dog…big man."

Evan glared at him and took a deep breath. "Claire…you and Jenn go up to the house and take Ginn with you."

"No Evan," Claire insisted. "Please?"

"I'll take Ginn for you." Andy's voice came from above. "Although I'd much prefer to stay here and watch this bastard get his ass whupped."

Steve looked up. The top of the steps was the gallery from which everyone was watching his demise.

"Forget it," he said. "I'm leaving. Don't be surprised if animal control comes to take the bitch away." He stared at Claire. "This time I'm talking about the dog."

He climbed slowly to the top of the steps and reached his hand to Mitchie. "Come on girl…let's get out of here."

"I don't think so…" She pulled back. "God, you're a jerk."

He laughed. "That's the best you can come up with? Quit the crap and get in the car."

"No."

"I'm warning you," he snarled, "come with me now or you're left here on your own."

"Excuse me Stevie-boy." Andy stepped between the two of them. "It appears that you're the one who's on his own."

"Look in a mirror lately sweetheart?"

"What's that supposed to mean?"

"You've been on your own for ten years because you couldn't keep somebody as simple as Jack happy. You used to make everybody happy, remember? Easy Andy wasn't it?"

Andy glared. "It's not going to work."

"Give it up girl. Oh that's right, you already have…for everybody but me."

"Even I have standards. And that comment about animal control? Don't even think about it."

"Yeah? Why not?"

"Assault and attempted rape should get things started."

"You're as big a bitch as ever."

"Yup. Now unless you want history to repeat itself I'd suggest you leave."

"Choke on it babe."

Andy's knee shot up between his legs at the same time her hand grabbed his throat. "Get your sorry ass out of here before I feed those tender little morsels to the wolf…babe!"

He doubled over then flailed his arm against hers, loosening her grip on him. With fists clenched he straightened and found himself staring into Danny's eyes.

"Let it go man," he said quietly. "It's over."

"Says who?"

"The guy who's busted your ass on more than one occasion. Trust me Steve, I can still do it."

They watched him limp along the walk and around the corner of the house. Andy put her arm around Danny's waist. "Thanks, I think I got in a little over my head." She turned to Marie. "Any more wine?"

Chapter 56

Evan sat with Ginn on the steps. "I think she's settled now…how about you two?"

"I think I am," Claire said, still hugging her daughter. "Jenn?"

She nodded and took a deep, shaky breath. "Yeah, I do feel a bit grubby though."

"We should get back and clean you up. Are you joining us Evan?"

"In a bit, Ginn and I are going to build a fire."

"Seems like the only logical thing to do," Claire said. "Why?"

Evan shrugged. "Because there isn't one?"

"Right." She knelt in front of him. "Nobody asked how you were."

"No, they didn't."

She leaned forward and kissed him. "Thanks for backing off, I know it was tough."

He stared into her eyes and put his hand against her cheek. "I think I'm settled now too," he whispered. They separated and held hands.

"Need some help with that fire?" she asked.

He chuckled. "No, it's doing just fine thank you."

"You know what I mean."

Jenn patted her mum on the shoulder. "I'm heading up. I'll be back in a bit."

"I'll go with you," Claire said.

"No, you stay and help Evan. You guys should have some time, you know?"

"Are you sure you're okay Jenn?" Claire hugged her and whispered, "Thanks."

"I'm fine Mum. See you in a while."

Jenn stepped passed them on the steps. She stopped at the top and looked at the couple at the bottom. She couldn't hear the words but their expressions said everything. Suddenly Steve didn't matter. There was so much good at the foot of the steps there was no room left for bad. She heard someone call her name then turned and made her way into the yard.

Danny and Carol stood waiting for her on the path to the house.

"Jenn," Danny said, "please accept our apologies?"

"For what?"

"Steve?"

"You didn't have anything to do with it Danny, but thanks anyway."

Carol stepped up to her. "What Danny is trying…we really should have been more aware. We all know him, what he's like. We just didn't think…."

"Carol, Danny…" She held up her hands. "I don't know what to say. I'm upset but I'm okay. This wasn't any of your doing. I know not to let my guard down but tonight was so easy and so much fun that I didn't see it coming. The signs were there, I just missed them."

"It wasn't your fault Jenn," Danny said, "don't blame yourself?"

Jenn nodded. "I'm not. I know it was none of my doing, I don't blame myself at all."

"We just wanted to make sure you were okay before we left. Man, Claire sure knows how to make neat kids."

Jenn giggled. "Thanks again, I'm sure Mum thanks you too. You're leaving?"

"Yeah, we're old…it's late." Danny leaned forward, hugged her and whispered, "And you really are a fox."

"And you're still a mule I trust?" she whispered back.

He stood upright, surprise covering his face. "You know about that?"

"You're a legend Danny," she said, "and a really nice guy. I hope we meet again soon?"

"Perhaps it'll be sooner than you think. Carol's suggested that we hang around Kamloops for a few days and catch up with Evan and Marie and maybe sort some things through. Hopefully we'll have a chance to finish our history lesson before you need to turn it in."

"I'd really like that."

"Me too. Say goodnight to Evan and your mum for us." He winked. "Wherever they are."

Jenn waved as they walked to the van then she joined Marie and Andy on the porch. "I didn't see Michelle," she asked as she leaned against the railing. "Did she go with Steve?"

"No she's already in the van," Andy said. "She was a little shook and felt a lot foolish."

"She actually seemed pretty nice."

"She is, just naive. It seems Steve had promised to help her put together a cd of her songs if she came out here with him."

"She bought that?"

"Like I said…naive. Danny is going to make sure she gets home safe and sound and maybe help her with her music. Are you okay?"

Jenn rubbed her arms. "A little cold but otherwise I'm fine."

"He didn't hurt you?"

"No, Ginn took care of him before he had a chance. I was pretty scared though."

Andy nodded. "No doubt. On behalf of the rest of the gang I'm sorry?"

"No need. Evan and I talked about that sort of thing earlier."

Marie looked at her. "What sort of thing?"

"About how some men haven't evolved from the caveman. I saw the proof tonight."

"Ah. By the way, where is the old philosopher?"

"He and Mum are lighting a fire on the beach."

Andy raised her hand. "Would that be a regular bon or a Jim Morrison kind of fire?"

"You can't help it can you?" Marie said.

"Help what?"

"Mixing, stirring things up. But if I don't see a glow over that bank in five minutes I'm heading down there with a bucket of cold water."

Jenn made her way across the porch and sat beside Marie. "Danny said that he and Carol are going to stick around for a bit. It'll be nice to get some more time with him."

"They're not leaving?" Andy asked. "I wouldn't mind hanging around for that show."

"What do you mean?"

"Carol voluntarily spending more time in the same province as Evan?"

Jenn nodded. "According to Danny it was her idea."

"Really? Curiouser and curiouser."

Marie spoke up. "Evan's never mentioned this. They don't get along?"

"Didn't used to," Andy said. "From day one they just got on each other's nerves. She thought Evan was serious with all the flirting and double entendre. She called him on it, which just made him push even more. Finally they agreed to do the peaceful co-existence thing but every so often the sparks flew. It was a personality clash more than anything, nothing serious, no blood spilled. Actually there were times when it was pretty funny."

"You're right this could be interesting. You look tired Jenn. Maybe you should head inside?"

"No, I need to unwind a little more. Ginn was pretty ugly down there. It looked like she was totally out of control."

"Better her than Evan," Andy said.

Marie looked across at her. "I'm guessing Steve would've chosen either one of them over you."

"What do you mean?" Jenn looked at Andy. "What happened?" She settled back on the couch and listened as Marie recapped the earlier moments.

Chapter 57

Evan lit the kindling and watched the flames quickly spread. Emotions finally in check he tried to piece together the evening. He realized that he was not unlike Lobo. He'd lived inside his own little part of the world and let the rest of it go by, knowing nothing about what went on outside.

Claire touched her hand to his shoulder. "What happened here tonight?"

He dropped a small branch into the flames and watched and the tiny sparks spiral skyward then disappear into the darkness. "The death of innocence," he mumbled.

"So it's a funeral pyre we're stoking?"

"It sure looks that way. What a night. All those familiar faces yet there was something missing, something just wasn't right. Maybe it is time to grow up."

"You remember the beach in that little cove by the motel in Oregon?"

He smiled as the images came back. "That was a night."

"Damn near froze our asses off."

He dropped a bigger branch into the flames. "Right, I remember the romance and you remember the temperature."

Claire shrugged. "Didn't affect you too much as I recall."

"So what's the point?"

"We wanted that moment to live forever. We never ever wanted to grow up and lose that feeling." She slid her hand down his arm. "It was the most beautiful moment of my life. I think about it often and when I do it all comes back…the moonlight, the ocean, the gentleness, the passion…the sand in my panties."

He laughed. "And the mouse or whatever the hell it was that ran across my leg at the most inopportune time."

"Oh, I'd say the timing was perfect." She grinned. "I look at the rest of us and realize how different we've become. I've seen most of them over the years but it took tonight, here with you, to see how different. You haven't let life change you. What you still have is something we've all lost along the way…you're still Evan Morris and there's nothing wrong with that."

"I'm too old to change now." He reached his arm around her.

"No, it'd be too easy." She moved away and sat on the sand beside him. "Thanks for helping Jenn with her project. I really appreciate it."

"You're welcome, it's been fun. She's a great girl although I think she has the impression that all we did was run around naked and make out every time we got the chance."

"I'm thinking somebody gave her that impression. How much did you tell her about us?"

"Probably more than I should have, more than you would have. She wanted to know the story and I think it's all part of the big picture."

"Surprisingly I agree with you Evan, I just wish I'd had a little warning. But you're right, I'm not sure I would've told her all of it. We did an interesting chat this afternoon though."

"About?"

"Pretty much everything…you told her about our hippie artwork?"

"It's a gritty tale of the struggle for survival and using your God-given resources to conquer adversity, how a peach saved our asses…you know."

"You do realize that not all of those stampings came from the produce aisle?"

"Oh?" He saw her smug smile. "Oh."

"We talked about those days near Sausalito. Did you know Andy wanted you back then?"

"No surprise, every woman wanted me back then."

Claire laughed. "Yeah, beating them off with a stick, right?"

"Something like that."

"Ever consider it? With Andy I mean."

"No."

"Ever want to?"

"Yeah."

"But alas, you loved me."

"The sixties supposedly drew the line between sex and love Claire."

"But alas, you loved me?"

"So how is Devon with you being here?"

"Swing and a miss." She shrugged her shoulders. "He says he's okay. The fact that Jenn's here has helped although I'm pretty sure he wouldn't be too thrilled about you telling her some of those stories."

"I can't believe I didn't think about that. I wouldn't be impressed either."

"So tell me…how often do you white wolf moon?" Claire smiled wickedly.

Evan felt a blush. "She told you huh?"

"Of course, in great detail. Marie figures that Jenn and I have an extra-special bond now."

He took a deep breath. "I don't want to hear about it."

"Wait!" She held her forefinger in the air. "I've just realized that all the women here share that special bond. That's got to be a bit of a rush for the old boy?"

"Can't any of you get past that?" he mumbled as he picked up another branch and tossed it into the flames.

There was a loud pop then sparks shot high but Claire didn't notice. She studied his face. In the firelight he reminded her of those nights on the beach, the sunset walks and a time when they were the only two people in the world. A lifetime passed through her mind, most of it without the sense of comfort they had nurtured so long ago. That same comfort she felt settling in around her now.

Claire stared at the moon. "You remember the last time we talked?"

"We were a million miles apart. Me here, you there…joined by a telephone line."

"On a night very much like this. We were both looking out our windows at the same full moon. Somehow that made you seem closer. I remember hanging up the phone..." She looked out over the river. "I've never felt so lonely. Did we make a mistake?"

"I don't think there's any way to answer that. When we finally recognized what it was, it was gone. That time is so confusing. I don't even remember breaking up."

"We didn't."

"Unfinished love," he said quietly. "Andy was interested in me?"

"You really didn't know?"

"No. I can't believe I didn't see any signs."

"She was pretty obvious. She even asked if she could take you out of the stable."

He chuckled. "Really? What did you say?"

"I told her to ask you."

"She didn't."

"I know. But if she had?"

"It would have been tempting, but alas...."

Claire lay on the sand, leaning back on her elbows.

"Me too."

Chapter 58

Evan looked up as Marie, Jenn, and Andy circled the fire, each carrying a blanket. As Jenn walked past him he took her hand. "You okay?" he asked.

"I will be as soon as everyone stops asking me. I'm sorry I created all that."

"You didn't. You are okay though?"

"Dammit yes." She squeezed his hand and smiled. "Just another of life's lessons, right? I really am fine Evan, thank you."

Claire stood and took the blanket from her daughter. "I assume everyone else has gone?"

"Andy cleaned house before I got up there." Jenn said. "She pretty much took care of Steve for all of us."

"What did she do?"

"Let's just say he won't be having any more kids." Jenn laughed.

Claire frowned at Andy. "Not again."

"Second verse, same as the first." She shrugged. "Besides, he called me 'babe'. Who brought the wine?"

"Nobody…you've had enough," Marie said.

"I figured you'd say that." Andy grinned, pulling a bottle from under her blanket and holding it high. "Cheers."

Evan watched them settle in around the flames. "This is cozy," he said. "I count four beautiful women and one willing old man. I like my chances tonight."

Marie punched his arm. "Keep that up and you'll have no chance tonight. How are you?"

"Okay, I think…just trying to put the evening to rest. I guess I was naive to think it'd be like it used to be." He pulled off his glasses and tucked them into his shirt pocket. "I feel pretty empty right now."

Claire nodded. "I knew it wouldn't be the same but I wasn't expecting that."

They all stared into the fire, trying to find words to ease the feelings.

Finally Jenn stood. "What the hell is wrong with you guys? I look around and I see some pretty special people here. Other than my mother I didn't know any of you a week ago. To be honest I'm not really sure I knew her all that well either."

Claire touched her arm. "Jenn…"

"No." Jenn pulled away and began pacing in front of them. "The important people are still here, the people who care about each other and love each other. Isn't that what this is all about? You're all forty-years older than me but it doesn't matter to any of you. I've been accepted as an equal, a peer. That's something special. You've shown me that love and acceptance has no barrier. Maybe that came out of the sixties somehow, I don't know and I don't really care. I only know that in my world I've never experienced this, but here it's all around me. It's not always what you say or what I hear…it's what I feel."

She stopped beside the flames and put her hands on her hips. "I used to think that sixty was ancient, that it had to be the end of life as I knew it. One day I realized my mum was sixty and there's a lot of life still in her…thankfully not as much as when she was twenty. I see how all of you are and I can really understand Evan's theory about being all ages. You carry on with the joking and flirting just like kids. It's such an eye-opener for me. You are who you are…and I love who you are."

Jenn looked at each of them then pointed intently at Evan. "You," she said. "The first time I saw you I thought you were some doped-out hippie stuck in the sixties and your attitude did little to change my opinion. You were distant, evasive, and downright miserable. But when you finally let me in I realized I couldn't have been more wrong. You have taught me more in the last few days than I think I could learn in a lifetime. But the most important thing has nothing to do with all we've talked about, it isn't all your philosophical banter…it's you. You're true to yourself, to who you are, and to what you are. You're caring and honest. You respected and trusted me and you taught me to believe in myself. I can't thank you enough for…for just being."

Jenn looked to his left. "Marie…when I first met you I couldn't understand how such a lovely person could be married to that old grouch. Then I figured that he couldn't really be an old grouch if you'd kept him around all those years. You carry love to the next level. You openly welcomed me into your home…hell, you even welcomed your husband's ex-girlfriend into your home. You guided me and advised me. You have become my best friend. I love you lady."

She looked out over the flames. "Andy…we just met but already you've shown me that it's okay to be female and tough, it's okay to speak your mind and Lord help anyone who disagrees with you. You're crazy, totally off the wall…but it's you. You love deeply but in a different way. I really hope we can become closer friends so I can understand more."

She turned and put her hand on Claire's shoulder. "And Mum…I can't tell you how much I love you, even after all the bizarre stuff I've heard lately. I've always loved you as a mother but now I appreciate you more as a person. I realize the values you've taught me came from your relationships with these people here tonight. I now see how your love grew although I must admit that some of it freaked me out."

Jenn faced the rest of the silent gathering. "The years don't matter, those other people don't matter." She stretched her arms. "This is what really matters…five people who truly care about each other. Who gives a damn what anyone else thinks?"

She sat down beside Claire. "Okay, I'm finished."

Claire touched a tear from her eye. "Well done Jenn, thanks." She wrapped her arm around her daughter. "My girl has certainly grown a little since she's been here." She looked at the faces around the fire. "Evan, Marie…even in such a short time I can see your influence on her and I couldn't be happier. She's right, you've made me feel so welcome in a situation that I was totally unsure about…scared as hell would be the best description. And Andy, what can I say about your questionable influence? I'm so glad she's had this opportunity and I have no qualms about you two getting to know each other better. Jenn's right, the truly important people are still here."

Marie nodded in agreement. "Well said Jenn…Claire." She poked Evan's shoulder. "And you hoped we'd get into a fight over you."

Claire glared at him. "What? You didn't tell me that! Evan you bugger!"

Evan raised his arms in resignation. "I was kidding, although it would liven up this gathering."

Claire looked disgusted as only Claire could. "That's it! Marie, you can have him."

"No, no, no…" Marie held up her hands. "You take him…I've had enough."

"Right, throw me the old cast-off? Bloody hell!"

"He was your cast-off when I got him. I'm just giving him back!"

Claire stood with her hands on her hips. "I don't want the jerk, you can keep him," she shouted.

Marie stood, adopted the same stance and snarled, "You wanna make something of it sister?"

Andy jumped between them and held up her hands. "Girls, girls, let's not brawl in front of the child," she said. "He's really not worth fighting over anyway so let's settle this diplomatically. If neither of you want him, I'll take him…okay?"

Claire grinned. "I agree, he's not worth the sweat." She stepped in front of Evan and extended her hand to Marie. "Truce?"

They performed a ritual, if somewhat exaggerated handshake.

Evan simply shrugged his shoulders. "So I'm guessing Andy takes me home?"

He waited for a response. When none came he looked up at her. Her face was pale even in the dim light. She was shaking, staring wide-eyed into the darkness. He stood and caught her as she collapsed into his arms.

She pressed her head into his shoulder and they wept.

Chapter 59

Andy sat on the last of the steps leading to the beach, Evan a step above…his arms and legs around her. She rested her head in the crook of his elbow watching the moon begin the climb over the mountain. "How long have I been crying?" she asked.

"Forever."

"Feels like it. I'm sorry."

"It's good Andy."

She snuggled down against him. "If you only knew how many times I've wanted a moment like this," she said softly.

He lowered his face to her cheek. "You okay?"

"Avoidance was always one of your strong points Evan. Yes, I'm okay." She watched Ginn running back and forth on the sand. "What's your dog doing?"

"Waiting for the right moment to howl."

"Maybe I should have done more waiting and less howling."

"You enjoyed life."

"That's a polite way of putting it."

"Any regrets?"

She shrugged. "A few, but I won't lose any sleep over them. You?"

"I'm sure if I think about it I'll come up with more than a few."

"Jack wanted me to be more like Ceejay."

"What?"

"Ceejay was classy, cute, sexy…little miss wonderful."

"Andy…"

"His words. You know how I feel about her Evan. I love that old girlfriend of yours."

"There's a lot of that going around lately."

"From both sides now. You two need closure…or a room."

"I don't want closure," he whispered.

"Neither does she. Seems like a terrible waste to me. I mean there are so many people out there who can't find love to save their souls and you two are hanging onto more than you'll ever be able to use."

He squeezed her gently. "I'm greedy. I want all I can get."

"Sounds promising." She sighed softly. "I really am going to miss him Evan. Suddenly the last ten years seem so unimportant. I keep wondering if I did something to cause this."

He remained silent and held her tighter.

She leaned back and looked into his eyes. "This is where you're supposed to jump in and say 'No Andy, you did nothing'."

"No Andy, you did nothing."

"Thanks. Tell me again why I need you here?"

"Jack made that decision. It was his choice, not yours. It wasn't your fault."

"Maybe he had no other options."

"There are always options if you have the desire and the courage to find them."

"He called me about two weeks before and left a message on the machine. He wanted to talk; to get together and try to work things out."

"Don't pull guilt out of that."

"I didn't call him back, now he's dead. How much more guilty can I be?"

"Has Collin talked to you?"

"Yeah but he's not any more help than you are." She felt his arms tense. "I'm sorry Evan. I know you're getting frustrated with me but I'm really messed up right now."

"What did Collin say?"

"Pretty much what you're saying but he's my son, I'd expect that from him."

"Step back and look at this as if it were someone else."

"None of that crap Evan, please?"

"Fine, then you really don't need me here." He released her and stood. "Until you come to grips with the fact that for whatever reason Jack decided he'd had enough and took his own life then there's nothing to talk about. You've got problems, I've got problems…we've all got fucking problems Andy but I don't see any of us jumping off the nearest tall building. We find a way to work them out. It was his decision. He took his own life."

"But if I'd just talked to him maybe he wouldn't have."

"And maybe he still would have. You don't know what he would have done."

"Maybe I could have found some help for him, somebody to talk to…someone who understands that sort of thing."

"Maybe he didn't want help."

"You don't know that."

"Any more than you know that he did. We can go around on this until the next full moon and it won't make a bit of difference. Get by that part."

"I can't get by it. I've seen him twice in five years and he was dead for one of them. I could have gone back…that might have changed things."

"At any time other than that phone call did he tell you he wanted you back?"

"I don't know."

"Yes you do."

"No, never." Andy stood and walked past him onto the sand then turned. "I called."

"What?"

"I don't know how many times but I called him. He was always too busy, just going somewhere…."

"There's one of those options we talked about, one that he chose to ignore. Lady you had absolutely nothing to do with what happened."

"I loved him Evan, I really did."

"I know. I don't know what happened over the last few years and to be honest I don't care. I only know that you're here and I'm here and that selfish son-of-a-bitch isn't."

"Evan?"

"I would've liked the chance to straighten him out for what he did but he's taken that away from me."

Andy stepped in front of him. "You would have done that?"

His eyes glistened as he looked up at the moon. "He was a Goddamn idiot to let you walk out of his life."

"Evan, he's gone. Let's not…"

"You're right." He reached and pulled her close. "I'm sorry."

She hugged him. "Thanks for rescuing me."

"What?"

"In the park…the summer of lust?"

"How long have you known?"

"Ceejay told me about it today. I was such a fool back then…and don't say I enjoyed life."

"Didn't you?"

"Yes, too much so." She put his hand on his chest and squeezed. "Nice tits."

"Is there anything you and Marie don't share?"

"I can think of something."

"Seriously what else has she told you?"

"I'll never tell, unless it's an appropriately embarrassing moment." She looked up into his face. "I miss the beard. But I hear it's on your butt?"

Evan laughed as Ginn raced up the beach then circled, brushing against them as she did.

Andy jumped. "Is she ready to howl yet?"

Evan dropped his forehead to hers. "Not quite."

"I am." She smiled then kissed him.

He closed his eyes trying to slow his thoughts, trying to not feel. "We should get back up to the house." His voice crackled.

"That would be the smart thing to do," she whispered, "but then I've never been accused of being smart."

"Andy…"

"I'm sorry Evan but I've waited forty years for this. Just hold me for another minute?"

Chapter 60

Jenn sat on the bench watching Ginn running circles in the sand as Andy and Evan climbed to the top of the steps. "How can she do that without getting dizzy?" she asked.

"She changes direction every so often," Evan said.

"Does that help?"

"I don't know." He looked across the yard. "Where are the other women in my life?"

"Two of them are sitting in the kitchen talking, I don't know about the rest…probably scattered all over the country."

Andy grimaced. "I think I should join the two in the kitchen." She nodded towards Jenn.

Evan sat on the bench, hands on his knees. "Nice night," he whispered.

"For some."

"Jennifer…" He reached for her.

"No." She slid to the end of the bench. "It's okay Evan, Marie and Mum didn't see anything."

"Oh, and what did you see?"

She looked at the moon. "I wanted to be the one that witnessed the wolf howl. Abundance of love, remember?"

"Jennifer?"

"I'd love to be held like that."

"You will."

"Not exactly like that." She turned to him. "I saw two old friends helping each other get by a tough spot. Is that good, in case anyone asks?"

"That's what you saw Jennifer. Don't read anything into something that hasn't been written."

"There was more than support happening there Evan. I'm sorry, I didn't mean to spy but…"

"I'm in love with Marie. Since she came into my life there has never been anyone else…never will be."

"I saw the way you looked at Mum tonight."

"No question there."

"You can't love them both, or all three of them."

"I don't have a choice in that matter. I do love them Jennifer, I just can't have them."

"Aren't you supposed to ignore those feelings?"

"Yes but they won't go away. You just can't let them run your life. It'll always be Marie I'm physically and emotionally with."

"So you're the one with the abundance of love. You've seen too many white wolf moons Mister Morris."

"That I have." He laughed. "Far too many."

"So how many women are you in love with right now?"

"One. And Marie's the name…."

"But Mum…"

"I love other women," he said, "but I'm in love with Marie."

"What's the difference?"

"Damned if I know."

"You're at a loss for words?"

"I'm afraid so. You never get too old to never be confused."

"I thought I had the market cornered."

"Emotions." He put his hands behind his head and gazed at the river. "You'll never figure them out. Just learn to deal with the fact that you can't always act on them whether they be love or otherwise."

"Marie says you're not good with matters of the heart."

"She's right, I'm not. Why?"

"You just always seem to…never mind."

"I seem to what?"

"I saw the difference between you and Steve tonight but can you honestly tell me that you're any better than he is?"

"I'm not sure I understand the question."

"The dirty old man bit, the women in your life…you joke about it. You obviously have the same thoughts as he does yet you don't play them out. You give every indication that you're no different from any other guy out there, yet you say you are. I've even seen that difference but…"

"What exactly are you looking for here?"

"I just want you to be straight with me. If that scene with Andy could have gone farther would you have let it?"

He leaned back on the bench. "No, but for a moment let's assume it did. I know that despite all her talk Andy wouldn't have let it get out of hand."

She closed her eyes. "I'm just so damned confused about you right now."

"Listen to me Jennifer…" He leaned forward, resting his elbows on his knees. "I still believe in love or at least an honest relationship before sex and still I believe in being true to Marie. You singling out Andy made my answer difficult. I love her and I love your mum but in the unlikely event that I seriously tried to take that extra step they'd both put a stop to it."

"What if there was no…I'm sorry, let's drop it. I'm getting pretty stupid here."

"What if there was no Marie?"

"Evan…"

"If there was no Marie there's no question, okay?" His voice had an edge she hadn't heard before.

"Please, I said I was sorry." Jenn buried her face in her hands. "This is really none of my business."

"No, it isn't and I'm still not sure where you were going with all that."

"The incident with Steve…" she softly said, "it wasn't the first. I have trust issues, or so guys have told me."

"There's nothing wrong with that."

"But if I don't trust how do I know I'm not missing the right one?"

"You'll know. Go with your feelings."

"They've screwed up before."

"But not as often lately, right?"

"How did you know?"

"Sixty years of experience, a lot of it garnered through mistaken feelings."

Jenn stared out to the beach watching Ginn. "I owe you an apology, I was out of line. You're nothing like Steve. The last few days have been incredible." She turned and smiled at him. "I met you and Marie and I fell into a different world. I accepted everything without question, with trust…even your moonlight madness. It was then I really began to relax with you."

"I'm flattered Jennifer, but that wasn't the right thing to do."

"I know but for reasons I don't think I'll ever understand you made it easy. Then Steve happened and tonight my life seems so damned complicated."

"Life is really very simple. You're born then you die. The stuff in the middle kind of screws you up if you let it, but it's not a big deal when you consider what's waiting for you."

"Way to raise the spirits old man." She nodded toward Ginn. "When's your dog going to speak up?"

He looked out on the beach. Ginn was sitting staring into the night sky. "Any minute now."

"I really am sorry for what I just said Evan, I don't know why I…"

"It's okay Jennifer. At some point it'll make sense to you then maybe you could explain it to me?"

"I will." She slid back across the bench and put her arm around him. "Are you okay with this?"

"If you are."

"I am." She watched Ginn stand and look down the beach. "It's like she's glowing. She really is beautiful."

"She is."

"She's okay? After the Steve thing I mean."

"She seems to have settled down but I'll have to keep a close eye on her for a while. I haven't seen that kind of wild since we brought her home."

Ginn suddenly stood still and raised her head.

"Now?" Jenn asked.

"Now."

Jenn tensed as the howl pierced the night. "Maybe I'll at least get the abundant harvest part," she said. "A girl can never have enough wheat."

"No Jennifer, you will have a lifetime of love. I envy the young man who's lucky enough to capture your heart. If he doesn't give you all the love you can handle have him call me and I'll damn well set him straight."

"I'm pretty sure I'll be taking you up on that." She rested her head on his shoulder. "You're really jealous of someone I haven't met yet?"

Evan kicked at the ground, throwing up a small cloud of dust. "I guess, yes."

"That's pretty nice, thank-you." She slowly caressed his arm. "Evan?"

"Jennifer?"

"I…really need to say something."

"You have my undivided attention."

"I…uh." She sat up straight. "Uh, about Andy…I know I acted like a child. I really am sorry."

"Please, no more apologies. You've had a pretty rough evening. Let it go?"

"Okay, thanks. I'm going to bed," she said, kissing his cheek. "Goodnight."

They both stood then Jenn made her way to the house.

Evan felt like a schoolboy, an embarrassed old schoolboy. He was truly envious of someone he would probably never meet over someone he had no right to feel this way about. He really wasn't good with matters of the heart. He still held on to a world that he should have let go long ago, clinging to emotions that should have been long forgotten. Only a fool would let his feelings feed off the presence of a girl who, at best, should be a passing acquaintance…a pleasant but minor intrusion. His mind had warned him but, as usual, his heart had tuned out his sensibilities.

Calling to Ginn he turned then shuffled along the worn path towards the house, head down, hands in his pockets. Marie walked down the porch steps and stopped a few feet in front of him. They stared at each other in the blue brightness of the moon.

"Andy…" Marie said.

Evan looked into her eyes. "We should talk."

"Yes, but not about that. She apologized, told me what happened. Under the circumstances I'm okay with it Evan. She said that Jenn was a little upset though?"

"Yeah…I think I know why."

"No, you don't. I imagine she's talking to them now. They're doing a candle-chat."

"Oh?" He looked at the flickering light in the kitchen window. "Then I'll stay out here."

"You have nothing to share?"

"Not with this crowd, they talk too much."

"Andy and Claire are staying over on the hide-a-bed. Claire wants to be close to Jenn in case she needs her. Of course Andy just wants a front row center seat in the event you decide to get a moonlight snack."

"Not a chance in hell now," he said, stepping forward. "So, we're fine?"

"We are, although I'm not so sure about me. We've talked about the before…I guess I didn't really understand."

"There's a reason it's called 'the before'."

"I think I'm feeling the same way Jenn felt when she heard about Claire's escapades. I never really thought about how close…how deep your relationships were."

"And still are to a certain extent. I do love them Marie but as much as they are my before, you are my now and my forever." He shifted his weight and opened his arms. "Ben E. King?" he whispered.

Marie closed the last of the space between them then wrapped her hands around his waist and drew him to her.

"Always," she whispered back.

Chapter 61

Claire stepped out onto the porch and squinted into the morning brightness. "Christ why isn't everyone in Kamloops blind?" she moaned. "Good morning Marie, have you seen Jenn?"

"She's off with Evan," Marie said. "He's taking her on one last walk. They'll probably do a bit of a photo hike through the woods."

"Lucky girl," Claire said as she sat in the armchair. "I remember the talks we'd have on those walks."

"It's a whole different world for him out there and it's really nice when you get to see it the way he does." Marie looked back at the doorway. "Where's Andy?"

"She's still purring in the hide-a-bed."

"You slept well?"

"Very well, considering the evening. How was Evan this morning?"

"I didn't see him, they just left a note. He usually hits the flea market first thing Sunday. I imagine he's dragged Jenn with him."

"He wouldn't have to drag her…she loves that sort of thing." Claire reached and touched Marie's hand. "I really want to thank you for everything this weekend. We just kind of took over your home and life."

"I've really enjoyed having you here but I'm damn glad you're all leaving today."

Claire laughed. "I'd feel the same way. Mostly I want to thank you for accepting Jenn the way you have although I didn't think she'd actually be moving into your home."

"It just made sense. I love Jenn…I hope we see her a few more times before she leaves."

"I know you will. She and Evan seem to have really hit it off."

"From the first second although I doubt he'll admit it. They've developed an interesting bond in such a short time. He's really going to miss her."

"And she him." Claire closed her eyes. "I'm not sure how to approach this Marie…"

"He hasn't changed. You probably know him as well as I do. Everything is fine."

"I know. I just needed to hear it from you. Thanks."

Chapter 62

Evan pulled the Rover into the turn-off then parked in the ditch. He let Jenn and Ginn out and pointed through the woods. "There's a path," he said, "that goes nowhere and everywhere. Ginn and I escape up here every now and then." He reached behind the driver's seat and pulled out a pair of battered knee-high moccasins.

Jenn watched as Ginn ran along the floor of the ditch and up onto a small beaten path on the other side.

"She's gone already," Jenn said. "You don't worry about her when she runs off like that?"

"No, she'll wait for me at the trail." He began lacing. "If I take too long to catch up she'll let out a howl."

Jenn watched him curiously. "Why the boots?"

"Moccasins, actually." He continued lacing. "Snakes."

"What? And I'm in sandals...why didn't you tell me?"

Evan laughed. "Don't worry Jennifer, I haven't seen one up here since the fires. I wear these for a little extra support on my calves. It can be a tough climb sometimes."

"Especially for an old guy with terminal LOFS."

While Jenn climbed out of the ditch and walked along the edge of the road toward the path Evan reached into the back of the Rover and retrieved a leather carry bag. He threw it over his shoulder then closed the door.

He followed behind her, his eyes drawn to her long tanned legs and denim cut-offs. Prurient interest was thriving in his tired body while his equally weary brain reprimanded him for this involuntary impulse, reminding him that he considered himself one of those who had supposedly evolved. But there were times....

Evan caught up to her as Jenn joined Ginn at the edge of the twisting overgrown pathway. He resisted the urge to put his arm around her, choosing to scratch the wolf behind the ears. He gave Ginn a pat and she started along the trail.

"This is what everything is about," he said. "Nature, life...it's everywhere but especially here."

"Why especially here?" Jenn asked.

"Because here is where we are."

She noticed the leather satchel hanging at his waist. "What's in the bag dad?"

"That doesn't even warrant comment." He opened the silver clasp and lifted the top. "Let's see...an old pipe and some very dry baccy, a book, voice recorder, a lighter, notepad and pencil, digital camera, a couple of granola bars and assorted sticks and stones that I've found on my trips."

"You need a housekeeper. Granola bars?"

"I'm holding for a friend."

"No cell phone?"

"I've never had one. Marie does but I'm not interested. There's no point in getting away from it all if you bring it with you."

"You have a digital camera? I thought you were a film man."

"For my larger work and the black and white I am but for the cards and bookmarks...the more commercial stuff, this suits my purposes fine."

"You do that sort of thing?"

"I'm not sure anyone could survive on selling their art unless you're a national name. There's always got to be an additional income. You hear about a sculptor getting fifteen grand for a commissioned statue but what you don't hear is that it's the only one he's sold and he'd worked on it for a year. Art has always been more of a labor of love and self-fulfillment. On the other hand I do enjoy the colour work and I love hearing people's comments as they pick up one of my cards. It's a pretty good ego boost."

"But you sold a few pieces at the showing where I first saw you."

"Ten to be precise. At two hundred apiece, subtracting taxes and expenses, it works out to be about twelve hundred dollars. That doesn't last long these days."

"In your art did you ever do figure studies?"

"Yes, I think almost everyone who has a love of photography has at one time or another tried to do a decent study. Why?"

"Oh I heard you were a pretty fair model in your day."

"Marie or Claire? Which one spilled that little secret?"

"I'm not telling."

"Originally it was for the money but later in return for my posing the university let me use their cameras and darkrooms to further my experience. It was a pretty fair trade. It also gave me an insight into what goes on in the mind and body of the person on the other side of the lens."

"Walk a mile in their shoes."

He smiled. "Or out of them, in this case. It was an interesting experience."

"So the commercial work is the trade-off for the art."

"Right."

Jenn reached into the satchel and pulled out the camera. "Do you mind?"

"Of course not."

They slowly walked the climbing pathway, Evan showing her how to use the camera; getting into detail about light and shadow, form and texture.

Jenn stopped beside a burnt tree and crouched at its base. A family of mushrooms had pushed their way up through the blackened earth, stark white against the charcoal trunk. "I'm thinking this is a good shot?" she asked.

"Then shoot it woman."

"No, I want your opinion. Is it good?"

"Your call Jennifer, I don't know what you see."

"White mushrooms, black tree...I like the contrast and the textures, especially the softness of the mushrooms against the hardness of the wood." She pressed the shutter release then, for good measure took three more pictures.

As she stood to continue the walk Evan stopped her. "What colour is the tree?"

She looked back down at the burned wood. "Black."

"Look closely and from this angle." He guided her to one side where the sun was at her back.

"Black," she said.

"Closer…"

As she drew within inches of the charred trunk, a rainbow of colours twinkled in the bright light. She raised the camera and took one more shot. "This is really beautiful."

"I'm not sure if you'll capture it the way you want, most of it is in your head."

"What?"

"A lot of it is illusion, like when you look at the full moon and it looms large in the sky. The moon never really changes size…it just appears that way. You'll get some of those colours but they won't be as bright and not quite so rich. A little creative manipulation on the computer will bring a lot of it back though."

They walked, alternating between shadow and light up the path, until they came to a hillside clearing overlooking a small valley. Ginn barked then with a low growl ran to the edge of the slope and disappeared.

"She's really into this isn't she?" Jenn said quietly.

He just nodded as he stared across the valley. The other side still showed the ravaged landscape left by the fire. Green was beginning to wrap the earth but the trees still stood as black skeletons serving mute sentry.

Jenn shaded her eyes. "The sun no longer shined so warm as it did before. Trees no longer grew so tall and flowers didn't grow at all. And bear too was broken, tired and with age."

His eyes narrowed as he looked at her. "Where did you hear that?" he asked.

"It's in an old binder Mum has."

"I thought I'd lost that in a move or something. She doesn't throw anything away does she?"

"Two peas in a pod. You wrote that?"

"'With knowing eyes bear watched in silence as they slithered like snakes into his valley…' one of my early bits of short prose. That's really all I can remember of it though."

"Damned freaky follows you everywhere doesn't it? I first read that about ten years ago. So many times I tried to understand what it was all about. A bear being attacked by…something. I never figured out what. And now here I am talking to you about it."

"What was your take?"

"I thought it might be a metaphor for the death of someone's dreams and how reality crept into his life and he didn't have the energy to fight to keep the dream alive anymore."

Evan shrugged his shoulders. "Not bad. I don't really remember what I was thinking at the time but there's nothing wrong with that interpretation, if you believe in metaphors."

"Let's not start that again. There has to be a couple of hundred pages in that binder…a lot it bordering on fantasy."

"It was my interest at the time. I still delve into it occasionally." He watched as Ginn slowly wound her way back up the side of the hill and flopped with a groan beside him. "She loves it up here. She's happy to have a home but she needs to recharge the wildness every now and then."

"Kinda like people."

"Kinda like." He reached and gently scratched Ginn on the back of her neck. "She reminds me of how we should all be."

"How so?"

"Regardless of her lineage this girl has a peaceful soul. She loves unconditionally and doesn't care whether you're fat, thin, old, young, tall or short. She accepts you on your terms and asks only that you accept her on hers."

"Sounds very flowerchild-like."

"I suppose it is."

"I've never thought of animals having expressions but she looks so relaxed and at peace with herself."

"A sheep in wolf's clothing." Evan stretched out beside Ginn and pulled his hat down over his face. "You too can be at peace like the wolf. It's easy and I'll show you how."

She moved around until her shadow wasn't in the frame then took a photograph of them. "So you taught her that too?"

"No, it comes naturally to her. Animals live in the now. When they hunt they give it their all, when they play they give it their all…and when they feel secure enough to rest they do it better than any human. If anything she taught me." He patted the ground beside him. "Lie back and close your eyes." He felt her touch against him as she lay down. "You okay?" he asked.

"Why wouldn't I be? So you've got me where you want me. Now what?"

"First you have to learn to appreciate yourself. Close your eyes and relax. Think about each part of your body. Concentrate all your energy and thought into that one area and as you do let those muscles relax. Start at your toes and gradually work up to your head. Feel from without…the sun bathing you in warmth and energy…the breeze taunting your skin. Hear all that surrounds you, the rustle of the leaves, that bird somewhere across the valley…even the grass twitching in the breeze beside you. Listen and you will hear. The smells, the slight odor of damp burned-out trees, the wildflowers…the dust. Let your mind go…let your senses guide your input. Feel all that you possess within…feel your light. Tune into the energy within you. Sense your own being then reach out and accept how this being relates to the rest of the world…to life. Appreciate yourself then you'll understand that you are a part of a greater entity. You are a part of all life and all life is part of you."

Jenn frowned at him. "You got all that from a wolf?"

"You're not trying," he mumbled through his hat.

"Sorry, but I thought you said you weren't into this sort of thing?"

"I said I didn't understand it."

"Sounds like you do. Okay, you want to run that by me again?"

"You'll try it this time?"

"I promise."

He repeated his words. This time Jenn let herself go…beginning with her toes as he instructed, relaxing each muscle until she began to feel the earth pulling her down. As she concentrated on her shoulders, she realized how tense she had been. She felt the sun wrapping her, the breeze touching her. Then she listened as the wind sound through the trees became clearer, louder. She resisted opening her eyes when she heard an unfamiliar syncopated swoosh. The 'caw' of a crow echoing across the valley told her what she had heard. A slight breeze whispered through the grass beside her ears. Then she caught the faint odor of burnt wood mingled with the sweetness of wildflowers. A bee buzzed somewhere near…or far. She couldn't tell which. Gradually she felt the earth releasing her, allowing her to become lighter…to be free.

She was looking down with closed eyes on the scene that surrounded her with a clarity she had never experienced. She drifted higher, the sounds blending together and becoming distant.

She slipped into sleep.

Chapter 63

Evan lay beside her watching her sleep. He resisted the urge to tame a delinquent wisp of hair that had settled across her eyes. Her lips, slightly parted, renewed forgotten yearnings for that first kiss, that first touch. He wanted to caress her cheek, to once again feel the joy, fear, and uncertainty that only first love brings. He'd willingly suffer the inevitable tragedy, pain, and tears…for just that first kiss.

Then reality yawned and stretched.

He stood then quietly walked along the hillside and into the valley as an old Lovin' Spoonful song kept a-rollin' across his mind.

A hawk flew a silent and deliberate path, surveying the earth below. Evan closed his eyes and soared with the hawk, peering into the shadows and light.

This was the now he cherished. All his yesterdays lay scattered through the valley concealed beneath the ragged brush and weeds. Some he sought out, the rest would stay hidden. Some he treasured, the rest didn't matter. He inhaled deeply and caught the distinct aroma of bacon frying. Apparently burnt toast indicates a stroke but what does bacon imply? Likely just another post-hippie syndrome sent to awaken snoozing mind-fodder.

A clumsy crow commandeered a log not five feet from where he sat. Evan marveled at the blue-blackness of its feathers, rich and regal. A face came to mind.

A soft-focused raven-haired girl with sepia skin and a fetching smile that wouldn't go away, like the hook in an old song…that unforgettable lyric that haunts your memory while the title remains forgotten. She was older than he, perhaps fourteen, wearing a red tartan skirt, white blouse and a soft, white sweater…her books clutched to her chest. She leaned against the rough red brick of the school, a gentle breeze lifting the subtleness of her perfume. For one moment their eyes locked in uncertainty then he fumbled a kiss. She laughed then told him she had to catch her bus. He watched her every movement until she disappeared behind the gymnasium.

He never saw her again. A lifetime later he would question whether she had been real or just the product of an over-active pre-teen imagination, a fantasy.

Evan settled back on the dried grass to consider the reality of the sleeping beauty that now occupied an inordinately large space in his mind and heart. Through the simple act of being she brought new life to feelings long dormant, buried beneath the scrub brush and tumbleweed, forgotten and unfinished. It warmed him that after all these years base emotions could still run rampant but he now suffered the weight of her trust upon his shoulders, a trust more overpowering than any selfish passion racing through him.

Suddenly the hawk quietly plummeted, its death-dive bearing darkness for some unwary creature on the valley floor.

Chapter 64

Jenn woke with a start and a kiss from Ginn. "Yuch…" she moaned, "wolfie breath. Well it's certain you're not my Prince Charming." She sat up and looked into those blue eyes. "I haven't thanked you for last night have I?"

Ginn dropped her head to one side.

"Thanks. Where's your soul mate?" she asked, scratching behind Ginn's ear.

Jenn stood and followed the wolf to the edge of the hill. Evan sat quietly, not moving. She lifted the camera and took a few photographs. He seemed so at peace with himself she hated to disturb him. After last night…after all she'd heard about his life she began to appreciate this side of him more.

She quietly slipped down the slope and sat beside him, linking her arm through his. "You left me alone up there," she said.

"You weren't alone; you had Ginn watching over you."

"Literally. Man, I must have been tired."

"It was a pretty emotional night. I'm surprised you were up so early this morning."

"How long was I asleep?"

"About twenty minutes."

"Is that all?" She stretched her legs. "I think I'll be trying that 'feel your toes' thing more often."

"By the way Ginn didn't teach me that. My first experience was on a beach on the Oregon coast."

"She really did sample from the buffet didn't she?"

"Big time, although I've never been able to make that little trick work."

"You really don't get into the new-age stuff do you?"

He chuckled. "About a year ago I had to deliver some advertising photo proofs to one of those spiritual awakening camps...Solstice something-or-other. I remember walking down the hall and hearing whales calling. I looked through the door and there were probably a dozen rather hefty women all wearing black and lying still on a deep blue carpet with the whale sounds blaring from the stereo." He peeled the wrapper off a granola bar. "I'll never get that image out of my mind."

"You know this is the first time I've actually seen you eat something other than supper and, uh, cereal?"

He smiled. "Actually I snack off and on throughout the day. I'm a believer in listening to my body. I eat when I'm hungry, drink when I'm dry, and sleep when I'm tired. But at my age I sometimes mix those last two up."

Jenn giggled then rubbed the sleeve of his shirt. "I haven't seen you wear flannel since that first day either."

"They make me look like a lumberjack."

"Ahh...but a pretty lumberjack."

He peered out from under his hat and grinned an evil grin. "You think I'm pretty?"

"You're not a lumberjack."

"What does that mean?"

"Shouldn't we be getting back?"

"Do you really want to?"

"No." Jenn looked out over the valley. "I'd like to stay here until the last possible minute. This has been quite an experience for me Evan."

He stretched his arms out in front of him. "Me too."

"I meant what I said last night, about learning so much from you over the last few days."

"Yes, I've been meaning to talk to you about that. 'Philosophical banter'?"

"Sorry, I was on a roll."

"That you were." He placed his hand on hers. "For months I've been trying to find that point in my life where I was truly happy and comfortable with myself. You came along and showed me I was looking in the wrong place. This experience has made me realize that there came a point where I grew jaded…when I accepted a lot of things I wouldn't even have considered back then. You and your mum have rekindled a lot more than you think. I suppose if you believe in such things it was fate that brought you to me just at a time when I was so screwed up that I wasn't sure that any of this was worth it anymore. Into everyone's rain a little life must fall, you are that life."

"I really did mean it Evan. You let me into your beautiful world. I honestly think I see things differently now."

"The most valuable gifts you can give another human being are your time and understanding. To share a part of your life is like sharing treasure."

"There's that philosophical banter again. But my time here with Mum backs that up. It's like I've discovered a friend that was always there but I didn't know." She picked up a twig and started drawing in the dirt. "I need to ask you something but I'll be okay if you don't want to answer."

"By now you should know if you're comfortable asking I'll answer."

"That's the problem. I'm not sure how to ask and I'm not sure how comfortable I'll be with what you say. I think I know what you're going to say but I need to…"

"Ask or not Jennifer, it's up to you."

"It was something Marie said. Promise you won't tell her I told you?"

"I can't, you know that."

"I know. Okay…" She hesitated then drew a deep breath. "She mentioned that she'd seen the way you looked at me and that in a different place and time, you know?"

"I think so."

"I said that feelings would have to be pretty strong to even consider it that way. Am I right?"

"Yes, you are."

"So…I guess my question is…" She lowered her eyes. "Do you love me?"

"Yes."

"Oh. You're sure you don't want to think about it for a while?"

"No."

Again she looked into the valley. "I don't know where we go from here."

"Nowhere. One of our basic needs is to be loved and sometimes that love comes from unexpected places. You truly are someone with whom I would like to share everything but that can't happen."

She looked down at her feet. "Those damned rules of society."

"That has nothing to do with it. I'm old and you're not, it's that simple. You've got a lifetime of love and discovery ahead of you. It's important that you do it on your own terms with someone on the same journey so you can learn and grow together."

"I'm sorry but that's a politically correct answer if I've ever heard one." Jenn turned and stared into his eyes. "Is that really the way you feel?"

"No." He put his arms around her and pressed his cheek against hers. "I do love you Jennifer and yes, the 'different time' notion has certainly crossed my mind. But for more reasons than I care to think about, obvious and otherwise…this is all there is."

"If you love her let her go?"

"Interesting thought but I can't let you go, I never had you."

"Oh you've got me and you're not going to get rid of me that easily."

"Sounds like there's a little bit of love coming my way?"

"A little bit," she whispered then rested her head on his shoulder. "I'm sorry…it was unfair of me to corner you like that."

"It was, but it was something you needed to know. Always get those questions out there Jenn. You'll regret it if you don't."

"Jenn again?"

"Jenn always."

Chapter 65

Evan carefully parked beside Andy's car, allowing her space to exit the driveway.

"Well," Jenn said, "I guess this is good-bye for a while. Hopefully I can come back and visit now and then."

"Anytime," Evan smiled, "you're always welcome." He looked through the windshield. "It appears the rest of my girls are leaving too."

"Your girls...like you're a Sultan or something."

"Something." He opened the door and stepped out, Ginn close behind.

Claire walked to the passenger side and helped Jenn out of the vehicle. "Good trip?" she asked.

"Yes," Jenn replied then whispered, "very good."

"I see." She brushed an errant strand of hair from her daughter's eyes. "Andy and I are heading back to the hotel. We're going to get an early start in the morning. I'd like it if you and I could have a quiet dinner this evening?"

"I'd like that too. I'll get my stuff and follow you back into town."

As Jenn headed toward the house Evan came around the front of the Rover and lifted himself up onto the hood. "So this is good-bye?"

"I guess...our first, really." She slapped the hood beside him. "So you finally got one of these suckers. Kind of butt ugly ain't she?"

"I don't know…I've seen some pretty nice butts in my time."

"Me too." She smiled. "We was good wasn't we?"

"Yes we was."

She rested her hands on his knees and looked into his eyes. There were so many things she could say but they were all things she couldn't say. She breathed deeply. "I guess I'd better get going."

"I don't want you to."

"I know. God this is tougher than I thought it would be."

He glanced over at Marie and Andy. "The rest of them are pretty busy, they'll never miss us. We could sneak off into the bushes…"

"I'd laugh if I didn't think it was such a good idea," she said quietly. "It wouldn't be enough Evan. When we hugged at the hotel it all resurfaced. I loved…love the life we had back then but I've got a pretty good one going now and so do you. As tough as it is to leave all the memories behind that's what we have to do. I can't even think of any words to describe how I feel right now but we each have our own special people to go to. It's as simple as that."

He reached and stroked her hair. As much as he wanted this moment to last forever, he wanted it to be over. How can feelings this old seem so new? "It's not that simple. Andy figures we need closure."

"Or a room…" She laughed as she brushed a tear from her cheek. "That wouldn't do it and you know it."

"I know." He slid off the hood and hugged her. "I'm just delaying the inevitable as long as possible."

"Please don't."

He bent to kiss her.

"No…I really have to go." She turned her face and pulled him close. "Good-bye."

"So this is it?"

"What?"

"We're finally breaking up?" His voice wavered.

She stepped back, smiled and winked. "We'll always have Scott McKenzie."

"Always," he whispered.

He watched her walk quickly through the gate, past Marie and Andy then stopping to say something to Jenn before she went behind the house. For the first time she was actually walking out of his life. For the first time he felt the hurt that a man feels when it's over.

He didn't like this feeling.

"You okay?" Andy asked, stepping into Claire's space in front of him.

"Not really. How about you?"

"Thanks to you I'm a bit okay. You look as destroyed as Ceejay. Pretty rough I guess."

"Pretty…" He couldn't stop the tears. "I'm sorry Andy."

"Don't be." She put her arms around him. "I only wish I could feel that much…about anything."

His voice trembled. "It's not all it's cracked up to be."

"I'd like to be able to decide that for myself." She slid her hand down his side and clasped his. "Walk with me for a minute?"

They wound their way along the path saying nothing until they reached the bench overlooking the river. He sat with his elbows on his knees, staring at the ground. "It was good to see you again Andy, although the circumstances might have been better."

"I know, and I appreciate everything you and Marie have done for me."

"That's what friends are for."

"Tsk, tsk, resorting to clichés again? So did Ceejay talk to you about Jenn?"

"No. What about her?"

"Be careful Evan, for some unknown reason she likes you."

"I like her too."

"You know what I mean."

"I know." He nodded. "We've talked."

"Good. I'd better get going, I've done my part."

"What part is that?"

"Jenn asked me to get you over here away from everyone else."

"Ah."

Andy placed a finger under his chin. "I'll miss you Evan but I'll be back soon. Jenn's little speech about this is where this nice people are? I figure if I want to learn how to be one of them I should study you guys a little more often. You okay with that?"

"Of course." He hugged her and kissed her cheek. "I love you Andy."

Her eyes filled as she forced a smile. "Damn you...why couldn't you have said that when we could've done something about it?"

He stretched out and closed his eyes, feeling the movement of the bench as she stood. Emptiness gripped inside him. Confusion twisted through his mind, racing as quickly as his heart.

"Mind if I sit down?" he heard Jenn ask.

"Would it make a difference?"

"No." She giggled.

"So why do you want me away from everyone else."

"I don't know. Mum asked me to tell Andy to get you down here then I was to come and talk to you. I'm supposed to ask if you remember the spiral staircase. Cryptic isn't it?"

"Not really, she's going to sneak out to the car and be gone before I get back."

"Oh, I'm sorry."

"Don't be, it's probably best. I'm not sure I could handle another good-bye."

"Neither could she. She looks so sad, so upset. I don't think I've ever seen her like this." She put her arm across his shoulder. "Spans the years doesn't it?"

"What does?"

"Love," she said, "...it knows not time. Isn't that out of one of your writings?"

"Pathetically prophetic but yes, it is."

"I've seen Mum and Dad. It's different with them."

"How so?" he asked.

"They love each other, that's pretty clear. But you and Mum...I can't explain it. There's this oneness about you two, a feeling. She still really loves you."

"I know."

"And you still really love her."

"I know."

"I can't imagine what that feels like."

"No, you can't."

Jenn looked back at the house. "You're right. They're leaving."

"I'm right more than I'm wrong."

"I've heard that. You aren't going to at least wave good-bye?"

He rubbed his eyes. "I can't."

"It's okay…I don't think she can either. So do you remember the spiral staircase?"

He nodded, smiled, and drew a deep breath, resisting the urge to look behind him. "When's your assignment due?"

"Wednesday. I'm okay."

"Yes, you are." He pointed down the river. "Look that way."

She turned then felt his hands on her neck. "What are you doing?"

She felt a weight fall against her chest and reached to find his pendant around her throat.

Evan gently rubbed her shoulder. "I want you to have this," he said. "A reminder of our time together."

Jenn turned and looked at his smile. "I don't need anything to remind me of this experience Evan."

"But you'll take it, right?"

"Just try and get it back." Jenn watched Andy's car pull out of the driveway. "I'd better get going too. I promised to meet Mum for dinner." She put her arms around his neck and hugged him. "Our talk on the hill? Thank-you."

He kissed her cheek. "And thank you…for a lot more than you'll ever know."

Jenn took a deep breath then stood. "Marie and Ginn at six-o'clock. I'd like to talk about the 'lot more' one day?"

"We will."

Evan watched her walk away then looked back down the beach, surprised that he still had room for more emptiness. Then he heard laughter. To his left Dobson and Marion were strolling the sand with matching plastic sandals and metal detectors.

He heard the good-byes behind him. As Ginn dropped at his feet he felt Marie's hands settle on his shoulders.

"You're one pretty lucky guy Evan," she said quietly.

"I've always thought so." He stared out over the river. "Why this time?"

"Of the three women that just left there wasn't one that wanted to. You've still got it."

"Don't want it."

"Uh huh." She gently kneaded his shoulders. "It's got to be a boost for the old ego though."

"You know I'm too great a man to have an ego Marie."

"Danny and Carol are hanging around for a bit. From what I've heard we may need a ref?"

"Don't believe everything you hear."

"Do you feel as drained as you sound?"

He drew a breath and sighed.

She dropped her arms to his chest and rested her chin on his neck. "Frog in a toilet?" she whispered.

"More like a blender." He chuckled then pointed to Marion and Dobson. "You see that?"

"Sweet isn't it? Lonely neighbors for all these years then finally they find each other."

"I might have to try out this 'cluck' thing."

"Like you need more chicks."

"Have we still got that old dryer in the storage shed?"

Marie kissed his cheek. "Welcome back."

Chapter 66

Evan twisted his neck in circles letting the hot water slowly trickle off his shoulders, moaning softly as the tension washed down his back. He wanted to free his mind; to let the moment take him away from the realities that had come rushing into his life and almost as quickly had left. He tried to simply be within himself; to find the peace that had become so much a part of him yet tonight was playing a mean game of hide-and-seek behind the emotions that now filled every part of him. He heard the shower curtain open and felt the cool air flood the enclosure. "Marie?" he asked.

"Who were you expecting?"

"It's just that you don't usually…you know?"

"I'm trying a little spontaneity. I've heard it's good for the old folks now and then."

He chuckled. "I think you heard right."

"That's not much of a shower you've got happening. I could barely hear the water running."

"It's not for cleansing the body, just the mind."

She smiled as she unbuttoned her shirt. "I'm afraid you're going to need more than a trickle for that."

"Agreed. So really…what are you doing?"

"I was planning on being spontaneous tomorrow night but that kind of goes against the whole concept."

He watched her intently. "You still can. I'll act surprised."

"With what I've got in mind you won't be acting old man. It seems like forever since we've been alone doesn't it?"

"It's just you and me Marie...us."

"I know." She dropped her shirt to the floor and separated the snap on her jeans. "It's not polite to stare. A real gentleman would look away."

He turned and closed his eyes then heard the sound of denim hitting the floor.

"Can I open them now?"

"No."

He listened as she moved around the bathroom. He heard the noise of a match strike. Even with eyes closed he sensed that it had gone dark. He heard the shower curtain draw shut and knew she was standing in front of him.

"Now?" he asked.

"Not yet."

"Why not?"

"I just want to look at you for a while, okay?"

He smiled and put his hands on his hips. "There's nothing here that you haven't seen before."

She giggled. "The boobs are new."

"Besides them."

The sound of the trickling water grew louder as he waited for her to say something.

"What are you thinking about?" he finally asked.

"I'm just remembering the first time we did this," she whispered.

"Unit 112." He opened his eyes and saw the tears on her cheeks. "In a shower quite similar to this. A little smaller though...we were much closer together."

Soft warm candlelight filtered through the curtain as she moved towards him. "We've put on a lot of mileage since then," she said.

He nodded. "But they were gentle miles, weren't they?"

"Mostly. Where did it all go Evan?"

"It's still here...it's just a tad sleepy."

She stepped up against him and nuzzled into his neck, her right hand in the small of his back, the other rubbing his chest. "I think I just need a little reassurance."

He put his arms around her, drawing her close. Kissing her cheek he held her tightly, the hot water trickling between them.

He moved his lips against her ear and whispered, "I love you."

"I know, honestly I do…and I love you. But seeing you with Claire…Christ, this is stupid. I keep telling myself I'm overreacting but I'm…"

He kissed her. The water washed away the years as they caressed, exploring each other as if for the first time. He pulled back, smiled, and then kissed her again.

She pressed her forehead against his chest and giggled. "Damn that's a helluva lot of reassurance you're packing there Wolfman." She looked up into his eyes. "Wash my back?"

She turned and leaned against him. He took the soap from the corner shelf and ran it across her shoulders. He watched the bubbles stream down her back then change course where their bodies touched.

He felt her tense then relax as he wrapped his arms around her waist. "What do you think of starting over?" he whispered, kissing her neck.

"I like it, one of his best."

"No…us. Tomorrow night, first date. Maybe dinner and a movie?"

"Like we used to in the early days. Sounds nice, but I have to be home by ten."

"A.m. or p.m.?"

She gave him a gentle nudge with her elbow. "Am I going out with Evan?"

"Of course. Starting over, right?"

"Won't Peter be a little pissed?"

"Let's not tell him."

"How will I explain where I've been?"

"I don't know…" Evan shrugged. "There was an emergency book club meeting?"

"Yeah, he'd buy it. So tonight…Floyd Cramer?"

"I suppose."

"Then I feel I should warn you Mister Morris, there are a lot of things I won't do on a first date." Marie reached back over her shoulder and pulled his face to hers. "But on a last date," she whispered, "pretty much anything goes."

Made in the USA
Charleston, SC
21 October 2016